# A HOSTILE STATE

# A HOSTILE STATE

## Adrian Magson

SEVERN
HOUSE

First world edition published in Great Britain and the USA in 2021
by Severn House, an imprint of Canongate Books Ltd,
14 High Street, Edinburgh EH1 1TE.

Trade paperback edition first published in Great Britain and the USA in 2022
by Severn House, an imprint of Canongate Books Ltd.

severnhouse.com

*British Library Cataloguing-in-Publication Data*
A CIP catalogue record for this title is available from the British Library.

ISBN-13: 9780727850270 (cased)
ISBN-13: 9781780297705 (trade paper)
ISBN-13: 9781448305087 (e-book)

*All Severn House titles are printed on acid-free paper.*

Typeset by Palimpsest Book Production Ltd.,
Falkirk, Stirlingshire, Scotland.
Printed and bound in Great Britain by
TJ Books Limited, Padstow, Cornwall.

To Ann. The best hunter-gatherer ever!
And BHT – gone but not forgotten.

# ONE

It's been claimed that you don't hear the sound of the bullet that kills you. Whoever said it wasn't speaking from experience. Idle thoughts like this tend to slide into your head when death comes too close for comfort.

What I did hear was the snap of a shot passing my face, leaving a ripple in the atmosphere. It was followed by the crack-and-whine as the bullet exploded off a rock three feet away. I ducked instinctively and way too late, feeling the spiteful sting of Lebanese sandstone peppering my cheek. A sound in the background might have been the rolling echo of the shot, but I ignored it. If I'd heard anything at all I was still good to go. I was also busy trying to compute where the shooter might be and whether I was rolling into a position where he could have another go at blowing my head off.

I kept moving, rolling to one side and hugging the earth. Sounds can be confusing in hilly areas, bouncing off rocks and coming back from somewhere different, leaving behind fragments you can't quite place and leading the unwary to pop up and look the wrong way. Bang, end of game. I hadn't caught any tell-tale muzzle smoke, but from the angle of the bullet striking the rock it had to have come from the high ground somewhere to my side and rear.

That thought made me go cold. Whoever had pulled the trigger had been looking down at me and I hadn't even been aware of their presence. But how? I'd been in the country barely twenty-four hours on a last-minute rush arrangement with instructions to sit and wait for a local intelligence source to show up. In that time I'd had minimal contacts and left no footprints. Those I had contacted wouldn't have been in any position to give me up as illicit gun dealing is frowned upon, even in Lebanon.

The source's name – it had to be a him because the locals

in this part of the world didn't have much time for women in positions of responsibility and therefore access to what was probably classified information – was top secret, but his DIA (Defence Intelligence Agency) code-name was Tango. Anything else about him was on a strict need-to-know basis and it had clearly been decided I wasn't on that list, which suited me fine. Using sources is like that; the fewer people who know their real name the less likely it is to blow back in everyone's face if they get rolled up.

But it didn't answer the fundamental question of the right-here-and-now. How the hell had someone got onto me so quickly? Had I inadvertently shown up on radar on the way here and tripped an alarm? Always possible but I wasn't so sure. I'd been extra careful coming here because that's the way I work. The only people who knew I was here were back in Langley, Virginia, the home of the CIA.

The here in question was on a hillside; a dry spit from the Yammoune nature reserve in the northern half of Lebanon. The briefing I'd had on the area told me it featured a lake and a Greco-Roman temple, but I didn't think I'd be doing any sightseeing on this trip. Violence had been sweeping the country for decades, from terrorist groups, Sunni and Shi'ite extremists and the twin forces of Hamas and Hezbollah, both outlawed by the international community and determined to retain some kind of stranglehold on the country.

Getting here had meant taking a dog-leg journey from the US through Geneva and hitching a ride out of Damascus with an air-taxi firm flying UN and aid volunteers into Tripoli's Kleyate airport. I figured I was likely to attract less interest with my cover as an aid volunteer than I would in the crowded and suspicion-riddled mess of Beirut's Rafic Hariri International, a feverish hunting ground for the Lebanese Government's General Directorate of State Security or the other force in the country, the Iranian-backed Hezbollah and their counter-intelligence unit.

On arrival I'd visited a recommended source of equipment in Tripoli (or Tarablus, to differentiate it from the city in Libya), to buy the kind of supplies that you won't find in your neighbour-hood tourist bazaar. In this case it was a used Kahr semi-automatic pistol and a spare magazine. I'd also got myself some wheels.

There were very few rentals here that didn't ask questions about where you were going and where you were from; details likely to end up under the suspicious gaze of the local General Security Office.

I'd chosen a beaten-up Land Cruiser that had seen better days but had a decent engine and good tyres. The man who'd sold it to me was a cousin of the man who'd supplied me with the semi-automatic, who also hadn't bothered asking questions. He had a weathered face and a nose like a hawk's beak, and had shaken his head when I'd asked about a rental price.

'Buy only. Not rent.' He'd chopped the air with his hand to signal his terms and conditions. Maybe he figured I was bound to come to grief and he'd never see me or the car again. He might have been right at that, so I wasn't in a position to argue. Besides, if I bought the car and had to drive any great distance after this job, I wouldn't have to go to the trouble of returning it. Leave it on any street or back alley and sooner or later it would be gone.

The deal-maker in him still had a shot at reading my mind. 'You bring back here, I give you a good price. Then I change the plates, give it a respray. Make it disappear.' He laughed at his own astuteness, snapped his fingers and spat on the ground. I decided not to negotiate further. He was a better businessman than me and I needed the ride.

I paid him what he asked, then got in the Land Cruiser and drove away.

But that was already history. I shrugged off the questions in my mind about what had led to this point and hugged dirt, grateful that the shooter's aim had been off even if his field-craft hadn't. You have to take what comfort you can from these things and move on. I slid into the cover of some big rocks and made a decision: I had to get out of here.

I counted to five to see if another shot would follow. When nothing happened I skidded further across the slope until I reached a dip in the ground and rolled onto my back, feeling the cushion of my day sack beneath me. It was slimmer than normal backpacks, holding some basic rations, a map, a compass and a bottle of water; essentials for a one-day trip into bandit country.

The plan had been to meet Tango on what passed as a road some 300 feet down the hill. It was more of a wide track but he'd apparently specified the location as safe. I could see a clear five-mile stretch from up here heading north, and the plan was simple: once I'd checked Tango was the right person and not a unit of Hezbollah, I was to get a memory stick from him and bug out for the airport. With a quick in-and-out trip like this, it made sense to travel extra-fast and extra-light.

It was one of the essentials in the backpack that I needed most right now, but getting it required a bit more space for movement than I had here without getting bits of me shot off. I needed to find better cover and a safe exit route out.

As I thought about tactics I found myself staring up at a vast expanse of blue, cloudless sky, with the thin contrail of an aircraft going who knew where. Blue meant calm but I didn't feel it. Being up there suddenly seemed a good place to be; better than down here with someone shooting at me. But that was wishing for the impossible.

I lay still for a moment, figuring out which way to go. Choosing the wrong exit route would make me an open target. Unfortunately I still wasn't sure of the shooter's location. Up the slope was no good as I'd be moving slowly and probably right onto his gun. Down was better, where I could move faster but I'd be right in line for a back-shot. I also had no way of knowing if the shooter had moved. A good one would have done so if there was a chance his location had been compromised. If he was still anywhere above me he had the advantage of elevation, and going right or left he could simply track me across the slope and wait for his moment to squeeze the trigger, like a plastic duck hunter in a fairground gallery.

The silence around me was complete; no bird noises, no wind, nothing, not even the sound of the plane. My breathing sounded way too loud. I made an effort to slow it down, along with the drumming of the pulse in my head. I reckoned I'd moved a mere twenty yards but felt and sounded as if I'd run a hundred.

Being shot at does that to the system; it accelerates the heartbeat and focusses everything right down to the moment, especially the demand for oxygen brought on by the rush of adrenalin and the heady realization that you've survived.

A mocking cry way up high pinpointed a lone hawk off to my right, circling on the thermals, a majestic master of the skies. He was either laughing at me for being such a sucker or dissing the shooter for not providing him with some easy pickings in the shape of my corpse. I shook my head at him and took another deep breath before rolling over and continuing across and down the slope in a fast crawl, using my elbows and feet to power me along on my belly like a lizard. It wasn't pretty nor was it entirely pain-free, but if it got me out from under the gun I'd be happy.

Then the air around me exploded and an array of dust and chippings fell around me like dry rain.

# TWO

*Moscow*

Building No 3, as it would have been known had it worn a nameplate, was an innocuous, concrete-and-glass office structure on the corner of Grizodubovoy Street in the Khoroshyovsky Administrative District in north-west Moscow. It was near to but not part of the central headquarters building of the Main Intelligence Directorate, known more commonly as the GRU – Russia's foreign military intelligence agency.

The location was a coincidence, since none of the people in the building were connected with the GRU, although they would have readily admitted to the same nation-state loyalties. The structure was guarded by a mobile security team and counter-surveillance systems, and anyone trying to gain access from the street, the roof or up through the basement would encounter fierce preventative measures to stop them.

In an austere room on the fourth level, which was the only one in use, a woman and four men had gathered. An armed guard stood outside the door with orders to admit nobody for any reason save, perhaps, President Vladimir Vladimirovich Putin himself, should he be in the unlikely position of making a personal visit.

No personal phones or electronic devices were permitted inside the room, which the occupants were well aware of, and no obvious records were kept of the discussions here. It was known, not unsurprisingly and with an element of dark humour by those who used it, as the 'dead room'.

The security in and around the building might have been regarded by many as considerable, even excessive, for it had limited use. The few discussions that took place here formed no part of Russia's general political activities or duties; those involved were not serving government officials, military or security officers; and none of them would have been recognized as ever appearing in media exercises, political campaigns or puff pieces for consumption by the general public.

In short, the four men and one woman were, to all intents and purposes, faceless and nameless. The security was in place to ensure they remained that way.

'Further to our previous discussions, I am pleased to announce that our affirmative action against the American CIA is about to go live. We are even now waiting for news of a successful outcome.'

The speaker was a slim man in a plain but expensive suit and crisp, white shirt. Konstantin Basalayev had small hands, thinning hair and an air of restless energy that regularly caused those around him a degree of unease, mostly, he was aware, because he bore more than a passing resemblance to the President, Vladimir Putin. Not that he cared one way or another; unease among others, he'd found, especially those on his own level who were invariably looking for dominance and upward mobility, bred uncertainty and allowed exploitation of their weaknesses.

Right now his words, spoken in a soft voice, caused two of the other men, who had been talking quietly while waiting for the meeting to begin, to fall instantly silent. 'Affirmative action' in the context Basalayev was using meant something final. Terminal. No publicity, no record; another small and dirty detail for which they had been gathered together more than once before in the name of Mother Russia.

'And we have a specific target?' The only woman, who was sitting at the opposite end of the table, was the first to break the silence. Irina Kolodka was in her forties, with dark eyes and glossy hair, and a figure which had caused the men in the room to study her arrival with carefully concealed interest. But that was all they did. She was, they knew, out of bounds to all. Off limits to anyone who cared for their life, their career . . . and their balls.

Basalayev tilted his head to one side. It could have been yes or no, but that was his way of speaking, of retaining attention, of keeping his audience guessing. This time it was unequivocal. 'We do. His identity was revealed and communicated to us recently by Agent Seraphim in Washington.'

'Seraphim?' Anatoly Dolmatov, a former FSB officer, sounded surprised. 'Is that where the information came from? I thought she'd retired to America and become a filthy capitalist.'

The comment caused a brief ripple of ironic laughter. As they were all well aware, one could find almost as many capitalists within spitting distance of this room as could be found in any hectare of the US capital.

'She did. She was reminded of her duty and agreed to help.'

This time the laughter was nervous. They all knew it was so but it demonstrated a level of caution they each recognized as necessary in these dangerous times. Any appearance of doubt was a contagion to be avoided at all costs.

Basalayev did not join in, but studied each person in turn. They were all members of a small and exclusive group dealing with highly secretive plans and projects, while remaining outside the normal run of the Moscow elite. Each had long ago given up their public roles in security, military and strategic operations, and their responsibilities now went far deeper than any normal matters of state.

'As you know it was decided that the time had come to send a message to those who threaten us, who seek to interfere in our activities to bolster trade and influence around the world.'

'About time, too.' The woman again, showing just a hint of impatience when the silence stretched beyond several seconds. Kolodka was the only one in the room who could get away with it, and they all knew it – even the chairman. You didn't mess with those who were blessed by the hand of the president, as this woman was. Nobody quite knew the details of her relationship with Putin, nor how much of a blessing his hand had been, whether personal, physical, or even spiritual. And none dared ask. The conferred status had been there for a long time and nobody questioned it.

'Indeed. There have been many suggestions raised about building a co-ordinated plan of attack aimed at the Pentagon and other US agencies, to undermine their confidence and sow a level of discord among their field operations. For too long now they have been running free, causing problems in various theatres and allowing other states to think that we are too weak to respond effectively. This has led to certain elements of our security and intelligence apparatus appearing vulnerable . . . even, dare I say, incompetent. After today that view will no longer be allowed to continue.' He raised a hand as if to pound the table, then seemed to think better of it.

Murmurs of assent went round the table. Basalayev was referring to recent failures by the GRU and other agencies in conducting operations against foreign states to silence traitors and agitators. Until now it was not a subject anyone had cared to raise, the events too recent and sufficiently sensitive to render them closed for discussion. The taint of failure was regarded with horror simply because, as they were all old enough to remember, some things in the new modern Russia had barely changed from the old, and the consequences of failure were chilling to contemplate.

'So what exactly is the plan?' Sergey Grishin, a former general, bore the characteristically blunt manner of many former high-ranking military men. Although as wary as anyone of treading on sensitive toes, he was known to forget himself occasionally. But his intimate experience and knowledge of the Russian military world made him invaluable to the group.

Basalayev smiled, a hint of rare warmth where there was often none. 'I must apologize to you all; I have not been entirely open about the progress of events so far because I did not have sufficient confidence that the information we required would be forthcoming. But now, thanks to arrangements by Anatoly, here,' he nodded to Dolmatov, 'we can be sure that action is about to be taken against the US operative.'

Grishin's eyebrows lifted in surprise. He glanced at Dolmatov. 'I have a question. Taking action can mean only one thing, can it not?'

Dolmatov nodded. 'It does. So?'

'Won't that be met with repercussions?'

'Maybe.' Basalayev gave a cool smile. 'If so we will respond further in kind. The Americans will soon understand that we mean business.'

'But . . . that's madness.' If Grishin wished for a brief moment that he could have swallowed his tongue, it was too late to go back. He forged on. 'A shooting war between our agencies and the Americans benefits nobody. At least, that has always been the considered thinking – or have I got that wrong?'

There were nods from the others, all looking at Basalayev for confirmation but relieved it had not been they who had come even close to challenging such a radical decision.

Before he could speak, Kolodka murmured with just a hint of query, 'Just to clarify, this suggestion comes from the highest level . . . does it not?'

It was an oddly-toned question and in most meetings would have been innocuous. But the word *highest* carried a special ring to it. In most organizations it could have been applied to any corporate CEO or a similar rank; here and now there was only one person to whom it could apply: President Putin himself. Nobody wanted to utter the name, not even, it seemed, Kolodka, even though the men in the room were under no doubts about her role here, which was to discreetly remind them of what they all suspected, in case there was any doubt.

'The highest,' Basaleyev said. 'We have full budget approval for this operation and clean, unattributed operatives tasked and briefed, ready to go. In fact they are already in place and have their orders.'

'How clean?' A thin-faced man named Oleg Voronin, recently recruited to the group and a former senior officer with the Russian Spetsgruppa 'V' unit of counter-terrorism and special ops forces, sat forward.

'Unattached clean,' Dolmatov put in quietly. With unusually heavy brows, coal-black hair and the powerful hands of a lumberjack, which he had once been, he wore the air of a permanently morose man. He was accustomed to varying levels of operatives, from the fully integrated and retained officers, to former operatives now contractors, all the way down to foreign hirelings from allied states such as Bulgaria and Albania. 'Don't worry – none of this comes back to this office or to this city.'

'Let us hope not.' Basalayev allowed the words to sink in before sliding a single briefing sheet to each person, their individual or collective tasks clearly highlighted beneath a printed photo of a man. 'Not for dissemination outside this room, of course, but for information only. This is the target.'

Kolodka leaned forward and picked up her copy. She studied

the photograph closely and said, 'Why this person? What is so special about him?'

One or two of the men studied her for a moment, as if trying to decide whether this was another deliberate insert or a genuine question. She, after all, would not be expected to soil her hands with any actual work; that was down to each of the men. That thought alone was a reminder that if they failed, they stood to incur the greatest penalty.

Voronin murmured, 'He's an enemy of the state. What other reason do we need to take him out?' He grinned, showing impeccable teeth and waved an apology. 'Sorry. I'm a simple patriot. You will have to forgive my lack of subtlety in these matters.'

Basaleyev explained, 'This man was chosen from a handful of American operatives. He has been a thorn in our side for some time. Unfortunately, until recently we knew very little about him save for the photograph before you. What we do know is that he's a ghost, working for the Central Intelligence Agency, yet with no direct connections with that agency. They appear to value him highly, according to our information, calling on him for specific tasks where the security of their agents is required but a larger force would attract too much attention.' He gave a thin smile. 'He seems an ideal candidate to use as a lesson for them that we will not accept such activity any longer.'

'He's a contractor, in blunt terms,' said Dolmatov with a sneer. 'A freelancer working for money. But given a few hours, not for much longer.'

Grishin snorted. 'We have many of those, too, don't we – contract fighters? But will the Americans miss him? Shouldn't we be aiming at one of their own instead, to ram home the message?'

'We could,' Basaleyev agreed mildly. 'But the message we're sending is far more important: we will not accept further interference by this man or any other. Any questions?'

'Does this man have a name?' Kolodka asked, tapping the paper before her.

Basalayev nodded. 'Indeed he does. Thanks to Agent Seraphim in Washington and her diligence, we now know much more about him. His code name is Watchman and his real name is Portman. Marc Portman.'

# THREE

The shooter must have been on edge. He'd let loose with a volley on full auto, the echoes bouncing around the hillside like a vicious drumbeat. Only the first three or four shots came near me before heading off to who knew where. But that was enough. The rest of the magazine poured down the slope and away, the shells' energy spent on ploughing up a line of holes in the earth and rocks.

I was fine with that. I was still in one piece and my attacker had just told me he didn't know exactly where I was. Using the spray-and-pray technique in the hopes that he'd hit something or scare me into showing myself was an old trick I wasn't about to fall for.

Sorry, pal; been there and done that. Didn't work then, either.

I kept on going down the slope, skidding and sliding and picking up a painful rash of cuts and digs until I reached the lip of a deep gulley I'd spotted on the way up. I rolled into the bottom and shrugged off my day sack, turning it on its head. To the casual eye it looked like a standard piece of hiking equipment you'd see on a hundred backs all over the world. But this one had been remodelled for me to provide a handy extra in the shape of a hidden compartment in the base. It was accessed by a zipper underneath, and wouldn't have stood close examination, but so far I hadn't had to test it. I ripped open the concealment flap held in place by a Velcro strip and tugged at the zipper.

Inside was a pocket holding the Kahr and spare magazine. The gun was neither big nor accurate enough at distance to scare off my attacker, who was using a rifle. But I'd picked it because it was small enough to conceal and would allow me to dump it easily if I ran into government military personnel or a militant group road block. Right now I was wishing it had a sixteen-inch barrel, a thirty-two-shot mag and a rapid rate of fire so I could spray the hell out of the hillside above and scare the crap out of whoever seemed to want me dead.

I checked the magazine and clicked it quietly back into place, then closed the flap of the backpack and took the bottle of water from the main compartment. It was warm and tasted like mud but it would keep me going for now. Dehydration can be a killer in hot climes like Lebanon, especially in a combat situation where the body temperature can go up like a rocket. Powered by the stress of the situation it can creep up unnoticed, the dryness of the mouth dismissed as nothing more than par for the course and you can always catch a drink later. Fact is, sometimes that later never comes, and anyway drinking the water was also a distraction exercise while I assessed my situation and my next move. Then I lay still and waited, listening.

Any hunter who takes a shot at a moving target is automatically disadvantaged by being governed by two powerful factors. If they don't see a body go down, curiosity makes them desperate to know if they got a hit or not. It's the not knowing that can eat away at them, especially if there's no subsequent movement. You shoot and expect the target to fall. Simple as. If it keeps running you try again. But if you can't see it, you eventually have to go take a closer look. And that's a dangerous gamble. The target might only be winged yet capable of fighting back. What usually overrides the shooter's need for caution is the pride thing; pride in their own marksmanship and the struggle to accept that they just might have missed when they held all the cards; that in the seconds between focussing their aim, judging wind-speed, elevation and angles and controlling the desire to get the job done, letting go that final slow outward breath might have been a fraction too quick, dumping enough air and muscle control to induce a faint wobble. And a wobble means a miss.

The scuff of leather against rock was my first indication that the gunman had moved. Common enough anywhere else, out in the hills the sound was alien, an intrusion that had no place here. There followed several seconds of silence, during which I guessed the shooter was cursing his clumsiness, freezing where he stood but desperate to move. His problem now was that he was probably exposed; he'd come out from where he'd been lying in wait and was standing out there somewhere trying to locate me. I couldn't see him over the lip of the gulley, but sticking my head up was asking to get it blown off. I needed to get him to move again. But how?

Simple plays best. It always works in films, anyway. I grabbed a small rock and twisted my body enough to wind up and snap it down the slope and away to the side. It hit and bounced, disappearing from view, the sound carrying clearly in the warm air and sounding surprisingly to me like someone making a fast exit down the hill.

The shooter must have thought so, too.

The first shot was loud, and closer than I'd expected. Much closer. He must have followed me down the slope by chance, the sounds of his movements muffled by my ass-sliding progress across the ground to this gulley. Another shot followed, neither of them coming near me. He was tracking the sound of the rock's progress down the slope. And he was nervous.

I drew in a deep breath and got to my knees and peered over the lip of the gulley. The guy was standing no more than thirty feet away, his head turning to follow the barrel of his gun as he tracked the direction of the rock. He was tall, dressed in a camo jacket and tan pants, and looked fit and capable. The weapon, an M16, and the way he held himself told me he was military or ex-military. It still didn't tell me who he was and why he was trying to kill me, but it gave me an indication of what I was up against.

He must have heard me move. He froze for a split second, before trying to turn and react all in the same moment. It made conflicting demands on an already tense mind and body and slowed him down. Swinging a rifle barrel away from where you've convinced yourself there is a target and onto another one isn't as simple as it looks. It involves a combination of several motor skills, requiring balance, speed and fluidity, and quickness of the eye. This guy was quick, but he was off-balance, one foot lower than the other, his body leaning back to counter the angle of the slope. He also wasn't sure exactly where I was, only that I was somewhere close.

There was no time to say anything, no time to see if he had any kind of back-up, although I doubted that was the case, otherwise I'd have heard something. Shooters in pairs have to be able to communicate silently even if they're in close line-of-sight. Even then it's almost impossible to remain totally quiet in a hostile situation because each man is relying on knowing what the other is going to do, yet keyed up to ensure they don't make a mistake that could be fatal to either of them.

I squeezed the trigger three times in quick succession. Accuracy at thirty feet with a pistol is a tough call, and although I'd had a test-firing session in the gun-dealer's underground range before coming here, it hadn't been sufficient to get to know how well the weapon would handle in a stress situation. But I got lucky.

The shooter stumbled, whether from a hit or not I couldn't tell yet. I was already moving sideways away from his rifle barrel, lining him up for another three-round volley and making him work harder to pull it round. Then the barrel dropped. He looked confused and shook his head and his body seemed to shake. I clambered out of the gulley and gestured at him with the pistol to drop his weapon. He didn't respond so I repeated the signal. Then he simply let go of the gun and sank to the ground.

I circled round to come at him from above. If he was still viable he'd find it tough to grab his rifle, locate me and shoot from a prone position. I could hear his breathing, which sounded hoarse and laboured, but I wasn't taking anything for granted. Wounded humans are no different to wounded animals, and are often at their most unpredictable and dangerous.

His rifle had fallen to one side and I stepped over and nudged it away with my foot, watching his hands to check he wasn't holding a stand-by weapon. The rifle looked surprisingly clean with a just trace of grease on the stock and no dents or dings from battlefield use. That didn't mean he was a new army recruit but pointed towards it being a recent acquisition from God knew where. Maybe a Lebanese or Syrian armoury.

I wondered who he was. He looked local enough in colour and build, although he could have come from further afield. Maybe he was a hunter who'd caught a glimpse of me and mistaken me for something else. Or maybe he'd decided to upgrade his life's experience and go man-hunting instead. Whatever he was and why he'd shot at me, he'd paid a serious price.

I squatted down beside him and moved his head until he was looking at me. His eyes were flickering and unfocussed and he was trembling with shock. I pulled his camo jacket open to expose his chest and saw he had blood seeping freely from a hole just below the throat. It bubbled and popped, which wasn't a good sign.

I checked his pockets for ID and found a pack of cheap cigarettes and a plastic lighter, a few coins and some dried fruit wrapped in greaseproof paper. A hip holster beneath his jacket held a Browning Hi-Power nine millimetre, also clean and in good condition. I tossed that aside and continued searching. One of his breast pockets held a black-and-white snapshot of a man entering a door of what might have been a commercial building. I recognized it immediately and my blood ran cold.

The man in the photo was me.

# FOUR

'd seen an identical photo to the one the gunman was carrying a few years ago. Back then it had been found on a Russian security contractor in Ukraine. It was a surprise then and was no more welcome now. Lightning clearly did strike twice.

I'd told myself more than once that it was bound to happen some day; the bright light of exposure beaming down on me in spite of the efforts I'd made to stay in the shadows. The world was now so infested with cameras recording our every move, staying out of sight was no longer as simple as it had once been. Sooner or later your likeness will pop up somewhere, caught by accident or intent and filed automatically, to be twinned eventually by a facial recognition software system in a law enforcement or intelligence agency data bank.

But this was no twin; it was an original. I knew that because I recognized the place where it had been taken: it was outside a CIA front office in New York City and I'd been on the way in to meet Brian Callahan, one of their Clandestine Service Officers. The shot had been lifted from the agency's security cameras at the entrance and I hadn't known then how it had got out to a Russian security contractor in Ukraine. Fact was, I still didn't know.

I put it in my pocket. There would be time to think about it in detail later. For now I had to get out of here to a place of safety. But first it would help if the shooter told me who he was and who he worked for.

I was too late. When I looked down his eyes had gone slack and dull and there was no chest movement. I bent close to him. He'd stopped breathing. I debated covering him with stones but the predators in these hills would soon rip them away. It would also take too much time which was something I might not have. If the shooter had someone waiting for him, say a back-up staying with whatever transport had got him here, they'd eventually come looking when he didn't report in. I thought it odd that he didn't have a phone or a radio on him, but maybe he'd forgotten it or left it behind for safe keeping.

I used my phone to take a photo of the man's face. It wasn't a trophy but a potential means of identifying him and the people behind him. If he was an official assassin it was possible there might be a picture of him on the vast databases which western intelligence agencies spend millions of dollars and man-hours building and feeding. It was a big if, but if he was in there it would eventually show up. Then I got the hell out of there. I paused long enough to survey my surroundings, then jogged across the hill to the track where I'd left my car.

I scanned the area where I'd left it in the lee of a rocky outcrop at the side of the track and waited. I couldn't see any other vehicles but I wasn't about to go rushing out there and get my head blown off. Wherever the shooter had left his ride it was out of sight somewhere and I didn't have time to look for it.

I crossed the track to see if anybody had touched the Land Cruiser. There were no broken windows, which was a good sign, and when I peered beneath the chassis I couldn't see any little black-box type surprises. I'd taken the precaution of throwing a handful of dust on the door handles before leaving for my observation point, but they were untouched. I jumped in and closed the door carefully.

Just as I pushed the key in the ignition I caught movement out of the corner of my eye.

A man had stepped out from a depression in the rock wall.

He was busy zipping up his pants so I guessed he hadn't heard me arrive or spotted me. Nor, it seemed, if he'd heard the shooting, had he been concerned enough to go take a look.

I eased back in my seat and watched him, assessing my chances. I knew he wasn't here for the scenery because he had an AK-74 assault rifle hanging from his shoulder on a webbing sling. If he had a back-up weapon it was probably out of sight beneath his jacket. Like the other man he was dressed in a camo jacket and pants, two peas out of the same military-style pod.

There was no time to get out and hide, but being inside the car was no protection either. If he saw me and got the rifle into play, the bullets would punch holes through both door panels and out the other side. On the way they would rip off shards of metal and other debris to spray the inside of the car with shrapnel and put me out of action.

I bit down on my impatience to move and waited for him to get closer. He'd have to unsling the rifle to do anything, and providing he wasn't too far off I had a good chance of taking him by surprise. When I heard the crunch of grit beneath his boots getting closer I clicked the door open and stepped out. It had occurred to me as soon as I saw him that there might be a third man somewhere and I didn't want to use the gun in my pocket if I could avoid it. I also wanted to get him to talk and find out what was going on here and why the shooter was carrying my photo.

He had his head down surveying the ground for footprints, and I figured he hadn't expected me to be here but lying dead somewhere on the hillside. When he finally became aware of me and looked up it was with a stunned expression and a grunting noise of disbelief. As he stopped and threw his shoulder forward to dislodge his rifle ready to open fire, I pushed myself away from the Land Cruiser and charged across the space between us.

He was quick, but off the pace. The rifle came into his hands while I was five steps away. Two more and he was bringing it up. Another two and he was struggling with the sling caught between his hand and the trigger. It was about as much of a break I was going to get so I launched myself at him and brought him down with a full body slam. He hit the ground hard on his back but he kept on rolling, shouting something and trying to scrabble away. He hadn't let go of the rifle, which was a worry, so I followed him using my knees to drive myself forward, grabbing the rifle as I caught up with him.

He was tough and lean, and coiled beneath me like a snake, grunting furiously. He let go of the rifle as a lost cause and began chopping at me with short, sharp strikes, one after the other, bucking in an effort to throw me off. A strike to my head was followed by another to the side of my neck and another to my upper chest, all delivered in a desperate volley. Each contact carried sting and power and I realized that if I didn't neutralize this guy very quickly I was going to be in real trouble.

He changed his approach and snapped his elbow around against my head. I went to block it but it was a feint, and he reached instead for the inside of his jacket. When he brought it out he was holding a pistol, a companion piece to the Browning I'd found on the first man.

I grabbed it before he could pull the trigger and twisted it back on him. We stared at each other for a split second, then he spat in my face, desperately trying to push the muzzle towards me. Being on top I had the advantage of weight and leverage.

He struggled like crazy, kicking his heels into the ground and shaking his whole body in an effort to dislodge me. Then I gave it one last effort and pushed the gun into him, hoping he'd see sense and give in because this was only going to end badly for one of us. And I really didn't want to kill him.

But he didn't see it the same way. He scrabbled frantically for the gun, piling on the pressure with his other hand, and I felt it beginning to slip from my grasp as our hands and the weapon became slick with greasy sweat. I could also feel the strength in my hands and wrists ebbing away. I took in a deep breath and gave it one last try, knowing it was now or nothing.

He swore, long and loud, then there was a muffled shot between us and I felt the heat against my chest as the blast rippled out from the muzzle.

I rolled off him, tearing the gun out of his hand and getting to my knees, bringing it to bear and ready to shoot in case he was faking it. But there was no need. He was dead.

I sat back, dropping the gun. I was trembling with the aftershock of the fight and knowing the situation could have so easily gone the other way. But the bigger shock was the realization that the man lying there was Russian.

Or had been.

# FIVE

I searched the dead man's pockets. Hearing him swear so fluently in Russian had done away with any idea that he might have been an innocent local hunter. When your life is so close to the edge you might call for God or your mother, but the last thing you do is adopt a language that is not your own. And the spare magazine for the pistol discounted the hunter idea even further. Other than that he was a carbon copy of the first man: no ID, nothing personal, just the photo of me in his jacket pocket. Which was as personal for me, at least, as it could get.

I dragged the body across to the depression in the rock face where I'd seen him emerge. A wet squiggle in the dust of the ground showed where he'd urinated, and a loosely screwed-up ball of greasy paper holding the remains of a shawarma sandwich lay nearby. I rolled the body into the gap and left him there.

Instinct and experience told me the Browning Hi-Power might come in useful, so I picked it up and walked back to the Land Cruiser. I started the engine and hit the gas, keeping an eye out for other vehicles and following the land downhill. I had to force myself to slow down; I was shaking with after-shock from the fight and my breathing was painful where he'd caught me on the side of the neck with a solid knuckle strike. I desperately wanted to take a slug of water but I needed to put distance between us before I could think of stopping. Having already been wrong about there being another man I didn't want to be wrong again.

A quarter mile later I spotted a pickup parked in a gap between two giant boulders. It was a Nissan and looked dusty and inconsequential, a go-anywhere vehicle that would attract little attention in this country. I skidded to a stop and jumped out. This had to be their ride.

The doors were locked so I smashed a window, apologizing

to any innocent folk this might be offending. Inside I found a paper bag with more sandwiches, bottles of water . . . and a cellphone in the armrest-lockbox.

Hold the excitement. It was a dud, well-used and with no history or numbers. A burner for one-time use, probably stolen and stripped. But it had a full charge so I knew it had to belong to one of the two men. Who else but a kill team would carry around one of these and nothing else? If caught they'd be identified. The solution was, don't carry anything more than you have to and nothing personal that could be back-tracked to a home or employer address. More than ever it made me think the men hadn't been local military or security forces, otherwise why worry about being so secretive in a country where being military was all the clout you ever needed? Whatever ID they'd had must have been left somewhere while they were engaged in their mission.

I got back in my car and gave it fifteen miles at a steady clip before I considered pulling over. So far I hadn't seen any signs of being followed, but that didn't mean I was alone. I'd seen a handful of vehicles coming the other way, but they were mostly small family-size sedans along with a couple of ancient pick-up trucks and three motorbikes each carrying a single elderly male rider with a variety of bundles on the rear panniers. Farmers or traders going about their business. Life going on as normal. A couple of them waved but that was local good manners. I waved back and kept going.

I stopped in the shelter of a large sandstone formation and killed the engine, then got out and took a walk. The fight had been brutal and I felt a wave of dizziness sweep through me as various pains in my body began coming awake. A bruising fight is nothing like they portray on film. For one, you don't automatically get up again if someone hits you, and while the shock of hard contact might be delayed, it soon catches up with you.

My breathing had slowed down and I could feel the adrenalin rush leaving me, but it would be some time yet before I could draw a straight line on paper or take a drink from a wine glass without spilling it. When I felt better I got back in the car and dropped the window so I could hear if anybody happened along. It was time to report in.

My current assignment was on behalf of the CIA and Brian Callahan – the same Callahan I'd first met in New York. I'd worked for him a few times now and trusted him implicitly, which is rare in this business. When you work undercover in hostile situations long enough, even your own handlers can fall into the bracket of those not to be fully trusted until proven otherwise. Most of that suspicion is internal, a natural blow-back of seeing everyone out there as a potential enemy until proven otherwise.

Callahan had explained in his briefing that this Lebanese mission had been on the cards for a couple of months, but had been placed on hold waiting for various factors to be in place. One of those factors – the main one as it turned out – was for a US Defence Intelligence Agency source – an official in Lebanese security – to load some information on a memory stick and get it away from watchers at the Office for State Security so he could pass it to his DIA handler. His position didn't allow for transmission of data other than strictly on an in-house network share, otherwise he'd have been able to send it by email and I could have saved myself a job.

The trip, according to Callahan, was well worth the effort to get hold of the memory stick, which was believed to include internal reports containing the identity of agents in the military suspected of selling information to, among others, the CIA and DIA. Sister agencies aren't always keen on sharing agendas until they're forced to, but in this case the DIA handler on the ground had fallen ill and been evacuated out of the country. That had left his bosses in the embarrassing situation of having to ask CIA Langley for help.

I could only hazard a guess at how that had gone down; there would have been considerable embarrassment on one side and some quiet jubilation on the other. But whatever the feelings in each camp, it was rated as an intelligence coup worth going for, especially if it saved the lives of other assets working on our behalf. Whether Hezbollah or the government, if the names on the memory stick got out, their lives would be forfeit. And if there's one thing guaranteed to attract good and reliable assets it's the knowledge that they will be looked after if their position becomes compromised.

The volatile nature of the region and the strength of the security apparatus locally didn't allow for a team to come in, but with none of their own Special Activities Centre or Global Response Staff available at short notice, Langley had hired me to meet up with Tango and make the pick-up. The last-minute nature of things had left me with no time to set up anything more sophisticated, but that's often the way. Unfortunately, it now looked like the meeting wasn't going to happen after all. It was a harsh conclusion to draw but when the collector of information – in this case me – finds himself on the wrong end of a sniper's gun, it has to be recognized that the game is over.

I texted Callahan a skeleton report along with snapshots of the dead shooters and the photo I'd found on them. I suggested he get the CIA's research bodies to check the databases to see if they could identify the men from known Russian personnel. It was a long shot but worth a try. Find out who they were and we might get to know who'd sent them after me.

A reply came surprisingly quickly. It was short and to the point.

*Copy that. Assignment terminated. Tango no longer in play. Suggest pull out. Report when clear. Further instructions follow.*

I acknowledged receipt and shut down the phone. If Tango had been compromised then he was lost for good and there was nothing I or anyone else could do for him. If they'd had him for more than a few hours, he'd have been drained of everything they could get out of him by now, including details of our proposed rendezvous and why we were meeting. The worst-case scenario was that they also had the memory stick, in which case the names on it were toast. But Callahan would know that and would be trying to pull them out already.

In one way it might explain why a couple of shooters had been sent to get me, but what was unusual was the implied finality – and why Russian? Maybe they were mercenaries brought in to do a dirty job. If so they hadn't exactly been the cream of the crop.

There was also the matter of missed opportunity. Any counter-espionage service faced with an opportunity to intercept and capture a spy or, as in my case, a support asset, would prefer to do it with the person alive. Trophies were always useful as collateral and as a demonstration of how effective the security was in the region to anyone else tempted to come this way. To do that and in this kind of open terrain the usual reaction would be to send in as many personnel as they felt it needed to close down an intruder's exit route. What they wouldn't do was send out a couple of snipers. It made no sense. Having a suitably battered and chastened-looking live person to show to the world via internet feeds and video news channels was pure gold. And the possibility of an eventual swap for some agreed benefit further down the line was always worth exploiting; more so than a dead body, which could be written off as fake news. They did it, we did it, it was part of the business.

I heard my phone beep and checked the screen. It was a text from Callahan.

*Proceed with urgency to emergency location (follows). Local contact Hunt. Stay safe.*

I pulled into the side of the road and took a long drink of water and had a think. *With urgency* was an expression I could have done without, along with being urged to stay safe. Callahan was an old hand at controlling assets and agents in the field and wasn't given to showing the mothering gene. If he'd felt it necessary to tell me to stay safe it meant there was something serious in the wind.

Most operatives who work undercover have a natural aversion to being high-profiled. It's part of the job to stay in the background, presenting only their work persona to the outside world. The threat of exposure is not just an inconvenience; it's life-threatening. And having your face displayed for anyone to see was more than just a bummer. Knowing these two men had been given my photo and whereabouts – and quite possibly my real name – was a huge concern. How many others had the same photo and the same instructions, to take what is euphemistically referred to in some quarters as 'extreme prejudice'?

Minutes later I got another beep and received three separate, random words which on the surface meant nothing at all. But they soon would. I called up an app on my phone and fed in the three words. That brought me a map and a pin-point location. The map showed the town of Aarsal, marked with a pin, lying some thirty miles to the north-east of my position. Touching the pin brought up the three random words to confirm the specific location.

That made me uneasy. It put me closer to the Syrian border than I would have liked, but clearly it was the kick-off to an exit route that would get me out of here. Going back to the airport and hoping to get a ride out was no longer an option. Whoever had tried to have me killed would probably by now have decided that their men's non-reappearance was not a good sign and would be watching for me to make a run for it back the way I'd come in.

I studied the map. Getting to Aarsal wasn't a problem if you were a crow. Thirty miles was a joy-ride to a bird on the wing, high up where earthly forces didn't get in your way and all you had to look out for other than the next meal was an even bigger bird doing the same. But the roads here weren't straight and I would have to cross the mountains and enter the Beqaa Valley. I had no sense of what the state of the road was like but I had a good idea of what to expect if I ran into trouble with one of the militant groups prowling the area. The only thing I had going for me was that I had a lot of time to get there.

The RV point on the digital map was the grandly-named Mansion Café & Restaurant close to the centre of town on the Laboueh Road. I had to be there by eleven a.m. the next day, where I would be approached by the nominated local contact, Hunt, whoever he was.

As I drove off, I hoped there was no significance in the fact that a point shown close to the RV on my map appeared to be the local cemetery.

# SIX

After many years in the CIA, first as a field officer and latterly as a controller running officers and agents, Brian Callahan recognized a serious problem when he saw one. Having an asset under fire wasn't exactly new; it went with the job, although thankfully, it didn't happen as often as some people thought. But place a man or woman in a hostile territory and there was always a possibility of them running into trouble.

Yet this was different. Marc Portman was different. He'd had his share of hot contacts, although he'd always managed to deal with them and come out relatively unscathed. What was unusual was that he'd run into a problem not long after arriving in-country, and worse, in a location where trouble should not have been waiting. Furthermore, if Portman was correct and the shooters were Russian, that brought in a whole new dimension of trouble.

He reached for the phone and set about following protocol, which meant informing the tight circle of people who needed to know what had happened, and the action to be taken. Top of the list was Senior Assistant Director, Jason Sewell. Experienced in the field of espionage and high-risk operations, Sewell had been a popular choice for the post among field officers and support workers alike, and liked to cut through the interdepartmental bullshit that often got in the way of operational expediency.

Following Sewell's advice he contacted a handful of others, who all set about doing their bit to plan for recovering the situation in Lebanon and getting Portman out from the country as quickly and as smoothly as possible.

Last on the list was Lindsay Citera, one of his communications support staff. She had worked with Portman on some high-risk assignments and they had proved to be an effective team. She hadn't been available for his current job in Lebanon, but that would have to change; if there was a problem getting Portman to safety and working out what had happened, he'd need a comms officer he knew and trusted.

Citera arrived a couple of minutes later, and sat down in front of him. She was slim, neat, with honey-blonde hair cut in a bob, and the direct gaze of someone with great inner confidence. She'd fitted in amazingly well to the often claustrophobic and intense atmosphere of mission-led comms, proving herself adept at soaking up a high degree of concentrated effort dealing with the complexities of video, wire and screen while absorbing report details and feeding background research to officers and assets on the move.

'This is just a briefing at this stage,' he told her. 'I know you've been tied up recently on other work, but I want you to be ready in case you're needed at short notice.'

'Of course,' she said.

He explained in outline about Portman's latest mission and the problem he faced. He kept it simple, the specific details of what had happened unnecessary at this stage. The fact that Portman had to leave the area with his mission aborted was sufficient for now. Painting a lurid picture with all the details of the attack would only serve to cloud the issue and wouldn't help accomplish what was uppermost in his mind: getting their man out to an area of safety.

'What can I do to help, sir?' she asked when he stopped speaking.

He smiled. As he'd expected, there were no unnecessary questions at this stage, no fuss or panic; she was ready to go, just as he'd suspected she would be. The realization gave him some comfort. In the next few hours or days he was likely to be stretched more than usual, especially getting Portman out of the country as well as dealing with the who and why of what had happened and who was responsible.

At least having someone like Lindsay involved, possessed of a clear mind and a strong desire to succeed, would be key to getting it done well and done fast.

Lindsay listened carefully. She was experienced enough to know that mission-fail was always a possibility. Whether by accident of location or events, by design on the part of the opposition, or simply bad luck, it was an ever-present shadow over the seemingly simplest of assignments. If the worst happened, it required maximum effort to rescue the agent in danger.

In doing so they had to cover the agent's tracks out to prevent the opposition following a lead back up the line and rolling up handlers, controllers and any other assets or sources that might have been involved in the operation. She, like any others involved in this, would have to be on top of her game if called on.

But having Marc Portman at the centre of the problem added another dimension. She had worked with him before, always remotely but in a way that had brought a closeness unlike any other. Directing movements to someone in the field, especially someone in danger, couldn't always be done with complete detachment. Every word, every comment focussed down the line carried an element that was intensely close, as if sharing every footstep, every move and every threat.

But *snipers*? The word kept coming back to her with a chilling feel that made her neck itch. Theirs was not an either-or situation, she knew that much; they weren't sent out to take prisoners or ask questions; they did not move in the open, in suits and shirts; they worked in isolation, stalking their targets. They had a simple task with no second-guessing.

Snipers killed people; it was what they were trained for.

# SEVEN

sobel Hunt was feeling queasy. A mixture of heavy traffic fumes, choking dust, a nearby open sewer threatening to bubble over into the street with horrific consequences, all presented a perfect storm of horror; and that was without the pain in her leg following a one-sided kicking match with a frenzied male camel three days ago. She was heavily sedated with painkillers but they hadn't been created with the backstreets of Aarsal, in northern Lebanon, in mind, nor the demands of her employers, who had insisted she get up and out no matter what the cost in discomfort.

Still, it could have been worse; the fucking camel might easily have broken her leg or bitten her which, according to the local doctor who had treated her, could have caused a maxillo-facial injury, whatever the hell that was, leading to a fatal infection if not treated. She hadn't wanted to know the grim details; her leg was so painful she couldn't focus for more than a few seconds without feeling nauseous and just wanted to get out of there.

'It is quite common,' he'd continued gravely, his dark eyes serious, 'especially during the mating season. The wise thing to do is stay away from them and leave them to the tourists.' His gaze was steady. 'You, however, are not a tourist, I think.' The almost-question was one she'd heard before; it could be interpreted as anything from suspicion to plain curiosity.

She was careful about her answer. Most doctors were keen to tread the middle line in political and religious matters, but she was aware that some leaned more towards the ruling groups than others, if only to avoid being dragged into anything that might threaten their livelihoods.

'No,' she'd agreed, and left it at that. 'I'm not.'

She was, in fact an employee of Her Majesty's Foreign, Commonwealth & Development Office in London, although she didn't tell him that. Beneath that overriding official umbrella, she worked for MI6 as a field operative, using the cover of a worker for various aid agencies in the region. The position allowed her to move around gathering information on local politicians, police, military and tribal factions, while also offering logistical support for colleagues whenever needed. Any information she picked up was passed back to her employers in London, but thus far there had been no demand for logistical support.

But evidently all that had changed a few minutes ago with the receipt of a text message couched in innocuous terms about her Uncle William's need for an urgent visit. Decoded into plain language it was direct and unmistakable.

*Get out. Now.*

She made a brief phone call, then took a last look around the small office which had been her base for the past six months. She wondered what lucky soul would be the next occupant. It contained a desk, a bookcase, a little-used filing cabinet and a desktop computer holding a raft of harmless information and emails about aid budgets, storage depots, refugee numbers and various proposals and requests for food, medical supplies and emergency facilities. The factual information was real, but most of the communications were fictitious, composed and regularly updated by Isobel and her handlers back in London just on the off-chance the office might one day be raided.

Placing a brown paper bag in her rucksack, she locked the door, hoping that whoever came to clear out the few personal effects she'd left behind would send them on quickly, if they bothered at all. She brushed a hand over the plastic sign on the outside wall. It indicated to the casual gaze that the building housed the regional representative for Accor, short for Action Coordination International, a non-governmental agency working on behalf of numerous charitable and non-governmental organizations through the continent.

In reality Isobel was the sole employee and anyone contacting the listed telephone or email address would find themselves communicating with a cheerfully helpful operator whose job it was to promise help while offering nothing immediately save a call from their local representative. It was a useful circular kiss-chase system but was usually enough to put them off taking their enquiries any further.

Combined with the orders to leave with all haste, she had received an immediate follow-up instruction to scoop up an asset in difficulty – AID in insider-speak – and get them both to a safe-house ready for onward extraction. The fact that the asset was an American called Watchman was beside the point. These days nationality was no barrier to working for MI6, and her duty was to obey. In any case, after the camel incident she had become disenchanted with this posting so she wasn't about to argue.

She knew nothing about Watchman nor what he was doing here, and it wasn't her place to ask. That he'd probably got what his countrymen referred to as his ass in a sling was a risk they all took. All she had to do was meet him – she guessed the code name denoted his gender although these days that point was fairly moot – and get them both on the fast road out of town.

Not for the first time she reminded herself that she should have been more careful about what she wished for. Meeting up with clandestine operators, which she guessed Watchman must be, was always akin to playing with fire. She could hardly blame anyone but herself, as she had known full well what she was signing up for when she took this posting.

Three years ago she had been swept up in a personnel cull deemed 'surplus to requirements' and forced to leave her research and support role in MI6, where the most dangerous task each day was replacing the paper and toner cartridges in the office printers.

With no family, pets or interest in growing old gracefully, she had soon become bored to death and in need of some outside stimulus. Having said as much to a former Service colleague in a catch-up lunch, she had been surprised to be called in for an interview, then accepted and sent on a number of short but intensive training courses. Her age and appearance, it seemed, had suddenly been seen as an advantage by controllers in the Service.

'It has to be said, you don't fit the usual profile of a clandestine operative,' one of the field controllers who'd interviewed her had said, lifting a hand to count off points on his fingers. He had the lined, leathered face of someone who had spent too much time in the tropics or had worked in too many stressful situations over the years. But he had a nice voice and sounded kind. 'You're of mature years, you look like someone's favourite granny and you don't look as if you've ever seen a weapon or a covert camera, let along handled one.'

'Thank you, sir.' She'd taken it as a compliment while wondering when the signal to end the interview would come. Suddenly, faced with this warrior lookalike, the thought of going back to an uneventful life seemed an even worse option.

'I like to say it as I see it,' he'd replied simply. If he'd thought HR might haul him into a retraining session for such a derogatory, sexist and demeaning statement, he didn't look as if he cared much. Instead he gave Isobel a blank stare before allowing a hint of a smile to touch his lips. 'You should do fine. I'm told you have a reputation for getting things done and have requested something challenging. Frankly I can't decide whether the people who decided to use you in this role are geniuses or morons. Let's hope you'll prove them the former, shall we?'

And here she was, re-suited and re-booted, as one of her instructors at the training base on the south coast of England had said, and ready to go forth to her next posting to do whatever was needed in the name of freedom, democracy and the Crown.

She ignored her small car, parked in the shadow of the building she had just left, and scanned her surroundings before ducking into a narrow alleyway which cut through to the next street. She was pretty sure she wasn't being followed, but the local security police were not above making random checks just for the hell of it to annoy foreigners, even older individuals like herself, working on behalf of aid organizations in the region.

What they might think a woman of late middle years with a gammy leg might get up to was anyone's guess, but you had to give them points for optimism. The poor buggers probably weren't paid much and liked to enhance their earnings with the occasional bribe. But so far she'd been lucky not to encounter more than the odd tickle for the sake of appearances.

Waving down a passing cab, a dusty and battered Mercedes, she climbed into the rear and gave the driver directions. Alongside him sat an older woman in black, who might have been his mother, and who talked at him non-stop without acknowledging Isobel's presence.

It was hotter than usual in the car, and if the air-con was working it was merely stirring the warm air like invisible soup.

She was glad she'd decided to wear light clothes; anything heavier would have been unbearable. She'd had to leave her ordinary travel clothes behind, the bug-out order meaning just that: don't stop to pack, it will slow you down and they'll know you're leaving. Walk out as if you're going shopping and don't look back.

The 'they' could only mean the local security police or whoever had put eyes on her. She wasn't about to argue; she valued her safety more than a few items of personal effects and they could always be replaced.

After a few minutes the driver pulled up at a pedestrian-infested corner where another elderly woman was waiting with her arm out. Amid an impatient cacophony of horns from other drivers, the woman took her time clambering in alongside Isobel, but instead of a greeting, raised the volume by joining in the conversation up front. Isobel didn't mind; cab-sharing had been a surprise discovery during her first week here, and something she had got used to, especially when the late joiners managed to hop out leaving the white woman to pay the fare.

The controllers in London HQ would have regarded this shared space as a potential security breach, but here it proved a useful source of cover during her trips around the city. A single European woman in a cab might attract attention from the authorities; two, even three women of different nationalities and ethnicity were less likely to do so. The local sisterhood system, apparently, was in fine working order.

She settled back to see out the ride, aware that this was prob-ably the last time she would set eyes on these streets. Bugging out like this hadn't been on the cards but neither had meeting an unknown American in the coffee shop RV she had nominated when asked by London. It made her wonder why she was also being told to get out, and hoped they were unconnected. Maybe someone higher up the ladder had got the jitters and decided to clear out whatever personnel were in the area as a matter of caution.

A volley of car horns made her check the street behind. A black car with a whip aerial had forced its way into the line of cars and was holding station three vehicles back. As they slowed to turn a corner past a mosque she caught a glimpse of a familiar

face in the front passenger seat. It was a police sergeant from
the local station. Ali something-or-other, a man who seemed to
view all foreigners as enemies of the state.

She turned to face the front, and caught the eye of the cab
driver in the mirror. He gave the barest shake of his head, which
she took as a clear indication that he'd also spotted the police car
and that she should not do anything to arouse their suspicion.

She asked the driver to drop her off three blocks away from
the RV and walked a circular route, eyeing her back-trail and
stopping occasionally to pick up small items of shopping. The
police car stayed on her for several minutes, before peeling off
and disappearing at speed.

She continued as before, knowing that if she was under
surveillance it would help to give off the impression that the
last thing she was about to do was to go on the run.

As a European, even one of a certain age, she knew that she
was bound to be on somebody's watch list simply because that
was the way of the world here. Complaining about it or trying
to plead discrimination would get her nowhere, even from her
overtly friendly local police chief, whom she made sure she
bumped into occasionally to brief him on her aid-related work.
That revelation alone, while back in London for a briefing
session, had drawn a sharp intake of breath from Iain Jacobsen,
her young office-based deputy field controller.

'That's idiotically risky and against all the rules of the game,'
he reminded her sternly, like a headmaster talking to an errant
pupil. 'You do not approach the security authorities under any
circumstances because that instantly puts you under the
spotlight.'

Isobel had toyed idly with taking out one of the line of pens
from his top pocket and stabbing him in the eye, but common
sense had prevailed. Instead she'd reminded him tersely that
she had worked at this 'game' long enough to know the dangers,
unlike some fast-track university types she could mention, and
when was the last time he'd been out in the field? Jacobsen, an
MBA-wielding management moron with a love of computers
and a comfortable work environment, had quickly changed the
subject.

She spotted the RV up ahead on the left. The Mansion

Café and Restaurant served as a go-to spot for wanderers, aid workers and transients, and nobody paid much attention as long as you paid your bill and didn't break the furniture. Isobel had used it often and was on good terms with Hadid, the owner, who had a lengthy list of cousins providing all manner of useful services such as electrical work, plumbing, driving and building repairs at absurdly low prices, some of which she'd been forced to use to keep the building habitable. He also served the best coffee in the area and made sure nobody pestered the little white lady who was here to help people.

She had no idea what the American she was meeting looked like but had been assured he would be in place when she arrived. She hoped he wasn't going to be the kind of muscle-bound contractor type dressed in multi-pocketed sleeveless jackets who regularly breezed through the region on the kind of business that meant someone down the line was going to be suborned, threatened or hurt. It would be like having a warning beacon tied around her neck, suspicious by association.

She crossed the street, hopping on her good foot to avoid an ancient pick-up truck belching smoke and rattling like a tin shed in a high wind, and entered the café. The interior was cool and sombre after the bright sunlight outside, but after a couple of seconds her eyes had adjusted and she scanned the tables, taking in everybody at a glance. A couple of backpackers, probably German or Dutch, one or two elderly men, passing time with tiny cups of treacle-like coffee, and a single man at a small table near the rear door who didn't pay her any attention. She noted a slim backpack on the floor between his feet.

She flapped a hand towards Hadid who smiled back and nodded, and she walked across to the single man's table. She didn't wait to be invited but sat down with a sigh, dragging her injured leg out of the way where it would be safe from a chance encounter with a passing customer.

Before she could speak Hadid delivered two cups of coffee. As soon as he faded away she said softly, 'You're on time, Watchman. That's good. I get the impression there's a shit-storm heading your way.'

# EIGHT

I had the woman who walked through the door of the café pegged as a tourist who'd got herself separated from the rest of her fun-time pack. I'd seen a couple of such groups on the way in, looking oddly out of place and ill-at-ease, which they had every right to be, given the current unrest in the country. She was dressed in pale voluminous pants and a floaty top, with a thin gossamer scarf around her neck, and was carrying a large rucksack in one hand. I noticed she had a serious limp. The rucksack didn't quite gel with the tourist bit, but what did I know? Tourists crazy enough to come here were probably dumb enough to carry unreasonable amounts of baggage.

Compact and neat, I put her age at somewhere on the north side of fifty, although it was hard to tell. She had short, silky-looking white hair and was nicely made up in spite of the heat and dust. German or American, I guessed, and gave it twenty seconds before she realized that this was no tourist hang-out and hauled a sharp U-turn to scoot back to the rest of the herd before she got robbed or trafficked into white slavery.

I was wrong on all counts. She eyed the other customers for a second, completely ignoring me, which was its own signal, before flicking two fingers at the guy behind the counter. He smiled and nodded and got busy at the coffee machine while she walked across to my table and sat herself down with a sigh.

She arranged herself carefully, her rucksack giving off an ominous clunk as she placed it against the table leg. The barman drifted across in no time with two cups of coffee and placed them in front of us. When I looked at him he gave me a shrug as if to say, *I know, but the crazy lady ordered them so what can I say?*

Then she delivered her greeting and I wondered why I didn't believe in unicorns.

'You're on time, Watchman. That's good. I get the impression there's a shit-storm heading your way.'

It was surreal hearing the word 'shit-storm' come out of the mouth of a sweet-looking little lady of middle years who dressed like a schoolteacher from Florida but sounded more like an escapee from England's home counties. It was also reassuring in a weird kind of way, hearing the calm way she spoke. It told me she was no beginner in this kind of environment. Still, I wasn't about to accept her at face value. Not yet.

'Do I know you?' You have to be careful, even with a person in the right place at the right time and with the correct recognizer – in this case my code name. I added, 'Only, you might have to vacate that seat soon because my wife's on her way here and she's the seriously jealous type.'

She gave me a look of mild scorn. 'Don't worry – you're not my type,' she said, dumping a lot of sugar into her coffee. 'My name's Isobel Hunt and I'm on your side . . . and I bet you're not the marrying type. Robert Vale can vouch for me.' she leaned across and said, 'You know Robert, of course?'

'No.' I knew a Tom Vale, but I figured she was simply being careful. I was right.

'Sorry. Did I say Robert? I meant Tom. Slip of the tongue.' She gave me a wily smile. 'He said you'd be very cautious. So you should; this is a risky part of the world. What about Doug Tober? I'm told you saved his life. Nice work. I could carry on dropping names all day but it wouldn't be appropriate and we do have to be moving as soon as I've had my coffee.' She punctuated this by taking a healthy sip followed by a shiver of appreciation.

I let her drink and kept a weather eye on the front door and the street outside. The Vale I knew worked for Britain's MI6 or Secret Intelligence Service. Or had done; it had been a while since I'd last seen him. Tober was one of their heavies from a group called The Basement, the equivalent of the CIA Special Activities Division. Tober and his colleagues were employed to do any heavy lifting required when other options were limited or non-existent.

But I still wasn't convinced.

'Sorry, lady, but you've lost me.' I got ready to leave. Anywhere else it would be considered rude, but right here and now in hostile territory it would be standard practice. If in doubt, don't sit waiting for the hammer to fall; just get up and go. One thing you don't do when the odds are against you is outstay your welcome.

She gave me her sweet smile and pushed her cup away. 'My apologies. How about Callahan and Citera – will that do you?'

'How do you know Vale?' I relaxed. She was on the side of the angels, having just mentioned a handful of names of people I'd worked with and trusted. The last two were from the CIA in Langley, Virginia and too well covered to have come to the notice of any casual outsiders.

'I've worked with him on various projects. He rates you very highly.'

That made her MI6. 'You're a field worker?' I used the innocuous term in case anyone was listening. She looked nothing like an operative, but unassuming ladies like her have been able to walk below the radar forever. The Russians, French and Israelis use them successfully all the time. Besides, there was the age thing at play here and I was trying to be tactful. I'd come across a handful of women field operatives in my time, and they were all extremely good at what they did. There were also plenty of older agents and assets in this business, but they were usually background operatives and surveillance workers, chosen because they could fit in almost anywhere and had the skills to merge and disappear. Like this one.

'Not always. I started out in research.'

I looked at our surroundings. 'This doesn't seem much like research work.'

'It's not far off it but I won't bore you with the details. I was dumped a few years ago in a budget squeeze and I didn't have any high-tech skills to keep me on. I got fed up and asked them to take me back before I did something unpleasant to my irritating neighbours.' She shrugged. 'I must have timed it right; the grey element among us were suddenly found to have value and they nearly took my arm off.'

It was a story I'd heard before about former operatives, although rarely the bit about being taken back. Many active service personnel found returning to a 'normal' life difficult, especially adjusting to no specific daily routine and a lack of excitement. Add in the demands of skirting around what they'd been doing for the past however many years with friends and neighbours and you had a different kind of stress. Most either knuckled under or took contracting work in somewhere like Afghanistan or Iraq until they realized they'd pushed their own personal envelope a bit too much and went back home for good. Not all of them made it.

'Good for you,' I said.

'Thank you. I managed to convince them I still had something to offer. Or maybe because they're ludicrously overstretched at the moment they agreed to take me on.' She gave me a steely look. 'Are you surprised?'

Actually, I was only surprised she was telling me. You don't usually open up on a first meeting like this to a complete stranger. But I put it down to operational stress. Once the green light is given for any aspect of rapid movement in the field, especially with the clock ticking, it's easy to find comfort in talking to someone who shares the same background. 'Is the limp real?' I asked, changing the subject.

'It is. I had a shin-kicking contest with a camel. The camel won. But enough about me . . . let's get down to business. What did they tell you?'

'They?'

She puffed out her lips. 'Your boss in Langley. Callahan.'

'Not much. I got targeted while on a pick-up assignment and he ordered me to bug out and to meet you here.'

'You got blown? I'm surprised you're not locked up.' Her expression became faintly suspicious, as if I'd been walking around with 'SPY' printed on the back of my jacket and might now be a double. 'Hezbollah don't usually let anyone slip out of their sticky little fingers once they zero in on them.'

'It was more terminal than that. They weren't trying to catch me.' I made the sign of a pistol and she looked shocked.

'Gosh, that's a bit mean-spirited. What did you do to earn that?'

'As far as I know, nothing. I'd only just arrived in the country.' I decided to change the subject. 'What's it like here?'

'Everything's been fine until just recently. Just your common-or-garden level of harassment and threatening looks from anyone in a uniform and a few without. The natives are friendly enough, and being called terrorists by the international community doesn't seem to bother them. In fact I think they regarded it as a badge of honour. But when my government decided to freeze their assets it seems to have hit a sore point. Now I'm not so sure it's a good place to be.' She gave me a sideways look. 'So what happened with the shooter?'

'He retired.'

She let that one lie and checked her watch. As she did so I looked towards the entrance. I'd become aware of a change in the street noises outside; there was less voice chatter than when I'd first come in and the traffic had dropped to zero, which was unnatural. We were sitting in a market town where busy and noisy was a way of life. A couple of women pedestrians hurried past, heads down, and across the other side of the street a man stuck his head out of a pharmacy doorway, took a look both ways, then ducked back inside and slammed the door.

That wasn't good.

'Damn', said Isobel calmly. 'I was followed for a while this morning but I thought they'd given up. They'll have probably blocked the street at both ends.' She reached for her rucksack. 'Do you have a vehicle?'

'A couple of blocks away. Nothing I can't leave behind.' I'd got my rucksack tucked between my feet and anything I'd left in the Land Cruiser was disposable and free of makers' labels. When you're on your way out of a situation in a hurry you have to reckon on leaving behind more than you came with, as long as it doesn't compromise you or point to your origins. I knew I was clean.

'Good.' She lifted out what looked like a bottle in a paper bag, and placed it on the table. The clunk I'd heard as she sat down. She nodded towards the rear of the room, to one side of the bar. 'See that door? We're going to walk across and go straight through. There's a rear door opening onto an alleyway. Outside will be a small jeep. I'll drive because I know the town and the area out of here. Are you all right with that?'

The way she said it suggested I had little choice but that was fine by me. I'd come here for one rush job and there hadn't been much time to study this particular area in case of a quick exit. 'I'm good. What about the barman – you trust him?'

'Hadid? He's OK, I promise. It's his jeep. I called him earlier and said I had to take a trip out of town. Would you mind paying – and leaving a *really* generous tip?'

I nodded and we both stood up. Isobel grabbed the bottle and led the way out towards the rear. Hadid watched us all the way from the corner of his eye and gave the faintest of nods as we passed by, then turned to the coffee machine and hit the steam button, sending a cloud of vapour into the air and shouting what sounded like a string of cuss words to attract attention away from our exit.

Isobel placed the bottle behind the bar and I did the same with a handful of notes.

Seconds later we were walking down a passageway and out into a shadow-filled alleyway lined with garbage bins, wooden crates and a couple of small dogs having a fight. A dun-coloured Suzuki jeep stood outside and Isobel climbed behind the wheel, dumped the rucksack by her feet and started the engine. It clattered a bit but sounded fine to me. As long it was moving we were in with a chance.

'Are you all right to drive?' I asked, and nodded at her leg.

'The bloody animal kicked me, it didn't disembowel me. Hold onto your seat.' With that we took off down the alleyway towards an intersection at the far end. The dogs abandoned hostilities and scooted out of our way with casual ease.

'In case you're wondering, Hadid doesn't drink alcohol. But whisky is a commodity to be traded here and every now and then he needs to offer something to smooth the way past some nonsense or other. This is one of those times.'

I found myself breathing in as the door handles of the jeep seemed to skim the walls on either side, and prayed no innocent householder stepped out for a stroll. Isobel seemed perfectly relaxed, however, steering with ease and pounding the horn while humming a tune I didn't recognize.

'Is he likely to talk?' I shouted over the racket as the engine noise boomed back off the buildings. It was like being in a fairground ride from hell and I could see the end of the track coming up way too fast.

She shook her head. 'No. He hates the regime and everything they stand for. And I think he's got a crush on me, the dirty old bugger.' She grinned and continued to lean on the horn as, without slowing she charged out onto the main street at the intersection, narrowly missing a donkey pulling a cart with huge rubber tyres. She bounced us off a kerbstone before correcting and straightening our line of travel while I held on and hoped we didn't run into a roadblock.

# NINE

The atmosphere in the fourth-floor meeting room in Building No 3 in Moscow was different to previous days; it now held an aura that the attendees found uncomfortable. They had been summoned at short notice by an irate Konstantin Basalayev, his voice on the phone containing a level of chill that did not bode well. The fact that he had called them personally rather than using his secretary was an additional cause for concern. It suggested the group's chairman was using a cut-out approach to keep whatever was ailing him to a limited number of people.

The door opened and Basalayev seemed to seep into the room like a shadow. He ignored the customary greetings and stood by his chair, one hand in his jacket pocket. His expression was about as friendly as the statue of Lenin in Kaluzhskaya Garden Square. Another bad sign.

'I am unhappy to report,' he said heavily, his free hand showing the white of his knuckles as he gripped the leathered back of his chair, 'that the attempted disposal of the American CIA contractor, Portman, who was traced to Lebanon on a mission, was carried out by imbeciles. Not only were they unable to kill a man who would have had no warning they were there, but they were killed by him.' His gaze swung to fix sharply on Anatoly Dolmatov. 'Perhaps we could discuss that.'

The silence in the room became intense until the former FSB man cleared his throat. 'I was badly advised,' he stated bluntly, his heavy brows dipping like angry caterpillars. 'I requested former special forces personnel, which they were, but they were clearly not of the calibre required.' He lifted one strong hand off the table. 'I apologize and have already put checks in place to make sure we use better people. We will get Portman next time and are already following his progress.'

Nobody else spoke, glancing at Dolmatov as if determining

whether this might be the last time they saw him here as a member of the group.

Basalayev rapped the table with his knuckles, drawing all eyes towards him.

'Mistakes were made. I accept that. But we have learned a useful lesson from this failure. Portman is clearly capable and ruthless, and does not hesitate to fight fire with fire. It means we must be even more determined to deal with him as soon as the next opportunity presents itself.' The way his eyes zeroed in on Dolmatov told everyone that there would be only one more opportunity.

'That's if he hasn't gone underground,' said Oleg Voronin, the former Spetsgruppa 'V' officer. 'If he's as good as they seem to think he is he will be accustomed to using multiple legends and routes in and out. Can we deal with that?'

'Indeed we can. Luckily for us we have access to an inside source who can follow his progress during the exit transition of his current assignment and provide Seraphim with a location whenever we need it. Seraphim will pass that detail to us the moment she has it.'

'Inside source?' Irina Kolodka queried. She lifted an elegant eyebrow. 'You mean inside Langley?'

'I cannot confirm that, and in any case it does not matter where the source is. Suffice to say we are being given information that will allow us to complete this task satisfactorily.' He looked at his watch. 'In fact, I understand we may already have a new location for Portman. Is that not so, Grishin?'

The former general, who had been given the task of collating and verifying the information received from the source in Washington, nodded. 'Correct. Portman is still in Lebanon in the company of a woman. We haven't yet identified her, but that is not important. We have his new location in the Bekaa Valley in the north-east of the country.' He nodded towards Dolmatov, subtly and effectively placing him once more in the spotlight. 'I believe Anatoly's new team will shortly be setting off on the next stage of the mission.'

Dolmatov said nothing, but nodded.

'Good,' Basalayev said. 'Back to work, gentlemen . . . and lady.'

# TEN

'Where are we going?' I asked as Isobel swerved to avoid another donkey, this one loaded with giant bales of something wrapped in tarpaulin. The man walking alongside waved angrily at us and showed a line of black teeth in a deeply tanned face. Whether it was because we'd frightened his donkey or because he disapproved of women drivers I wasn't sure.

'There's a safe-house outside town. Why, do you have somewhere else you'd rather be?'

'The nearest international airport and a flight out would be top of my list. And I'd like to get there in one piece.'

She waved my concerns away with one hand and hooked a hard right turn down a narrow street, pounding on the horn to clear the way of pedestrians, kids and scavenging dogs.

'The only international airport of any note would be too dangerous. With the number of protests and the level of violence going on at the moment, all foreigners are being scrutinized carefully. Paranoia rules. Anyway, it isn't all about you, you know. I have to get out of here, too. Do you have a real name, by the way? I can't keep calling you Watchman; it makes you sound like one of those super-hero movie characters. You're not wearing Spandex under those clothes, are you?'

'Not this trip. It's Marc. With a cee.'

'Fine. Marc-with-a-cee. The other thing is, this my ride. So, as you Americans would say.'

'So?'

'So I get to call the shots.' She threw me an engaging smile which changed her face entirely, and I got the feeling she was enjoying herself acting out a little. 'Actually, that's not strictly true; it is mostly about you and I'm just hitching a lift on your coat-tails. But I do know the location of the safe-house so that's my main input to this trip. It won't be quick getting there, I can tell you that. It's not very far but the roads can be God-awful with traffic and we'll probably get held up or stopped more than once.'

'But once we do get there?'

'We wait for someone to pick us up. From there we'll be taken to a location where a plane will be waiting. At least, that's the plan.'

It sounded too simple and probably wasn't, but I'd heard worse plans and even worked on a few with less obvious signs of potential success. 'Good to know.' After a few minutes of silence I asked, 'I know why I'm getting out, but what's next for you?'

'Hell, I don't know. Orders is orders . . . and I think my time's up, anyway. It happens. All I can tell you is that my controller said to drop what I was doing and leave right now, today, and to pick you up on the way. I think we're both *persona non grata*, so that's the end of our stay here.'

'It happens.'

'Not to me it doesn't. A couple of others I know, in other locations, but that was a while back.' She gave me a look. 'My cover was as an agency for assisting aid efforts in the region. It worked, too, for a while. But I had a feeling it couldn't last. Hezbollah are so fucking suspicious of anyone and everyone, even little old ladies who get kicked by shitty camels.'

'What changed?' I nearly laughed at her choice of language, but held it in.

'The local security office kicked out a couple of small aid agencies recently for "suspicious activities not consistent with their stated aims", if you can believe that. They didn't grease the right palms is probably the real reason. I did but it clearly wasn't enough.' A short pause, then, 'What did you do wrong to get you under the gun?'

'I don't know. I came in under the radar and other than buying some supplies, I stayed out of everyone's way. Then I didn't.' I saw no need to tell her that the 'supplies' I'd bought included a gun and ammunition from a local armourer who did favours for the right kind of money. It had occurred to me briefly that he might have been the leak but that didn't fit.

Logistically there simply hadn't been time for him to contact anyone and get them on my tail because he didn't know where

I was headed. Ergo, not him and probably not his hawk-faced cousin the car dealer, either. But who?

'Well, sweetie,' she said philosophically in a truly terrible American accent, 'shit happens and nobody asks our permission. Ain't that the way?' She yanked on the wheel to dodge a car broken down at the side of the road outside a small supermarket and waved cheerfully to the owner who stood open-mouthed, spanner in hand and watched us go.

'The ordinary Lebanese civilians are a lovely people,' she continued, waving a hand in apology. 'Unfortunately they're under the hammer here on all sides, from the government, Hezbollah, terrorists, militants and the presence of Palestinian and Syrian refugees. You might as well throw in Hamas further south, I suppose. All that has knocked the country off-balance and there are regular protests in built-up areas and cities which bring everything to a stop but achieve very little. Aarsal looked calm enough just now but there's been a lot of violence there, too. Don't be surprised if we come across armed patrols and roadblocks.'

'Is that all?'

'No. There's violence all over this area of the Bekaa Valley. It's sporadic and unpredictable and sectarian as well as terrorist-fuelled. Foreigners are targets at any time where there isn't a heavy police or army presence, and sometimes when there is. They like to hit restaurants, cafés and markets, wherever they think they can score some shock value for whatever cause they espouse.' She shook her head. 'But you probably know that.'

I did. I'd been to other places with similar problems, like Somalia and the Gulf regions, where the sheer unpredictability was a part of daily life, something you had to expect and accept, otherwise you'd never go anywhere. Trying to factor in who might kill you next was an exercise in futility and fuel for paranoia.

As we drove I could sense the looming influence of Hezbollah everywhere, on every hoarding and telegraph pole, with flags or posters bearing the familiar AK-47 symbol on a red, green or yellow background, contrasting with political posters bearing unsmiling faces and slogans no doubt urging the populace to vote if they knew what was good for them. And everywhere there were signs that violence had passed this way like a bulldozer, with wrecks of vehicles and houses, of walls and infrastructure, and the collateral damage of blackened rubble lying everywhere. Yet all around, daily life seemed to go on, albeit at a pace unique to the local area.

Isobel pulled off the road at regular intervals. Once was to buy water and fruit, the other stops were at a filling station and other roadside pull-ins to allow other vehicles to go by. That and the crazy attitude of drivers on the road slowed our rate of progress but I wasn't about to argue; we had plenty of time and she knew the country better than I did. It also demonstrated that she believed in a reassuring level of caution.

At the town of Laboue we turned north onto the Baalbek–Qaa Highway. Once out of the town we could see the hills rolling away into the distance, patterned with the regular shapes of a farmed landscape which was Lebanon's agricultural heart. Settlements covered the slopes like a rash, the pale structures reflecting the sun and faintly misted under the heat rising from the parched earth.

'Don't be fooled by what you see,' Isobel said at one point, and nodded to the east where a hillside a couple of miles away was dotted with white and blue squares in neat rows. She pulled off the road into a make-shift truck stop, and we studied the far hillside. The mist hung over the scene, screening the fine detail of what lay there. The coloured squares might have been an agricultural layout but I had a feeling it was nothing of the sort. 'It looks almost peaceful, doesn't it?'

'I'm guessing it's not.'

'It's a Syrian refugee camp. One of many around here. They slip across the border through the mountains. Not all of them make it during the winter months. It's like a never-ending tide and it's taking a lot of the country's resources to deal with them.' She put the jeep into gear and moved out into the flow of traffic. 'And the sad thing is, even if they wanted to, there's precious little for them to go back to.'

It made my problems seem almost minor by comparison. At least I had a means of getting out of the country, which the refugees did not without considerable risk. As we continued north, passing more military trucks and local traffic, I saw other settlements and camps along the way, some with a solid building as a focal point, and clear signs of order in the layout.

'Aid agencies at work,' said Isobel, reading my mind. 'That one's new . . . *Médecins Sans Frontières*, I think. There are plenty more. MSF has the political muscle to resist getting pushed around too much, but even that's no guarantee.'

Moments later, as we rounded a hillside we ran into a roadblock.

# ELEVEN

Lindsay Citera was enjoying a late salad lunch in the CIA Langley comms section cafeteria when a tall, elegant woman approached her table, carrying a tray.

'Mind if I join you?' the newcomer asked, sliding effortlessly into a seat across from Lindsay, bringing with her hint of expensive perfume. Her tray held a bottle of water, a thin sandwich and an apple, the standard low-calorie lunch of figure-conscious champions.

Lindsay nodded and drank some apple juice. She didn't need to look around her to see that the cafeteria was quiet, with a lot of empty tables; maybe the woman needed company, although she doubted it.

Carly Ledhoffen was in her early forties, tall and willowy, with enviable legs and the kind of high-end dress sense that seemed to get her invited to all the 'right' parties, according to the sisterhood washroom cat-chat. Employed in the agency's Directorate of Support, she was reputed to have private family means and a cool apartment in Woodley Park, although nobody was sure where the family money came from. She was smart, with a bagful of degrees including law and mathematics, and had been around in the agency for a good while occupying a vague but clearly middle-management role. Like many other government organizations the CIA had a level of pecking-order snobbery, and 'Laid-often' as she was known down-river, was reputed to play it like a flute. Nobody had proof of anything to substantiate the nickname, but all agreed that she certainly had a talent for sucking up to people of influence. The fact that she rarely appeared to speak to anyone outside her own tight circle unless her work demanded – and certainly not to low-graders like Lindsay – made this approach unusual.

'It's Lindsay, right?' Ledhoffen uncapped her bottle of water and took a tiny sip, eyes flicking around at the adjacent tables, all unoccupied. When she looked back at Lindsay, her gaze was piercing. 'Comms section.'

'Citera. Correct,' Lindsay confirmed, and felt a ripple of nerves. She knew enough about the Directorate of Support to know they dealt with internal security among other things, and wondered if Ledhoffen had sought her out on some obscure kind of fishing trip. Why on earth would she be of interest to them . . . unless it was considered that she had stuffed up in some way?

'Uh-huh.' Ledhoffen smiled, showing surface warmth only, as if her facial muscles were merely activated as part of an auto-response mechanism required of the situation, colleague-to-colleague. Then she placed the bottle on the table and looked around, before leaning an inch or two closer as if they were long-time buddies.

'You've probably heard the news,' she said quietly, 'about an agency asset burned in Lebanon? There's quite a storm raging about it upstairs.' The way she flicked her eyes towards the ceiling, indicating the upper reaches of the organization, was meant to convey that she was, of course, privy to the kind of upper-management scuttlebutt not available to most others on the lower floors. 'I just wanted to check if there has been any talk about it down here.'

'I haven't heard any,' said Lindsay. 'I don't think I'm on the right wavelength for hearing that kind of detail anyway.' She felt the ripple increase in tempo, and wondered where this was leading. There were always stories circulating, even in this ultra-secret organization or maybe because of it. But she preferred not to be fed by the rumour-mill because that way lay the risk of being seen by senior personnel as indiscreet. And her job in the comms section demanded the highest level of discretion at all times.

'Really?' Ledhoffen looked surprised. 'How strange. I thought all ops division staff would be on top of the latest buzz, seeing as how you're all . . . well, pretty closely involved.'

'Only if it involves a team on an ongoing mission.' Lindsay wondered how much explaining she should do. Say too much and she could be accused of blabbing; say too little and someone might think she had something to hide. God, was she being paranoid? 'I've been busy in closed-comms sessions elsewhere,' she said, 'so I guess I'm out of the loop. Was it anyone we know?'

It wasn't a question she wanted to ask, in view of what Callahan had told her, but she figured it might look odd if she didn't show at least a modicum of interest. Without outlets and input gossips don't have anything to pass on.

Ledhoffen shrugged. 'I really shouldn't say.' She made the zipper gesture across her lips, a gesture Lindsay found oddly childish. Yet the way it was done in a slow, almost teasing motion would probably have some of the male officers around here swallowing their tongues. 'But the way I'm hearing it, it's not good news, although I don't have *all* the dirty details just yet.' Ledhoffen gave a ghost of a smile to indicate that she knew of course but really couldn't divulge anything at this point to anyone in the lower orders.

She was bluffing, Lindsay decided; trawling for details after she'd picked up a hint of something upstairs. She pushed her salad around her plate, her appetite gone and wary of being drawn into something. Cafeteria talk existed here as it did in any other work situation; it was even considered healthy amid such high-pressure personnel, as long as certain boundaries were observed. Curiosity was a natural trait and showing concern for a fellow worker was natural, even if they were unknown to you.

She took another sip of juice, trying to read in the older woman's face just how much she knew. 'Was it an asset or officer?' There was a difference; officers were insiders, assets were not. But both were valuable.

Ledhoffen didn't respond immediately, but picked at her sub, peeling back one half to reveal something pale and lifeless that might have been turkey or pork or a dead fish. She let it drop and reached instead for the apple, which she rolled around in her fingers. Lindsay wondered when she would come to the point.

Eventually Ledhoffen said, 'I hear it's an asset.'

Lindsay's heartbeat went up a notch but she kept her face blank. Was she referring to Marc Portman? Maybe, maybe not. Portman wasn't the only one out there; other agency sub-contractor missions were currently ongoing with assets whose activities she also helped monitor as and when needed.

'You really didn't know?' The touch of incredulity in Ledhoffen's voice was carefully controlled, but evident.

'How could I? Closed-comms means just that. The day before that was the same and in between I took breaks in the dorm downstairs.' Closed or restricted comms meant nobody came or went from a comms room while an operation was in progress unless to take a necessary sleep or meal break, both snatched within the building. This was to guard against loss of focus and continuity on the part of comms operators who had live personnel on the end of the line; personnel whose safety could be put at risk by a moment's inattention. It didn't stop there; there was often an outside support network involved with the potential to roll back up the line like dominoes falling. It was a brutal part of the work requiring absolute commitment but she enjoyed it. 'It's the first I've heard.'

'Holy shit.' The word was somehow devoid of vulgarity coming off Ledhoffen's lips, as if the rouged skin was Teflon-coated. 'Better forget I said anything, then. We don't want anyone coming after us for tittle-tattling, do we?'

With that she gave a wink and stood up, leaving her tray and walking out of the cafeteria without looking back, her sleek figure the focus of three people just entering, one set of eyes male and two female. Ledhoffen's gyrating ass, it seemed, inspired equal parts admiration and envy by both sexes.

What the hell, Lindsay thought. She was showboating. Had to be. But why come and dump the knowledge on me? She cleared away her tray, feeling faintly and inexplicably unsettled. Maybe Ledhoffen had been in need of a boost in personal morale, and had chosen Lindsay as the first pair of ears she'd seen to show off what she knew.

She walked back to the comms section with a feeling of unease – and she wasn't just thinking about Portman. There could be another, more sinister reason for the approach, although it had come across as a bit clumsy. Unless that was part of the technique: make it too smooth and it would fool nobody. What if the leggy security officer had been sent down to sow a wild seed, drop a snippet of gossip in the comm's ear, to test where it might lead? If the snippet became a flow around the building after speaking to Lindsay, it wouldn't take much to pinpoint the beginning of a line of indiscretion.

But why choose the comms section to run a test? Had there been a leak pinpointed in the department somewhere? Or had Ledhoffen been blowing smoke just for the hell of it to feed her own sense of self-importance?

She unlocked her office door and scooped up a pencil from the floor beneath her desk with a huff of irritation. She hated untidiness around her workstation and wondered how she'd missed it. Like her boss, Brian Callahan, a senior Clandestine Service Officer who spent most of his time at his desk running officers and assets rather than out in the field, she preferred everything tidy and controlled. She didn't have quite his level of what some people claimed was OCD but she'd learned early on here that distractions in the office could lead to an eye off the ball for those people outside; people like Portman who depended on maximum focus to complete their missions.

The screens and servers were all quiet, her latest assignment now over, and she just had to fill out a report to submit to Callahan, as part of the process of getting it signed off. She adjusted the position of her keyboard and tilted the monitor back a touch to its normal position.

A copy of a security memo lay in the centre of her desk, and she scanned it briefly before realizing she'd seen it already. She made a mental note to speak to the janitorial section to ask them not to touch stuff in here. Coming in on a rush job meant being able to use everything that was hers without having to resettle it first. Like jumping in her car and having to move the seat back into its slot, something she always had to do if one of her house-mates borrowed it for a date.

She'd discovered before that if anyone else used her work station while she was away or on vacation, they never left things as they'd found them. Instead there would be a mess of drawers churned over, coffee rings on the desk top, headphone wires tangled like spaghetti or screens left on when they were no longer in use. Damn, she better not start picking up their bad habits, otherwise Callahan might decide to get in someone matching his own levels of major-orderliness.

She picked up an A4 legal notepad on the corner of her desk. It wasn't a comms pad which had to be stripped of notes at the end of each day and locked in the safe in the corner of her office, but a plain paper pad she used for innocuous in-house tasks such as noting upcoming courses, times and dates, keeping on top of knowledge streams and job development programmes. Getting ahead in the agency meant not standing still, even if you didn't aspire to the upper echelons of the organization.

She opened the pad where the corner of a page was folded back and straightened it out. It was a blank page apart from a square doodle in one corner. Squares. She was always drawing squares, often with elaborate borders and containing words usually related to something on her mind. A roommate at college had noticed it and once said it was a classic demonstration of anxiety syndrome. Lindsay hadn't been able to fault her. Yes, she had anxiety issues like every other person on the planet, but nothing out of the ordinary. At least, she hadn't considered a desire for success in exams and course work at all unusual.

*Watchman.*

The word was written in the centre of this particular square.

Damn. How careless could she be? She ripped out the page and fed it into the shredder in the corner. A brief buzz and it was gone, reduced to a mini-confetti in the drum beneath, unreadable and beyond any attempt at reconstruction.

She felt a pulse throbbing in her temple, and told herself to get a grip. OK, that was a mistake, leaving a code name on a notepad ready for anyone to see. Especially that particular code name. She turned and scanned the rest of the small room. Was that all she'd left on show? God, she needed to get her head in order. The recent closed comms sessions had been demanding, but this wasn't the first time she'd done them, nor would it be the last.

She checked the desk drawers, telling herself she was letting her imagination get the better of her. A pencil on the floor was no biggy; it could have rolled off the desk as she was getting up to go to lunch and hit the carpet without a sound. And the pad was . . . well, yes, she'd been beyond careless doodling an operative's code name on it. She would have to mention it to Callahan, just in case. In case of what – in case someone had been in here and might report it? But who would that have been?

She paced the office, trying to steady her thoughts. She knew what was happening: she'd been in a position once before where someone – a senator in the all-powerful Intelligence Community – had come into her office and subsequently attempted to bully and threaten her for no other reason than to undermine the CIA. He hadn't succeeded, but it had been an unsettling experience that had left her feeling vulnerable.

She checked her watch. Twenty-eight minutes, give or take one. That was how long she'd been gone. Easily enough time for . . . and now she really was being paranoid. Is that what this place did to you in the end? A job involving endless smoke and mirrors, staring at screens and imagining all manner of scenarios going on in the big outside world, working like a rat in a science lab.

She left the room, locking it behind her and walked along the corridor to Callahan's office. He was just leaving and opened the door as she was about to knock.

'Sorry,' he said, stepping around her. 'Big meeting on.' He paused and smiled. 'Can it be quick?'

'No.' She shook her head, noting his sense of urgency. She desperately wanted to say that, no it couldn't wait, but decided not to. 'I'll catch you later.'

'Great.' He started to turn away, then paused. 'I've heard you did good work the last few days. Glad to hear it.'

'Thank you, sir.' She flushed at the compliment. 'It was a bit intense but interesting.'

'What's it been, ten-hour stretches at a time?'

She smiled. Callahan knew how long it was to the minute. 'Eight, actually.'

'Long enough. Go. I'll see you tomorrow.' With that he waved and was gone.

# TWELVE

C allahan hurried up two flights of stairs to a meeting he could have happily done without this late in the afternoon. He would have preferred going for a coffee somewhere well away from here and staring at the traffic for a couple of hours instead. Something mundane where he wouldn't have to think about life-or-death situations where an agent's existence might hang in the balance. He liked seeing the ordinary world going about its business, and a part of him wondered how easily he might find it to one day settle into a life of everyday domestic routine instead of the push-and-shove of intelligence work.

But duty called and, if what he'd heard earlier from Portman was true, this was no blow-in flash of panic, of the kind you got from an inexperienced agent in the field who'd sailed too close and carelessly to the wind, or who thought they'd been blown after spotting the same face twice or receiving a phone call followed by an immediate hang-up.

What had happened to Portman had been of the highest-level threat and would call for the same degree of reaction.

Not that Portman did panic. He didn't have ice in his veins, but Callahan was pretty sure that whatever flowed in them was permanently set at a low temperature and not easily disturbed.

He arrived at the nominated meeting room on the heels of a small group of other attendees who'd been summoned by Assistant Director Sewell. Sewell was already seated, he noted, as was his custom. He'd been around too long to waste everyone's time and they all knew it.

While the six other attendees arranged themselves in order of importance, Callahan arrowed in on a seat near the far end of the table, where the shrapnel of blame, if any was in the air, usually took a little longer to reach. Not that he felt it was likely here. He knew what the meeting was about, but it was too early to guess where it was headed. For now it was probably going to be listen a lot and say no more than you had to.

Sewell raised a hand and conversation died. He was a comfortable-looking man in his mid-fifties, with a genial smile and the watchful eyes of someone who had been around the block a few times and knew all the moves in this vast den of secrecy and intrigue. However, for a man of his rank to be here in person instead of on the other end of a video-conference line, Callahan figured it had the potential to be a real zinger.

'You all know each other, I guess,' said Sewell, his voice soft but with a core of authority, 'so I won't waste time on introductions except for,' he nodded at a woman to his immediate right, 'Carly Ledhoffen representing the security section of the Directorate of Support. Her head of section is unavailable so they've asked her to sit in on this.'

Ledhoffen responded with a cool smile at nobody in particular and said nothing.

Spartan in appearance, the room was devoid of windows, pictures or other adornments. Although there were none of the usual cluster of wires and electronic devices that dominated so many parts of this building, with telephones carrying direct links to certain strategic numbers, of listening and recording devices linked to other rooms where words and reactions would be transcribed, recorded and remembered for all time, it didn't mean they weren't there.

The CIA, like most other intelligence agencies, had long ago learned that words were weapons, as much used against itself as outside enemies, and if someone somewhere was going to trip over their feet and cause a major fuck-up of Titanic proportions, politically speaking, it was worth having a note of who said what and when.

Callahan knew each person present, with the exception of Ledhoffen. He'd seen her around the building but not to speak to. Other than that the group was the usual mix of representatives with expertise on a broad range of issues. Sewell would have chosen those he considered most relevant without making the attendance list too unwieldy. He lifted a hand to acknowledge their presence.

There was James Cardew from the Middle-East desk; George Jackson from the Defence Intelligence Agency; Fred Groll from the National Security Agency; Craig Breakman from Special

Activities and the only other woman, Gina Patel from Political Analysis.

Sewell looked down at a scratchpad in front of him and said, 'There are others who were unable to attend at short notice. They'll be informed in due course.'

Murmurs and nods around the table showed the gathering settling down and shifting into business mode.

'Brian,' said Sewell, 'perhaps you could give us a brief background on what happened?'

Callahan nodded and cleared his throat. He disliked this kind of verbal delivery; so much of what was said on the hoof could be taken out of context and used against you if someone had an axe to grind. Not that he expected that here, but you never knew. Give him a keyboard any day and he could have composed something informative, to the point and free of potential misunderstandings. He decided to keep it brief.

'This morning I received news from an asset code-named Watchman on the ground in Lebanon. An attempt was made on his life by a sniper. It was entirely unexpected, as was the discovery that the shooter was clean. He had no phone, no ID or any other documentation. What he did have, which raises serious questions about this matter, was a photo of Watchman himself.'

The mood in the room went still as the implications sank in.

'That wasn't all,' Callahan continued. 'There was a second man who he believes was a back-up. He was the same: clean with no ID. Watchman came across him while evacuating the area. He described both men as either serving or former military and armed with automatic weapons. The real kicker was that the second man swore at him in fluent Russian.'

Someone in the room muttered a quiet oath, echoed by feet shifting under the table as the implication of that sank in.

'Their vehicle was clean, apart from some rations and a used cellphone, probably a burner. No numbers or call history, no way of telling where it was from.' He barely lifted his hands off the table. 'That's all we have at the moment. I have photos of the two shooters and we're currently trying to identify them from our files.'

Cardew, a professorial individual in his fifties, with thick spectacles and thinning hair, was the first to speak. 'This Watchman,' he said, once he was sure Callahan had finished. 'Can I ask why he was there?'

Callahan nodded. 'He was tasked with collecting some information from a local DIA source, code-named Tango. A rendezvous had been agreed previously with the source's DIA handler, but the handler fell ill and had to be air-lifted to an isolation hospital on Cyprus. The DIA asked if we had anyone available to go in for them at very short notice. It was a simple collect-and-go assignment, the sort we engage in all the time. We were happy to oblige.' He paused and nodded at Jackson from the DIA. 'As a result of the attack we're both contacting a handful of other assets in the region to pull them out as a safety measure.'

'Isn't it unusual, sending in a substitution when dealing with a source?' said Groll.

Callahan passed the ball to Jackson, who said, 'It's not the way any of us likes to do things, that's true. Sources like to know who they're dealing with – and that works both ways. We had Tango's firm assurances that what he had was vitally important and needed getting out. Luckily for us you guys had someone near enough to give it a try.'

'And the asset was OK with that?' Breakman, from Special Activities, asked. 'It would have been risky for him.'

'It was,' said Callahan, 'but considered worthwhile. We've used him on several assignments before and he's very experienced in high-risk situations. He was operating alone and wouldn't have agreed if he thought the odds were stacked against him.'

'Is he local?'

'No.'

Breakman asked, 'How long had he been on the ground in-country?'

'About twenty hours. The assignment was estimated to take less than twenty-four, all going well.'

'So he hadn't been there long enough to have picked up tails, then,' Cardew surmised.

Callahan nodded. 'Correct. His end of the mission had been put together at very short notice. Tango had advised that he was

nervous about being under surveillance and insisted on a change
of RV for the handover.'

'Was this Tango person trustworthy?' asked Sewell. 'He
couldn't have been burned and turned or had a change of heart?'

Jackson interjected. 'We don't think so. He passed the code
tests we'd set him to make sure he wasn't being controlled or
coerced to communicate under duress. He was due to be pulled
out in the next few weeks and relocated with his family to a
place of safety so he had everything to lose by switching sides.
As for the asset, nobody was supposed to know he was there,
much less what he looked like.'

'Yet two shooters were waiting for him. And Russians at
that.' This from Breakman and the room went still again.

'Do we know when the photo carried by the attacker was
taken?' Groll, the NSA representative, was heavyset with dark,
wavy hair and an intense look. Callahan knew him for having
a keen eye for detail and an analytical approach to problems.

'We do. As far as I'm aware it's the only photo of Watchman
in existence. It was recorded by the security cameras at our
New York front office about four years ago.'

'What was he doing *there*?' Carly Ledhoffen hadn't said
anything so far, watching and listening as each person spoke.
She waved a hand laden with a gold bracelet and the emphasis
laid on the last word carried no small hint of surprise. 'And
don't we carry photos of all such external personnel? It could
have come from anywhere.'

'To answer your first question, he was there to be interviewed by me for an assignment – a short-term contract. As
for the second, it's not CIA practice to have a bragging wall
of contractors past or present for everyone to see.'

'So this person is an American? Does he have a name?'

'I can't reveal that,' Callahan replied, adding quickly as
Ledhoffen's mouth opened, 'nor his nationality.' His instincts
were against relaying any other information if he didn't have
to. It might come out sooner or later because there were others
on the code-circulation list, but that was down to others to
control.

'But he's a contractor?'

'Correct.'

'Ex-military?' She glanced towards Breakman with a faint hint of distaste as if classifying his kind as some sort of unwelcome outsider. The Special Activities officer scowled in return but said nothing.

'I think with the kind of work we ask him to do, that speaks for itself.'

She continued, 'If he's not a trained field operative, but gets around a lot, might he not have been spotted on his way there or when he arrived in-country?'

The question received a few nods around the table, but Callahan ignored them. It was a valid question but would lead the discussion nowhere fast. 'Your point being?'

'From the few I've seen these contractors tend to stand out in a normal crowd. Couldn't local security have read this Watchman for what he is, or maybe someone recognized him from some previous activity?'

Callahan was beaten to the punch by Sewell, who said firmly, 'Not this one. It was his first time in Lebanon. It's possible he might have been spotted by chance by someone from outside the country, but it's a long shot. The short time frame involved setting it up makes it very unlikely.'

'How so?'

'To spot him coming in, acquire a photo ID from whatever records were available, get a two-man team together and on his tail armed and ready to take him out all within twenty-four hours . . . that happens in films, not real life.'

Cardew leaned forward and added, 'Correct. And neither the Lebanese government nor Hezbollah, who are the real strength in the country, has the resources to do that. The worrying thing is this photo must have been accessed from our records. Can we find out when?'

'We already know the answer to that.' Callahan wasn't keen to add anything further for general discussion, but if what he knew came out later, there might be some questions asked about why he'd remained silent. 'That photo was originally found in the possession of a Russian security operative in Ukraine a few years ago. We believe it was sourced by someone with inside access, but we have no way of tracing that original source.'

'Let us move on, please,' said Sewell. 'Any further questions about where we go from here?'

Callahan closed his mouth, relieved to see that line of discussion shut down. He noticed the dark look Ledhoffen threw at him and decided to ignore her. The last thing he wanted to do was to get into a pissing contest on specifics with any of these people, especially one like Ledhoffen who was rumoured to have friends in high places. In any case she appeared to be less than well-informed about the kind of work they did out in the field, which might excuse her manner as a case of eagerness overcoming tact.

'Is there a political aspect tied to this . . . collection of information?' queried Gina Patel. She was a slim woman in her late twenties or early thirties and spoke softly with a faint accent.

'That's a good question,' Sewell interjected smoothly, no doubt also relieved at the change of direction. 'There's always the potential for a political angle in these events, but it doesn't seem likely this time . . . at least, I can't see one with the Russian angle.' He smiled in Patel's direction. 'But that's something I'd like you to monitor for us from here on in, Gina, in case anything should blow up.'

Callahan explained further, 'The source, Tango, was employed in a senior administrative role in the security police. But their system has cut-outs so that only preferred and senior rank officers get to report on a governmental level. It's how they get known and favoured when it comes to gaining key positions and promotions.'

'Was?' Ledhoffen again. 'You think Tango is dead, then?'

'We have to assume that, yes. Under the circumstances there's every likelihood he was intercepted. If true it would probably have been by Hezbollah's counter-intelligence unit. They're not known for treating people kindly, especially suspected traitors.'

'What about your contractor?' she shot back. 'What was his reaction when this happened?'

'He did as I ordered: he left the area immediately.'

'Without checking up on the source? That's cold.'

Breakman made a noise and shook his head, but a look from Sewell stopped him saying what he thought.

'I think,' Sewell said, raising a hand, 'there are two aspects here that we all have to be aware of. The first is to ascertain what happened to the source, Tango.' He looked at Callahan and Jackson. 'I take it you two have a way of doing that via someone on the ground?'

Jackson nodded. 'It's already underway. But they're not active service personnel so it will have to be low-level and may take time.'

'Same here,' Callahan said. 'If it was Hezbollah behind the shooting they tend not to broadcast the news until they're ready to use it. They prefer to hide their bodies unless they can use them.'

'Fine. Do what you can. The second aspect is more worrying for our whole community. Put simply, one of our experienced assets has found himself on somebody's kill list. With the kind of work he does that's not impossible but it is unusual. That means we all have to take note. This person operates alone and undercover so as not to get made by anyone – or, at least he hasn't until now. And nobody sends out two shooters each with a target's photo just on the off-chance they might stumble on him in the street. This has all the marks of a planned operation.'

'Does this kind of thing happen often?' asked Groll.

'Less than you might think, thank God,' Callahan replied. 'If it did we'd have a war on our hands, which is why we train everyone to be as effective as they can. If they sense they've been compromised they get out and we work on finding a replacement once the dust has settled.'

'So what,' asked Ledhoffen, a frown edging her eyes, 'is the agency's view on what happened to the two shooters?'

Callahan looked at her but said nothing. He wasn't sure if she was there solely to raise awkward questions or if it was another display of her inexperience. Whichever it was, it made him wonder what the point was and why she was being confrontational. He glanced at Sewell, but the senior man seemed unaffected by the exchange.

'Two nil to us is my guess,' growled Breakman, in the brief silence.

Ledhoffen bristled at that and said to Callahan, 'Are you not going to tell us?'

'I think we all know the answer to that, Ms Ledhoffen.'
Sewell sat back. He looked tired. 'Let's not pursue it further.'
He looked around the table. 'This was intended as a general
briefing only until more details emerge. My concern is that the
asset's presence in the country, planned at short notice, seems
to have been realized very quickly and acted upon. That's pretty
unusual. Needless to say we do not discuss this with anyone
else at this time. If you should come across anything further
which might add to the discussion, let me know.' He nodded
at Callahan, Cardew and Groll in turn. 'You three are our ears,
so if you come across any chatter going on out there, report it
to me for evaluation. Brian, I guess you'll be debriefing
Watchman as soon as he's out of there?' At Callahan's nod he
looked round and stood up. 'Thank you, folks.'

Callahan made his excuses and left the room as soon as he
could. On the way back to his office, it occurred to him with
a sense of uneasiness how events could come back to haunt
you long after first occurring. In this case it was the photo of
Marc Portman resurfacing.

The original person who'd instigated it was no longer
alive to talk about the how, and the person who had retrieved
it from the CIA system had vanished like mist. It was too late
to do anything about it except to think of a way of finding out
where it had come from on this occasion and who had punted
it into circulation with an active kill team.

One thing his instincts told him was that it hadn't been lying
around in a foreign security service archive, waiting to be used
again. Whoever had let it loose again had done so for a specific
purpose.

And therein, he thought, lay an oddity. In such a prime
nest of secrets and suspicions as Langley, where everything
and anything was fair game to be tabled at moments of forensic
foraging like the attempted assassination of an important
asset, nobody around the table just now had raised the most
unmentionable of all subjects.

Was there an active leak inside the CIA?

# THIRTEEN

We were on a stretch of road with no side turnings and no way of avoiding the roadblock. Going back would look too suspicious and the soldiers would be on us within minutes. Half a dozen armed soldiers in military fatigues were standing around a couple of olive-coloured Humvees parked across the centre of the road in a vee-formation.

They'd chosen a good spot; the road here was bordered by a wall of rock on one side and a steep drop into a dried-out river gulley – a wadi – on the other. If we tried to push our way through the narrow gap and misjudged it, this little Suzuki would ping off the heavier vehicles and we'd end up with our faces buried in the rock wall or lying upside down in the wadi being shot up by the soldier manning an FN MAG machine gun on one of the Humvees.

'They're not after us,' Isobel said calmly, and began to slow down. 'They're regular army. It's a security thing they have to do all the time. Are you carrying a weapon?'

'Yes.' I didn't tell her I actually had two because one was plenty enough to worry about in this situation. Anything more would be showing off.

'Better pray they don't decide to search us, then. Let me do the talking.'

We drew to a stop behind half a dozen other vehicles, a mix of trucks and small, battered sedans. The south-bound queue looked a lot longer, and a group of soldiers was clustered on the other side of the two Humvees checking documents and drivers. The men nearest to us didn't appear quite so busy but their body language showed they were on edge as they quickly checked the trucks in front of us and waved them on, spending a little more time on the cars.

Then it was our turn and the soldiers spread out around us with professional ease. I wondered what they were looking for. I guess we'd soon find out.

A man with three dark stripes on his uniform stepped up alongside and eyed the Suzuki carefully. He even gave one of the tyres a kick as if it might be up for sale. I put him in his forties, a career soldier and nobody's fool. The dark stripes made him a sergeant 1st class and I guessed this little exercise was his team's current assignment for the day.

Isobel wound down her window and said a soft hello in French. She received a half smile in return which almost reached his dark eyes. He replied in French and asked where we were going and what was our reason for being here. So far so calm.

'I'm a regional organizer for the UN aid missions here,' Isobel replied carefully, and produced a sheet of official looking paper. 'We're trying to monitor the refugee situation in this area, as agreed with your government through Prime Minister Saad Hariri.' She smiled and added, 'I realize, of course that he is no longer in charge, but I understand the new administration wishes for that agreement to continue. So do we.'

In true military fashion the sergeant didn't look impressed by the name-dropping. He was either allied to a different section of the various power groups in this country or he simply didn't give a damn because he had a job to do. He looked at me. 'And this man? Who is he?'

'He's my guard,' Isobel said, and waved a dismissive hand. 'I was advised by Major General Imad Osman of the police that I should travel with him because of the troubles.' She finished with a faint snort of derision which I took to signify that she had no need of a guard and that I was surplus to requirements but what could she do?

The sergeant sniffed and studied me for a moment. While he did that another soldier, an older man with the wizened toughness of a long-time veteran, wandered up to the rear of the Suzuki and peered in the rear window. He rubbed a hand on the dusty glass for a better view, and I was beginning to wonder if the chit-chat with his sergeant had been a ploy to put us off-guard.

I turned my head to see what he might be looking for and hoped there wasn't anything back there to make him go for his gun. Then my blood ran cold. Lying on the back seat where it had slid out from my bag was the spare magazine for the Hi-Power.

'American?' the sergeant asked me in English.

'Absolutely not,' I said, laying on a touch of outrage. '*Français.*' Luckily, I had a passport to back that up. But if the other man spotted the spare magazine no passport on earth was going to help us. I tapped Isobel on the leg and gestured to the rear, and she pretended to be adjusting her seat belt to have a quick look. She was quick on the uptake and with amazing coolness took the scarf from around her neck and tossed it into the back, covering the magazine.

'It's so hot,' she murmured to no-one in particular.

'Military?' The sergeant flicked his eyes to her, then back on me. I made sure to keep my hands in full view all the time.

'I was, a long time ago.' It was pointless denying it because who else but someone with military experience would be employed as a guard in this country? In any case, most three-stripers the world over can spot a former soldier at fifty paces. It's in the stance, the eyes and the body language, and almost impossible to eradicate completely.

'With?' Damn, he wasn't going to let this go. I glanced at Isobel, but she was calmly fanning her face as if this kind of delay was all in a day's work when you knew the country and nothing to worry about.

'The Legion.' I wasn't concerned about him being able to check it out because I knew the French Foreign Legion doesn't reveal that kind of information to outsiders.

'Really?' His face cracked with the beginnings of a grin. 'My uncle was with them for ten years. Which brigade were you with?'

'The best – the 13th Demi.' A bit of bragging between army units never goes amiss and it would come across to him as completely natural.

He pulled a mock-sympathetic face and said. 'No, sorry, my friend, but my *uncle* was in the best – the 2nd Foreign Parachute Brigade.'

'Then he has my profound respect. How are his knees?'

That made him laugh. He said, 'Not good. Too many jumps. He's still tough as leather but he walks like a duck.' He rattled off a translation for the benefit of his colleagues, who gave what I guessed were whoops of Lebanese one-upmanship. The

older man peering into the jeep turned and joined in, giving a
descending whistle noise while with his free hand he mimed
a high dive towards the ground, before turning and walking
away to much laughter from the other men.

The sergeant handed Isobel her authorization document and
said, 'Travel safely, *m'sieur*, *madame*. Be aware it is dangerous
to leave this road, especially towards the border. We cannot
help you if you do.' Then he stepped back and waved us on.
Isobel thanked him politely and edged us carefully past the
Humvees and we were through.

'The Foreign *Legion*?' She stared at me. 'That was one heck
of a bluff.'

'It wasn't.'

'Seriously? Why the hell did you join them? Were you on
the run?'

'It's a long story.' It was one I didn't want to go into, another
part of my life and long gone. Thankfully she didn't push me
on it and we sank into a long bout of silence, both relieved that
the roadblock had gone as well as it had. It took another ten
miles of silence before the tension began to evaporate.

Eventually Isobel slowed before turning right onto a rough,
rubble-strewn track climbing into the hills. There were no signs
so I guessed this wasn't going to end up at a decent four-star
hotel with room service and a pool. The jeep's suspension
creaked and groaned as we climbed, the wheels dipping into
crevices which couldn't be avoided, and I hoped it didn't give
out on us out of sheer fatigue. We were already beyond help
unless a friendly truck driver happened along.

'What are we supposed to do with this when we're done?'
I asked, nodding at the dashboard. My tip had been generous
as she'd asked, but not big enough to buy a replacement.

'We dump it,' Isobel said. 'Hadid has a side deal on used
cars and this one's not registered to him. If asked he'll say it
was stolen by militants. They're always on the lookout for
vehicles and run a trade in knock-offs to fund local
operations.'

The track wound around the side of the hill, and as we
climbed I spotted the top edge of a square structure standing
out against the surrounding sandstone. It must have been the

only building for miles and I wondered who had built such a place out here. It wasn't exactly on a major bus route, although there wouldn't be much of a problem with noisy neighbours.

'Is that it?' I asked. 'The safe-house?'

Isobel nodded. 'Home from home. It used to belong to a local government minister. He thought it would be a good place to establish a base for weekend hunting parties. Migrant bird hunting is a big thing around here. When he realized nobody else was interested because of the risks involved with the changing situation he abandoned the project. MI6 bought it through a middleman in case it ever came in handy. It's a bit obvious but nice and remote and it's only for one night. We get airlifted out in the morning.'

The track wound its way across a momentarily flat area, then lifted us up a steep gradient riddled with potholes and cracks that made the suspension of the jeep groan even louder. Two hundred yards later the scenery changed dramatically and Isobel swore and pulled to a stop, a vague ghost of trailing dust brushing past us in the air and momentarily shrouding us like a veil.

'Christ,' Isobel muttered and cut the engine. 'If I'd known the family was coming to stay I'd have dusted first.'

The side of the hill all around the house was a mass of makeshift shelters, weather-worn tents hung with washing, and campfires. And people. Hundreds of people. There were men, mostly old, but hugely outnumbered by women and children. A mist of dark grey smoke from the numerous fires drifted over the scene, eddying and swirling with the movement of the breeze and lending it the kind of surreal quality any Hollywood film-maker would have given their right arm to be able to emulate.

But you can't replicate that kind of scene. It was misery in the flesh, a setting right out of the news but with the added quality that only seeing it first-hand can bring, rather than through the lens of a television camera.

Neither of us spoke; it was all too sudden and shocking. I'd seen worse, but usually when I'd been expecting it. And even though I knew perfectly well what the refugee situation was like all over the Middle East, my guard had been let down while focussing on getting away from the men who'd tried to kill me.

Then the smoke at one end of the encampment shifted and swirled, like a curtain moving aside. It revealed among the flood of humanity three men in military uniform emerging from one tent and pushing into another. They were accompanied by several soldiers armed with automatic rifles, shoving aside anyone taking too long to move out of their way.

The people outside the tent could only comply and stare, their faces dull and empty of expression. Any instinctive protest at the invasion was no doubt suppressed for fear of drawing the attention of the soldiers when all they wanted to do was sink into this unwelcoming landscape and find somewhere to hide.

The soldiers reappeared and moved to the next tent, flanked by their guards. There was something about the way they were focussed which indicated they were looking for someone specific but I didn't think it was us. At least I hoped not.

When the three men came out this time they were bundling a man before them. He struggled to get free, but one of the armed soldiers clubbed him with the butt of his rifle and his comrades dragged the man away, pursued by a handful of women and children, all pleading with them to let him go.

When the scene was swallowed up by a denser curtain of smoke moving across I knew that was our signal to move. If they saw our vehicle they'd be down on us in force, our appearance in this remote place too unusual to ignore.

'Back up,' I said. 'But slowly.'

# FOURTEEN

sobel took her foot off the brake. The gradient did the rest, drawing us back soundlessly down the slope until we were out of sight of the encampment. With a quick spin of the wheel we were facing downwards and building up momentum until we reached the road, where Isobel hit the starter and turned right.

'I suppose we shouldn't be surprised,' she muttered. 'Why wouldn't they be here, poor buggers. The house is isolated, it's empty, it's shelter and they have nothing. No doubt the military will move them on eventually. I'd better inform London as soon as I can in case anyone else is thinking of using the house.'

'How often do they check it?'

'It's been on the books for years. They're supposed to get someone to call by every now and then, but I doubt they were able to do anything faced with all those people.' She changed gear and put her foot down, leaving a cloud of dust behind us. 'There's a space I know further on. It's not shelter as such but hopefully it'll be deserted.'

'Why do they keep the house on?'

'Who knows? It's probably a hangover from way back and they never got round to shutting it down. Our civil service is hooked on property-owning, even though it's not theirs. There are vast tracts of Britain owned by the government but not used for anything apart from lobbing missiles and shells at targets. Are you a property hound?'

'I am.' In fact I had three properties to my name, all city apartments in different capitals and little more than temporary bolt-holes-cum-investments. I spent little time in any of them and would turn them all in if the need arose and I had to disappear.

We drove for an hour, passing more columns of military traffic interspersed with motorbikes, mopeds and pickups. The troops gave us the eye as they swept by but made no move to

stop us. Eventually Isobel pulled off the road onto a narrow
track through a rocky outcrop surrounded by stunted olive trees
and dried grass. It didn't look as if much traffic came this
way and I guessed it was a deserted farm track leading
nowhere. Once in among the rocks she turned the car around
and cut off the engine.

'We need shut-eye,' she said, and slid her seat back. 'Can
you take first watch? The next stop is a couple of hours away.'

I took a short walk to keep myself awake and checked out
our surroundings. It wasn't scenic and the heat was hitting me
from both directions, weighing on my head and coming off the
ground like an open oven. After forty minutes I gave her a
nudge and we changed places.

It didn't last long enough, and I was jerked awake by her
hand on my arm.

'I think we've got company,' she said, and nodded through
the windscreen.

A dusty 4WD was trundling slowly towards us, disappearing
occasionally as it followed the winding track, the sun glancing
off the windscreen and obscuring the inside. Then it turned and
stopped, and three men climbed out.

They were dressed in dirty combat pants, plain shirts
and scruffy trainers and each carried an AK-47 assault rifle
swinging by their side. They were young, skinny and I put
their ages in their twenties. Thugs looking for trouble and
easy money.

'Bandits,' Isobel confirmed. 'They watch the road from up
on one of the slopes and hope to pick off anyone who looks
vulnerable.'

I checked the Hi-Power and the Kahr and handed the Kahr
to Isobel. She took it and checked it over. Whoever the men
were it didn't look good, but the more fire-power we could
show them the better. We had no way out of here except past
them and I doubted they were going to let us go with a smile
and a wave.

They strolled towards us with a swagger. They didn't look
particularly wary, but I put that down to inexperience or arro-
gance. They'd seen us go by and decided to try their luck. This
was their territory and they could do whatever they liked.

Anyway, what could two people in a little jeep do to stop them? To them we must have looked like easy prey.

I said, 'Lower your window. When I say, step out, use the door for cover and show them your gun. I'll do the same. If they look like shooting, shoot back.' I wasn't sure it would work but we didn't have any option. This was the brutal reality of a country where factional groups like this ruled in spite of the military presence because they had the weaponry and the ability to disappear into the countryside like smoke. They lived by their own rules simply because there were no others they respected.

I let them come on until they were less than fifty feet away. Anything further back and our handguns would be useless. I didn't know what kind of markswoman Isobel was, but the men were grouped close enough together on the narrow track to present a decent target for both of us if hell broke loose.

I said, 'Now,' and stepped out, kicking the door back on its hinges and settling my gun hand on the edge of the window frame. I aimed at the man in the centre because a flick either way would cover the other two.

They stopped, confused. Three surprised faces in a neat line as they saw the guns and realized they were out in the open with no easy way back. The man on the right of the group recovered first, shouting and swinging his rifle up. Isobel opened fire with the Kahr, letting off two shots. She missed him but hit the man in the middle, who skipped round with a scream and fell over, dropping his gun. I switched aim and centred on the first man as a hail of wild shots went over our heads and disappeared towards Syria. I fired three times, knocking him off his feet.

The man on the left decided not to join the party. Instead he dodged sideways and scurried into the rocks at the side of the track like a rabbit followed by more shots from Isobel's gun. I got the feeling she was annoyed.

'I'll go after him,' I said. 'Stay here and watch your back.'

I was taking a chance on the lesser of evils. If we drove down the track he'd be able to pick us off as we went by. What he wouldn't expect us to do was follow him into the maze of rocky outcrops where he'd have the advantage and lots of cover.

First I ran forward and checked both the men we'd shot. The

one in the centre was wounded, with blood oozing from a shoulder wound. His eyes were glassy and he was out of it. I checked him for secondary weapons but he was clean. The man who'd fired first was dead.

Instead of following number three into the rocks I ran further up the track until I reached higher ground. The air seemed thinner up here, although maybe that was the rush of adrenalin messing with my breathing. There was no sign of the gunman but with the extent of rocks and crevices he could be hiding anywhere. I slid into a gap between two massive outcrops and waited, listening.

A predator bird high up in the sky above me gave a lonely call, no doubt telling others that there were good pickings to be had down here and just to wait. I ignored it and stepped forward, feeling the heat coming off the rock and seeing a snake slithering away into a hole. I preferred not to think about snakes and stepped past it quickly.

There was a natural path here, with animal prints in the soft wind-blown surface. No man prints, though. I moved forward towards a bend in the path around an out-jutting rock the size of a house. Then I heard a scuff of noise from nearby. Someone wasn't accustomed to moving quietly.

I bent and picked up a piece of rock the size of a golf ball and tossed it ahead of me along the path. There was an immediate blast of shots, tearing up the ground and zinging off the rocks in a mad hailstorm of lead.

I gave a groan and waited. The feathered predator up top had fallen silent, maybe out of expectation or surprise. I wondered if the shooting could be heard from the road. If any military traffic came along and heard it, they might take it on themselves to venture up here. I hoped not. They wouldn't necessarily stop the gunman and would start asking us some serious questions about what we were doing here. That's if they didn't come in shooting in which case we'd all be losers.

There's a time for waiting and a time for precipitating action. I figured we'd been here long enough and had better get moving. As I stepped forward three paces I caught a glimpse of a shadow to my right. But it wasn't at my level. It was higher and looking down at me.

I spun round and dropped to the ground to reduce the target. The third man was standing on the rocks above me. He'd been casting around looking for me, and had just turned my way, bringing his rifle to bear on the path where I'd been standing.

He sprayed the area with a volley of shots, but the rifle barrel was too high and the shots ricocheted off the hard surfaces like angry hornets, one of them clipping my right leg. By the time he adjusted his aim it was too late. One shot and he went down, tumbling off his perch to land across the path in front of me.

I got to my feet and watched him. He wasn't dead and tried to get up, a patch of blood spreading across his side. I used my gun to motion him to stay down and he put up both hands to show he understood. I stepped closer and checked the wound. It had torn a groove in his side but it wasn't a life or death issue. He stared up at me with eyes like puddles of ink and I knew what he was thinking: this kind of situation went one of two ways. Either I was going to finish him off or let him go – and by his expression he wasn't an optimist.

I patted him down. His shirt pocket contained a pack of cigarettes, crumpled where he'd fall off the rock, and his pants pockets held a few small notes, a lighter and a driver's licence with another man's face.

But there was no photo of me, which was good.

Satisfied he wasn't about to jump me I checked where the stray shot had nicked my leg. It was a graze which stung rather than hurt but could have been a lot worse. I was still mobile. What was it in the Monty Python film – always look on the bright side?

I took the man's rifle and extracted the magazine, then threw the gun over one side of the rocks and the magazine over the other. If he got a second wind he'd have to go searching all over before he got to be a threat.

I motioned for him to stay where he was. He nodded compliance with what looked like cautious relief, so I walked back to the Suzuki where Isobel was sitting in the shade of the car. She was holding the gun but didn't look happy.

I said, 'Have you been hit?'

She took a while to acknowledge me, then shook her head.

I knelt down in front of her. She'd been crying, tear tracks
showing in the dust down her cheeks.

'What's wrong?'

She brushed away the tears and said, 'Sorry . . . I've never
done that before. Shot anyone, I mean.' Her voice was shaky
and she looked at me with wide eyes. 'I can't believe it.'

'Don't worry,' I said. 'It gets easier. Just try not to make a
habit of it.'

'But I missed! I mean, how could I do that? I could have
got us both killed.'

'You didn't. OK, you missed him but the other man got in
the way. Same outcome. It happens.' It was kinder than saying
her shooting was off. I eased the Kahr out of her hand and
placed it in the car. Shock does strange things to people
and doesn't always mix well with a loaded gun.

We drove on, Isobel insisting on driving to occupy her mind.
Having no focus other than reflecting on having just killed a
man – even someone who'd been trying to kill you – can lead
to a desperate downward spiral that does nobody any good. But
I didn't waste time trying to engage her in conversation. She
didn't need it and I had little to say that would help.

The evening was beginning to close in now and we saw few
signs of life off the road other than the occasional flicker of
house lights or camp fires or a plume of dust as a vehicle
followed a track across the side of a hill. I kept one eye on our
rear for signs of vehicles coming up fast but we seemed to have
the road to ourselves in this direction.

We passed a steady stream of pick-ups and small trucks going
the other way, and even a few military vehicles, but they showed
no interest in us. Isobel gave them a wide berth, which seemed
wise considering the way they held the centre-line of the road.

Not long after we passed a battered sign on our left to El
Hermel, she turned off the road and drove up another steep and
rugged track into an extensive grove of olive trees with a tiny
wooden hut. As we passed by I could see the door of the hut
hanging open but there was nobody inside.

The headlights cast a flurry of shadows among the branches
and down the twisted and gnarled trunks of the trees, creating
the impression of movement where there was none. With our

recent run-in with the three men behind us I had the Kahr out down by my feet, so I lifted it and got ready in case we ran into any opposition. In this deserted spot we might not get much warning of a roadblock even this late and I doubted it would be official.

We topped a rise between a collection of large rocks which looked like the end of the road. Isobel stopped and reversed into a deep gap before switching off the engine. The ticking as the metal cooled was the only sound, and even winding the window down offered just the sound of the breeze. The sky was huge, showing a vast array of stars, and I once more felt awed by the sheer size of the space above our heads.

'There's a flat area just down there,' she said, pointing back down towards the olive grove. 'Easy for a chopper to land. I'll give them the new coordinates and they'll pick us up before dawn.' With that she took out her cellphone and began tapping at the keys.

I didn't bother asking how she knew this. Isobel was becoming more of a revelation as time passed, a contrast to the image she presented to the world, and I wondered how much of her career and experience she had glossed over. Probably a great deal more than I would ever discover. She was a professional.

I climbed out of the jeep and did a quick recce of the area to make sure we weren't sharing this space with a unit of Hezbollah on night exercises. I moved carefully among the rocks, wary of stumbling down a hole, until I reached higher and more open ground with a good view across what I hoped was unoccupied rolling hills. Not that I could see much in the dark, but when light falls you have to rely on other senses.

I stood and tuned into the night, listening to various noises and discounting anything to worry about. Goats I recognized easily enough, along with the smell, but a host of other night-time sounds had me beat.

I returned to the car and found Isobel gone. I stayed close by, waiting. When she did appear it was like a ghost. She climbed in the car and opened a glove-box, and the small inside light revealed that she was holding a semi-automatic pistol.

'I did some training when they took me back,' she said quietly. 'Communications and surveillance – that sort of thing. One was a small arms course. They said I might need it for self-defence. I didn't want to do it but it was orders, so . . .'

'Good thing you did,' I said. 'For both of us.'

She smiled gratefully. 'I mentioned the course to my maiden aunt before coming out here. She's in her nineties and was in the WRNS – the woman's branch of the Royal Navy – during the war. She has a pithy sense of humour, as you'd expect. She said, "Just because I don't, doesn't mean I can't."'

'She's a wise lady,' I said. 'Did they do weapons training in the WRNS?'

'I think she was talking about sex, but I suppose the same rule applies.'

# FIFTEEN

She looked down at the gun as if seeing it for the first time and put it back. 'Sorry I wobbled. It's not the same when you do it for real, is it?'

'No. It's not.' I let it go. At least now I knew what else had clunked against the table leg back at the Mansion Café. It made me wonder what she'd have done if the soldiers back at the roadblock had insisted on searching the jeep. Probably sweet-talked them about being lost or maybe gone all nuclear and blown them away. She was turning into a bundle of surprises.

I walked away back up the slope a little to regain my night-vision and listen to the night. If anyone did turn up uninvited I didn't want to get caught out. It wasn't just myself I had to think about, either; Isobel was as much my responsibility as I was hers. It's what you do in the field – you watch each other's back.

A scrape of sound nearby me had me turning with the Kahr levelled and ready to shoot. Isobel was twenty yards away, her white clothing barely visible in what little ambient light there was. She didn't appear to be the least put out at having me pointing a gun at her head. She was carrying her rucksack.

'I cleared out what little food I thought would be useful,' she explained, and extracted what turned out to be a mixture of biscuits, dried fruit, local goats' cheese and bottles of water. 'I didn't see the point in letting everything go to waste.' She looked around. 'Everything quiet?'

'Nobody here but us. Not even any scorpions.'

We sat on the ground and ate. It was almost serene apart from the occasional bird call and the hiss of the breeze, and should have seemed intimate, an ordinary picnic, the kind of thing you do with family or friends – although here and now it was neither intimate nor ordinary.

'Why were you in Aarsal?' I asked, to break the silence. 'Seems a little out of the way of anything strategic.'

She nodded and flicked a piece of date stalk away. 'I know. Some bright spark analyst deep in the bowels of SIS with a bunch of university degrees and zero experience on the ground decided that monitoring an area so near the Syrian border would provide useful information on the movements of cross-border insurgents, refugees and government forces.'

'And has it?'

'Hell, no. I've seen graveyards with more excitement. Maybe that's why they decided to pull me out – that and budget constraints.' She gave me an oblique look. 'My orders referred to you as an asset. From the way Vale spoke of you, I'm guessing you're not on the US government's regular payroll.'

I shook my head. 'It's been a long time since I was on anybody's regular payroll.'

The truth was I preferred being free to take work or reject it. It meant I wasn't bound by someone else's idea of duty or their desire to score points on a promotions ladder. I didn't turn down many assignments unless I was already tied up on something else, but the time would surely come when it would be wiser to step back from a job that I could see promised no chance of a good outcome. Analysts with bright ideas and no field experience existed in both Washington and London, and were to be viewed with caution.

After we'd finished eating Isobel held up her phone and announced it was time to contact her controller for information. I had to do the same, and after checking our location, texted the three-word locator to Callahan and signed off. If he wanted to talk he would get back to me, but there was no reason to waste air time unless it was important.

With that done I made my way further up the slope for a hundred yards or so and sat on the ground in the lee of a large boulder, from where I could watch the area towards the track and beyond. I was looking for a hint of dust; even in poor light it carried a faint luminescence and would be the first sign in this kind of landscape of anyone approaching. But aside from the faintest sighing of a breeze sweeping the area and a couple of birds passing overhead, I was alone.

I hadn't asked Isobel how exactly we were going to exit the

area, but I guess I'd know soon enough once she received confirmation from whoever was running this op. If Callahan was in on the strategy I figured he'd have a close eye on things, but I had no doubts that SIS's involvement would run smoothly enough. They had years of experience running personnel around the Middle East, and they'd know all the wrinkles. For now it was sit and wait and watch the horizon.

After a while I began to pick up a distant droning sound off to the east. Was that a helicopter or a ground-based vehicle? It was too faint to tell. I couldn't see any lights but there was a lot of dead ground out there with hills to blank them out. If trouble was coming it could be ten miles off or just over the next piece of mountainside. Night-time plays havoc with sound, spreading it like jam on bread. You know a sound is there but precision is not an option until the source gets closer and identifiable.

Leave it too late and it could be right on top of you before you know it.

I heard another noise, this one much closer among the trees. Somebody was moving, the soft scrape of a careless footfall, a foot nudging a rock, a shuffling sound cut off suddenly by a hiss. I eased off the safety and waited. If the person knew we were here they had an advantage. The question was, how many were out there and were we already surrounded?

Then a figure appeared out of the blackness walking across my front about eighty yards off but not looking my way. I had the gun up ready to squeeze off a couple of shots when I hesitated. Whoever it was had come dressed in sombre clothing, the detail almost swallowed up by the night, yet pale enough to show a vague outline.

Not military, that was all I could tell. But not every military force in this area dressed the part. The man was carrying something out in front of him – was that a rifle, pointing at the ground? I lifted the gun again, ready to take him out if he turned my way. But he didn't. He just continued moving, something about his gait telling me it was a man, tall and rangy, floating steadily across the ground as if he were on wheels, but careful of where he was treading.

Then I realized the rifle was actually a heavy stick, and he was probing the path in front of him, testing for holes and obstacles. He was followed closely by another figure and another, a line of similar shapes, all treading in his footsteps. But these later ones moved differently, and I realized they were mostly women, some with smaller ones that had to be children.

Nobody spoke, nobody looked our way. Some of the female shapes carried small bundles slung across their fronts and I guessed these were babies. But they made no sound, either, silenced by some deep-seated instinct for survival. It was like watching a silent tableaux of spirits walking by, there but somehow disconnected from the world Isobel and I were in; the living passing from one world into the next.

They moved on what was plainly a predetermined path, treading with care as if stepping through a minefield, yet unable to alter course because they'd consigned their fate to whichever god they favoured and the man out front.

The line finally began to thin out and ended with a short gap and an elderly figure scurrying along to keep up, turning occasionally to look behind, the nominated back-marker with the unenviable task of making sure he spotted trouble before it came rampaging out of the gloom to engulf them.

'You've not seen this before?' Isobel had moved silently up the hill to join me, wary of spooking the people in the trees.

'Plenty. But not like this, at night.'

'They're Syrians. They'll have crossed the border just east of here, guided by smugglers. The man in the lead will take them only so far, then tell them to keep going west before ducking out and leaving them to their own devices. We should get back to the car in case they're spotted by the border patrols. That many people will be leaving a big heat signature.'

We slipped away and moved back down the slope to the car, and sat down to wait for daylight and keep our eyes and ears open.

# SIXTEEN

We were woken before first light by the roar of large engines passing close overhead. It had grown too cold to stay outside during the night so we'd climbed into the jeep and settled down for a restless sleep on the Suzuki's utilitarian seats. It wasn't the best place from which to keep watch, but we hadn't got much choice.

The helicopter was moving slightly north of our position, its downdraft fanning the foliage of the olive trees and kicking up a swirl of dust and dried leaves from the ground. I figured it was down to a couple of hundred feet, but not quite close enough to leave us exposed. But that could change in an instant if he took a chance on coming any lower.

I peered up and for a moment saw the vague silhouette of what looked like an Agusta against the sky. I didn't like the look of that; the local forces had Agusta machines along with a few other models, and a beast that size wasn't something you hired by the day if you were on a private hunting trip.

As it moved towards the upper slopes I wondered if it was carrying border guards searching for the group of ghostly individuals who'd passed us during the night. If so I felt sorry for them; they'd come so far and were now about to be corralled and herded into a camp somewhere before being processed, their journey cut short and their future even more uncertain.

Then the Agusta dipped its nose and slowed to a hover, setting up a dust storm further up the slope. There were trees all around and I wondered what they were doing. I soon had my answer: coils of ropes dropped to the ground from the fuselage, followed by black figures rappelling down. Their silhouettes were etched momentarily against the sky along with the assault rifles on their backs, and the speed with which they moved showed this was no first-time thing or a training exercise. The pilot had all along been scouting a clear location where he could drop the men.

Just to be sure, I said, 'Did your people say what they were sending to pull us out?' I had to shout because of the engine noise, but I knew they would never hear me. I was sure Isobel's people wouldn't send anything so large or obvious, especially in this region. Exfils or extractions in hostile areas are supposed to be as unobtrusive as you can make them and often carried out at speed and with the ability to drop out of sight if necessary. Sending in what amounted to a gunship was altogether too big a toy to join the party and would eventually draw the attention of someone who was paid to do something about it.

Isobel shook her head. 'Nothing that big. A scout, maybe, like a Gazelle. It's billed as an aid mission flight – and that's definitely not it.'

It was all I needed to know. If it wasn't our ride it had to be Lebanese government forces, Hezbollah . . . or someone else in the region with some muscle and the freedom to go wherever they pleased and frighten the neighbours.

'Come on – let's go,' I said. We grabbed our bags and moved down the slope among the trees. I immediately felt exposed, which was always the case when under the spotlight of an air search, and hoped that the pilot and men who'd rappelled to the ground were looking the other way.

Whichever. If they were searching for us, how the hell had they got onto our location? And what did they want?

That thought was made violently redundant as a long volley of gunfire lit up the area behind us like a firework display, adding to the clatter of the helicopter's engines to further shatter the early dawn. I risked a quick glance back. The flashes of gunfire were coming from all around the area where we had been sitting moments ago. The attackers weren't taking any chances and were going in full bore, a scorched earth approach to get the job done and dusted.

The battering of the combined assault seemed to shake the ground and trees and any birds that hadn't already flown out of their roosts took off and looped frantically away to the south, while rabbits and other ground-based mammals ran frantically from almost under our feet in a desperate attempt to get away.

Trying to run in half-light among trees with low branches and over rough ground is not easy. Especially with thoughts that those following you might be using night-vision glasses or thermal imaging equipment to pick up heat sources. I had no idea what the helicopter might be equipped with, but instinct told me that if they were using machine guns they probably had some high-tech equipment on board as well. Staying where we were would not end well.

I ran alongside Isobel, who moved with surprising ease to begin with. But she quickly began to flag after stumbling two or three times over hollows in the ground and half-buried tree roots. I grabbed her bag so she could focus on keeping her balance, and we made good progress down the slope towards where she had indicated we would be picked up.

Eventually, as I knew we would, we reached the edge of the olive grove and the track we'd followed up here. We were forced to stop. Moving out of here now would be suicidal.

I turned and looked north. The gunfire had ceased and the helicopter had disappeared from sight behind the trees, reducing the engine to a muffled roar. My guess was they were putting down more men to see the results of the shooting and conduct a ground search if they didn't like the results.

'I don't get it,' Isobel gasped, out of breath. She was crouched down on one knee, a hand on her chest as she tried to draw in her breath in great whooping gasps. Eventually she coughed and got back to normal. 'How did they get here? And who the hell are they?'

'Beats me. Can you get in touch with your controller? If our ride arrives now they'll be in trouble.' I didn't like to think of what would happen, but instinct told me that if the people in the Agusta were happy to drill the local countryside with machine-gun fire, they wouldn't think twice about taking out anyone they considered a threat, including another helicopter intruding on their party. Shoot first, ask questions later was a common maxim in this part of the world.

Isobel dialled up and waited, then asked the question, explaining in the briefest terms what our problem was. I didn't hear the other side of the conversation but it didn't sound good, and she closed the connection and looked at me.

'We're too late to stop them,' she said. 'Our ride is already on his way in from the west. They'll try to warn him but radio

contact is patchy.' She pointed down the slope to an area
the size of a small football pitch surround by a few olive trees.
'We need to be down there otherwise he'll never see us among
these trees.'

And coming up here to find us would be too risky. I hoped
the pilot had balls because if he spotted the Agusta or his
controller got through to him to let him know the dangers, he'd
need them. We couldn't wait here, that much was obvious. But
getting down to the area Isobel had pointed out was across open
ground with virtually nil cover, and for us, just as dangerous.

A muffled explosion came from up the slope behind us. Right
where we'd left the Suzuki. It wouldn't take much searching
to reveal that there were no bodies inside or anywhere nearby,
and the crew of the Agusta would start spreading their search
net much wider.

It was do or die. 'Come on,' I said, slinging Isobel's rucksack
over my shoulder and grabbing her hand. 'This time we walk,
but get ready to drop when I say and lie very still.' In uncertain
light and this terrain our pale clothes might help us blend in
against the earth and dried grass.

We walked quickly, staying low. I kept a weather eye on the
area behind us, waiting for the tell-tale roar of the overcharged
twin engines getting the Agusta off the ground. I knew we had
a little time but the trek to the trees seemed to take way too
long.

Suddenly another shape appeared coming from the west. It
was skimming the ground, a giant dragonfly with a splash of
early sun flaring off the glass of the cabin. It began drifting our
way across the open ground, skirting a clump of trees with
almost elegant ease. Then the pilot spotted us and headed our
way, dropping to near ground-level. I hoped he'd been warned
about the Agusta and that he was going to hold his nerve long
enough to get us on board.

I put on speed, dragging and half-carrying Isobel with me,
and we stumbled over the dry grass as the Gazelle skimmed
the earth. The moment the skids touched down the side door
flipped open and the pilot was gesturing for us to get inside
double-quick.

He gestured to us to put on our seatbelts, then faced forward and hit the gas, lifting off with a gut-wrenching turn back down the slope, hugging the ground all the way and flying through the occasional gap between the olive trees in a way that had Isobel yelling and clutching her seat. Not that I was enjoying it; I'd been in this situation before – and worse – but I was resigned to the fact that being this close to a crash landing was something I'd never get used to.

The pilot glanced back at me and tapped his flying helmet. I looked round but all I could see was two sets of earphones in a netting pocket. I put on one set and handed the other set to Isobel. She nodded, looking slightly green, and dropped them in her lap.

'Sorry about that,' the pilot said with amazing calm. He sounded young and British. 'I'm Max. I normally go through a pre-flight check to welcome people aboard, but I sensed we didn't have time for that. You two OK?' I caught him looking back at us and showing some teeth in a grin. Damn, he looked about eighteen and just out of school. If he was wondering what we'd been doing down on the ground he wasn't asking any questions.

'We're fine,' I said. 'You saw the Agusta?'

'I saw the smoke from a fire. Looked a bit serious. I was told to expect hostiles. Are they local forces?'

'Not sure but I doubt it. Can you outrun them?'

'On paper, yes. There's not that much in it, but we should be all right – as long as they don't follow us across country.'

'Where are we going?'

'I have to make a stop to deliver the meds on the seat or I'll be in trouble with the local ATC. They get a bit serious if we go off-plan.'

I looked across from me where a small stack of cardboard boxes was strapped to one of the other seats, and remembered Isobel mentioning that he'd come in under the guise of a humanitarian run to one of the camps in the area. If he was having to make a genuine delivery I couldn't see what the guise was, but I guess they had to play the game here or pay the consequences.

'You do what you have to,' I said. 'And thank you.'

'No prob. It's about forty miles north-west of here so I hope

we can lose them on the way. If they have an overflight
agreement they'll be able to follow us in. That might be
problematic but we'll see how it goes.'

*Problematic?* It was a hell of a word for what could be the end
of this trip. If the people in the Agusta were a Lebanese or
Hezbollah security group they had already demonstrated a willingness to open fire on a vehicle in poor light without checking first
who might be in it. They certainly wouldn't be too concerned
about going on the offensive near a crowd of Syrian refugees.

For now all they had to do was sit on our tail and keep us
in sight, and they'd catch us as we slowed ready to land. I kept
my eye on our rear but I couldn't see any signs of pursuit.

Max seemed unconcerned. 'Sit back and enjoy the ride. I'll
let you know if there's a change of plan.'

'Good point,' I said. 'What is the plan?' I looked at Isobel
but she hadn't put on her earphones and looked about ready to
throw up.

'I have instructions to get you to Akrotiri in Cyprus. Beyond
that it's not my place to know.'

# SEVENTEEN

Another meeting, this one called at short notice, and another round of faces. Brian Callahan took a seat in one of the sub-level rooms in the CIA Langley Headquarters and wondered what was in the wind. He hoped it would be some planned reaction to the attempt on Portman's life, but somehow he doubted it. There seemed to be a lack of movement on that score, which he couldn't understand but was hoping this meeting would explain.

He felt the urge to get up and run back to his desk. Having Portman and Hunt out there and under the hammer from God knew who was making him impatient and jumpy, and a meeting like this was wasting his time and taking his eye off efforts to get things resolved. But orders were orders. He gritted his teeth and checked out the faces in the room.

Ten or so bodies, some he knew, at least three he did not. He sighed inwardly. It was pointless asking who they were because it was unlikely he'd be told. Some, he was sure, were people who would soon learn about certain activities of the CIA when all good sense suggested they should not. Head of these, he decided, was a man just taking a chair at the end of the table nearest the door.

Walter M. Broderick, Deputy Assistant Secretary and at least two rungs beneath the current US Secretary of State, was smooth, coiffed and wore his expensive imported suit as if he'd been born in it. Good suits were a common enough cloak of armour in Washington's political circles, where wealth was on a par with substance and often higher than ability, but this one came across as a little ostentatious in the secretive surroundings of Langley, where affectation was frowned upon as a matter of instinct and training.

He knew Broderick from some past contact, and had little regard for the man. He was too ambitious and cared nothing for the people below him. He had both hands firmly on the

State Department ladder and in all likelihood would take over the top spot there one day. Callahan wasn't impressed. Here in the world of secret intelligence and security, ambition was fine but also a little suspect when it might lead to some people making rash decisions.

The main chair at the table was occupied by Jason Sewell. He welcomed Broderick with a quick, no-nonsense nod but avoided looking at anyone else. That alone, Callahan worried, was telling if you knew the signs. Not everyone was welcome as a friend here and you had best beware the wolf in smart clothing if they had any kind of agenda.

Among the more familiar faces were James Cardew, Jackson, Fred Groll, Craig Breakman, Gina Patel and, squeezing in alongside Broderick with a sun-burst smile that threatened to light up the area around him and him only, Carly Ledhoffen.

'I'll keep this brief,' Sewell said, knuckling the table to still conversation. 'The last time we met was to discuss the development of what appeared to be an attack on one of our contractors, code-named Watchman, on assignment in Lebanon. I won't go into more detail on that right now.' He glanced around at the newcomers, adding, 'I'll be circulating a summary record later to confirm the background. As of minutes ago a decision has been made that significantly changes our attitude of response to the attack.' He paused, and Callahan recognized by the set of Sewell's face that he was far from happy. Whatever the decision was, it had plainly been made without his input and didn't bode well for somebody.

Callahan waited for Sewell to continue. The man was usually unflappable, out-and-out in his loyalty to the CIA, more old-school than new, and had made no bones about the fact that protecting their own – even contractors – should be embedded in the organization's culture. If you were attached to the CIA team and prepared to put your life on the line for it and the country, you got the same level of care and effort as everyone else.

Sewell inclined his head sideways towards the man from the State Department. 'Deputy Assistant Secretary Broderick has kindly come along to advise on the direction we're taking on the Watchman situation.' He stopped there and waved a hand to cede the floor without further ado.

Broderick looked surprised by the abrupt hand-over, but recovered quickly.

'Thank you, James. As you all know, the situation vis-a-vis our relationship with Moscow is a little changeable at this time. The White House and State Department are doing all we can to stabilize the co-operation between us and get over the occasional bumps along the way.' He showed his teeth in what was supposed to be a grin but it lacked humour. 'It's been made a little more difficult with China's growing role on the world stage and its military surge. But we have to address the most obvious threats first. I don't need to tell you about Moscow's current developments in the Middle East – especially Syria and Iran – and their influence elsewhere, namely Latin America and their focus on gaining traction in Venezuela's oil-producing sector. Their increasing investment programme in the African continent is accelerating, too, so we need to ensure that we keep a level head when talking to our counterparts in the Kremlin. Make no mistake, that does not mean we're prepared to roll over in any way.' He tapped the table with a hefty forefinger to emphasize the point. 'Not one bit. President Putin admires strength and takes advantage wherever he can when opponents show any sign of weakness. We cannot and will not allow that to happen.'

There was a 'but' coming. Callahan could hear it like a runaway truck in a shopping mall. *Jesus, where is this going?*

'In short,' Broderick continued, 'while we recognize the *alleged* threat made to the operative known as Watchman, we also have to temper our instinctive reactions to it by not going around making wild accusations which cannot be substantiated. We cannot allow one man – a sub-contractor, no less, not one of our own – to drag us into taking any kind of reckless action that could have unforeseen consequences down the line.'

'Alleged?' Callahan couldn't help it; the word was out before he could haul it back. But it was too late and too instinctive. 'What does that mean?'

Broderick looked at him with a cold, fish-eyed expression that probably worked well with State Department juniors who knew their place, but Callahan was too riled to care.

'I don't think I caught your name or position, Mr—?'

'It's Callahan, Mr Deputy.' He was damned if he was going to dignify the man with a 'sir'. 'Brian Callahan. I'm a CSO here in Langley.'

Broderick looked puzzled by the acronym until Carly Ledhoffen leaned across and explained in a stage whisper, 'Clandestine Service Officer, sir. He's Watchman's controller.' She smiled at Callahan and shrugged, eyes wide in a 'What else could I do?' expression.

'Thank you, Callahan, for your question. Let me be perfectly clear on this matter. This "incident" should not have happened. It comes at a difficult time and our involvement in this particular Lebanon mission should be shut down immediately. The fact is, we cannot allow further US incursions in clearing up this man's mess to get in the way of ongoing discussions.'

'But we need to get him out of there!' Callahan protested. 'This was a real and active threat against one of our people on a sanctioned mission to retrieve vital information. There was no "alleged" about it. Snipers do not simply go out and look for a random person to take out for the hell of it. These men had his photo in their possession and knew who they were looking for. Furthermore, I don't see how us calling it like it is in any way endangers our foreign policy. The sniper was Russian and he attacked a US citizen—'

'You only have your man's report on that,' Broderick broke in. 'How do we know he wasn't mistaken?'

'Well, in my experience,' said Craig Breakman from Special Activities, 'men wounded in combat don't usually adopt a language that is not their own. Just saying.'

Callahan looked to Sewell for help, but his boss avoided meeting his eye. It was instantly clear to Callahan that Sewell had received his orders on the subject and was in no position to counter them.

'Well, Callahan,' Broderick said coolly, 'your comments are clear and understood. However, we do not require you to worry about US foreign policy, nor are you mandated to do so. We have many highly effective people around DC to do that for us. And just for the sake of record let me remind you that your man knew the risks when he took the job, did he not?'

'He's a professional, yes—'

'Good. The fact is he's a hired gun. No more, no less. I assume he works for the private sector as well as the CIA?'

'Yes, but—'

'Then he chose his line of work and has to understand that we're under no obligation to help him if he got careless and picked up some attention in whatever else he's been involved in. We cannot endanger the current US negotiating position with Moscow to get him out of whatever jam he's gotten himself into.'

Callahan took a deep breath and said as calmly as he could, 'He's anything but a hired gun.' He sensed some warning looks from others at the table for pursuing this, not least Sewell, and knew he was pushing his luck. He ignored them. It was too late for that. Fuck 'em. He continued, 'Watchman has performed several dangerous assignments on our behalf in many situations where we could not send accredited staff operatives. He even saved the life of a State Department employee – a colleague of yours, incidentally – by pulling him out of a lockup in Ukraine at great personal risk to himself.'

Broderick wasn't listening. He shook his head in a dismissive manner. 'Be that as it may, the decision has been taken at the very top, Callahan.' In case there was any doubt as to what he meant, he raised a single finger in the air. 'And I mean, the top.' He stared balefully at Callahan. 'If you feel unable to accept that decision I suggest you need to consider your next comments very carefully.'

The silence that followed such a clear threat was total, punctuated only by the shuffling of feet as others got ready to vacate their chairs. Some were no doubt keen to move away from any potential collateral damage heading in Callahan's direction. Most had their heads down, whether from passivity or embarrassment Callahan couldn't tell.

Then George Jackson from the Defence Intelligence Agency spoke up. 'Notwithstanding all that,' he said carefully, 'and I'm sure those at the top have given it careful thought, but has this decision been run past the various committees of the National Intelligence Community? I ask that because the asset on the ground in this case was ours and there are serious ramifications we all have to consider here, namely that your proposal suggests

leaving the contractor Watchman – an American citizen, as
Mr Callahan has reminded us – out in the cold. That's pretty
damned outrageous in my view, and threatens the safe conduct
and conclusion of any future assignments where we have to
employ contractors rather than our own field officers.'

There were mutters of agreement around the table. In response
Broderick gave a smile that barely moved the skin around his
mouth. 'Thank you for your input, Mr Jackson. I'll be sure to
pass your comments upstairs.' His eyes swept the room like
twin barrels of a gun. 'However, in case anyone else here shares
your doubts, I can assure you that all the necessary approvals
and oversight procedures have been carefully dealt with.' He
looked at Jackson and said, 'In addition, to correct a point you
made, I understand this man is not solely a US citizen but has
dual nationality status with Britain. So I suggest we let them
look after him. We have more than enough to do.'

Jackson looked as if he was about to respond, but clamped
his mouth shut and glanced at Callahan with a look of apology.

'Shut down all communications with this man, Callahan,'
Broderick ordered bluntly. 'As of now he's on his own.'

Callahan said nothing. He got to his feet and walked to the
door. There was nothing left to say. He was grateful for
the support from Jackson and Breakman but was too angry to
speak let alone excuse himself. It was no good appealing
to Sewell, who remained in his seat, eyes fixed on the table.
The assistant director looked stunned and Callahan figured
the orders really had come from on high, and that all the possible
arguments had been put forward and knocked back.

It made him wonder, though, about the eventual effects when
this decision became known in the wider intelligence community, as it surely would. Passing off responsibility for someone
you employed, no matter how tangentially, never reflected well
on an organization, especially one which valued loyalty and
service as highly as did the CIA.

Broderick looked surprised by his move and barked, 'Where
are you going?'

Callahan paused, his hand on the door. 'I'm going to give
Watchman his final orders, Mr Deputy, as you requested. Just
so he doesn't become an embarrassment to the State Department

or the White House. And I'll make sure to tell him that he'd better get on with saving his own ass because it looks like we no longer have the moral guts to do it for him in case we upset those friendly folks over in the Kremlin.'

The door closed behind him leaving a roomful of stunned people and a heavy silence.

# EIGHTEEN

Callahan strode back to his office in a mood of white hot anger. Broderick and his kind were doing nothing less than throwing Portman to the dogs, all in the name of political expediency. Was this the new mantra – don't anyone rock the boat even if we allow a good man to go down in the process? If so it was cowardly and counter-productive. When other contractors got wind of it, the likelihood was that it would frighten away good operatives; nobody wanted to work for an employer who was prepared to leave them hanging when things got tough.

He put his head in the main outer office where Lindsay was sitting at a monitor assisting another comms operator. He caught her eye and gestured for her to follow him when she was free.

While he was waiting he checked his messages and found two. One was from Vale, advising him that the plan was for Portman and Hunt to be flown out of Lebanon to a location in Cyprus, precise details to follow.

The second message was from Portman himself, consisting of a three-word locator signalling his position. He almost smiled at the brevity and felt even worse for the position they'd both been forced into. This wasn't how professionals should be treated.

'Close the door,' he said softly, when Lindsay appeared minutes later. He sat down and gestured for her to do the same.

'Is everything all right, sir?' she asked, a tiny frown forming.

He realized she knew his moods better than most people and could tell when things were piling up. Right now he guessed he must look like a pot about to simmer over. A lot had been happening in the background as far as Portman was concerned, and he had to think of the best way of bringing Lindsay up to date on the situation.

'Portman's on his way out of Lebanon,' he said. 'London's coordinating that with their operative on the ground, a woman named Hunt.' Rather than us, he felt like saying, but decided against it. There was no need to bring Lindsay in on his conflict with the State Department. That would be a mismatch made in hell.

'How do we get involved, sir?'

'We don't, not yet. If there's a change of plan for any reason they will keep on top of it.' And fingers crossed on that, he thought. Changes of plan were common to all intelligence assignments, usually governed by forces outside the operative's control. As he'd learned very early on in his career, having a plan B was essential because plan A was always open to going wrong.

'As of this moment I want you to be ready to drop what you're doing and focus on supporting them where necessary. For now all we can do is provide an oversight role, but we must be ready to step in if we can find a way of doing so without any fanfare echoing further than this room. You understand?'

'Sir. That doesn't sound good.'

'It's not good, it's anything but good.' He breathed deep and scowled for a moment as if coming to a momentous decision. Then he said, 'This is for your ears only, Lindsay. As of the meeting a few minutes ago Watchman is on his own. That means we don't speak to him, we don't support him, we don't send back-up and we don't do anything to rock the political boat vis-à-vis our current relations with Moscow. By "our" I mean the State Department and the White House.'

She looked stunned. 'But that's . . . I don't understand.'

'You will in time. As of now we use absolute care when communicating with Portman, we do not disseminate copies of comms records and we use exclusive-restricted channels only. You don't mention having any connections with Portman or use the Watchman code name and be very careful who you speak to.'

'I understand.'

'Good. You wanted to speak to me yesterday. I'm sorry I couldn't stop right then. What was it about?'

'That's all right, sir. It wasn't important. I think I was concerned for Portman, that's all. As you've said before, he's part of the team.'

'And rightly so. Because of that it's even more important that we be honest with each other. What was worrying you?'

Put so directly there was no way out. She had intended

forgetting all about Carly Ledhoffen's odd approach in the cafeteria and brushing it off as the woman's attempt at spreading her circle of contacts among the lower orders. She still hadn't figured out why, nor what Ledhoffen thought she could gain by it; but then, she had never understood people of Ledhoffen's kind of ambition and the tortuous extents to which they would go to achieve their goals. Now she was wondering if there had been an odd convergence of events that led to this moment, and realized she had better come clean about it.

First she described the feeling that someone had been in her workspace, and included an apology for her carelessness at leaving the code word out for anyone to see.

'Do you think your computer was accessed?' Callahan asked when she finished. It was an instinctive question given their situation.

'It wasn't. I checked with security. The last access codes used were mine earlier in the day. In any case, there's nothing on there that could be useful. It was more a feeling of things having been moved. It's never happened before. I hope I was imagining it.'

'Could it have been the janitors?'

'I thought about that but I don't think so. They're short-staffed at the moment and are focussing on the most-used areas where there's a concentration of traffic and waste. I haven't used my space much over the last week or so while I've been helping out with the other comms operators.'

Callahan chewed his lip, then said. 'What else?'

She related her conversation with Carly Ledhoffen and how unusual it had seemed, and how Ledhoffen had never even spoken to her before. 'I'm sorry,' she concluded. 'I didn't want to seem like I was telling tales.'

To her surprise, Callahan looked almost nonplussed. 'I understand. Did she mention who this asset might be?'

'No. She didn't use a name. What I don't understand is why she should have approached me. Is there any way she would know I've been Portman's comms support?'

'It's possible. I would always prefer anything conducted in this section stays here, but that's not in my control. Because of potential overlap some details of mission reports have to be disseminated to other sections and agencies.' She knew he was probably referring to the NSA, Air Force Intelligence, Army Intel, Naval Intel, FBI, DEA and a lot of others in between the bricks and mortar of the US Intelligence community. In this instance a physical threat against a contractor on CIA business automatically called for a warning to be sent out to others in the field to watch their backs and tighten up their personal security.

Then something occurred to her. 'Would that include the Support Directorate?'

He gave a thin smile. 'Ledhoffen was included to sit in on the briefing list for this one by the head of security in the Directorate, yes.'

He didn't clarify further and Lindsay didn't ask. It wasn't their position to query what was discussed with other divisions or why.

'Forget it,' he said with a sigh. 'There's a lot going on here and we're all on edge. Let's focus on the task in hand.'

She was glad of the change of subject and said, 'Sir, is there really nothing we can do to help Portman but wait?'

'Not yet. The three-word code I just gave you is his current location in Lebanon. He and the MI6 officer, Hunt, are making their way to an eventual site in Cyprus. All we can do is wait and see if they make it safely past all the stops along the way.'

'Can't they be picked up and fly direct?'

'Not easily. They would have to pass over heavily restricted areas and we know from experience that overflight permission would not be granted. An area further north offers a clearer corridor, and I just heard that the British are putting that in place right now. Once they're on the island they should be home and dry.'

'I hope he's all right. I was thinking what you said about the snipers.' Callahan's mention of them earlier had stayed with her. He hadn't included specific details, which she suspected was deliberate, but it added an extra dimension of threat when she thought about their methods of stalking, lying in wait and long-distance kills . . . and how their targets rarely knew they were coming until it was too late.

Callahan waved it off. 'He'll be fine. I can't say the same for the two snipers, however.' He gave a grim smile and murmured, 'Sorry – forget I said that. I'd have the Support Section down on my neck for talking out of turn and frightening the children.'

She preferred not to think about it and blocked the unwelcome images from her mind. 'I still don't understand how they found him,' she said. 'The photo, I mean. I thought he was off the radar.'

'He is – was. It's a long story but these two appear to have been waiting for him . . . or, at least, they knew precisely where to find him, which is just as bad. We have to assume they might not be the only ones sent after him. We don't yet know who sent them so we're having to work on identifying the shooters from our database of known operatives. Hopefully it will give us a heads-up.'

Lindsay felt a chill wind about her that was almost personal. She'd spoken to Portman a lot on comms while supporting him and monitoring his activities and movements and, in spite of the clipped way they were forced to converse due to mission pressures, she felt they had established a friendly working relationship. She had met him only once, which had been in Washington. Callahan had asked her to debrief him after a particularly arduous mission, and she'd been surprised by how unremarkable he was.

For someone whose life had been on the line more than a few times in some of the world's toughest trouble spots, times when she'd been able to talk him through a situation and even provide active back-up when needed, he seemed about as far from the usual man of action she had seen around Langley, such as in the Special Activities Division, as it was possible to get. But she knew enough about him to know that he was one of the most effective contractors out there.

'Is it possible Portman made a mistake or was it bad luck?' she asked. She knew Portman's skill was in being able to move around covertly and avoiding being pinged or noticed. It was what made him invaluable to the CIA and other agencies, especially for missions where they either didn't have enough of their own people or deniability meant bringing in a skilled outsider like him.

'I'd like to think it was bad luck,' Callahan said eventually.

'But since both snipers had the same photo of him, it's unlikely. It must have been pre-arranged. Who by, we don't know, but it must have been someone with resources.'

'But how would they have known where he was, if this assignment was set up at the last minute?'

'That's what we're all asking. To date I don't have an answer.'

Lindsay felt shocked by the stark possibility presented. She didn't know anything about Portman's mission in Lebanon other than what Callahan had told her. It would have been different had she been his comms support, as she would have had a detailed agenda of his movements and locations, tracked and filled in carefully on her screen so as not to lose sight of any potential threats in the same area of operations.

But the circle of other people involved would not have been extensive; the old need-to-know dictum beloved of security officials still counted for much. An individual or even a group would find it difficult to track a man like Portman without some serious back-up facilities. And that kind of pull fell into the realm of a state-operated agency rather than an individual player.

'What else can we do?' The question was out before she could stop it. 'Sorry – I didn't mean to imply you're not already . . .'

Callahan smiled warmly. 'That's all right. There's nothing we're going to be authorized to do. But it doesn't mean I'm prepared to leave him to his own devices. I owe him more than that.' He reached for a small notepad and pen, tore off a sheet and wrote down three words with the date and time received and passed the note across the desk. 'I have to go out in a little while. While I'm gone, this is the latest locator from Portman. I want you to take it back to your desk as it is and leave it there in plain sight.'

'Sir?' She gave him a look.

He replied with a wry smile, 'Don't worry. I'm just trying something. I'll explain another time.' He hesitated then added, 'We're putting what we have through the grinder right now to see what comes up. In the meantime, if Ledhoffen or anyone else speaks to you on the subject, let me know immediately.'

# NINETEEN

The CIA in Langley didn't actively discourage old Cold War warriors from visiting, especially if they had anything to offer in the way of valuable insights into the thoughts and methodology of the nation's common enemy. But Russell Hoffman, once one of the most highly regarded, if secretive operators in the old CIA, had long ago blotted his copybook in criticizing the administration and its soft approach to Moscow's continued interference.

It had been enough to make him persona non grata to the overly sensitive higher management, keen to protect the new echelons from the hawkish views of what they regarded as gung-ho oldsters from a long-gone era. Not that Hoffman went that far back; he'd been too young for the original Office of Strategic Services, changed in 1947 to the CIA, but not so far back that he hadn't learned a great deal from the life and operational experiences passed down by its instructors and field personnel.

Strictly speaking, Brian Callahan knew he would have been criticized for meeting up with the former spook. But right now he didn't care; he had an asset under threat and wanted an outsider's perspective on the situation, unvarnished and free of any ambition for higher office. Anything that helped him pull Portman from out under the hammer was worth considering. Furthermore, he was coming round to the uncomfortable conclusion that he no longer felt able to confide his worries to his colleagues. Too many of them appeared to be in search of a quieter life without ripples.

Even more worrying was his growing suspicion that information about Portman had originated from inside Langley itself. He had no idea if that was right, but he hoped to find out shortly. He just hoped he hadn't roped Lindsay Citera into something they would both regret by getting her to leave his note on her desk.

'So how can I help the new CIA, Brian?' Hoffman greeted him as they sat down across from each other in a bar a short spit from Logan Circle in downtown Washington.

The way he smiled robbed the question of abruptness, and Callahan was pleased to see that the former spy had lost none of his sense of humour. He was looking old, though, and shrunken, with a florid complexion and a spider-work of veins in his cheeks. He still had a full head of hair but the grey had settled into near-white, giving him the air of an aging college professor.

'Is it that obvious?' he asked, and raised his glass in salute. The bar hadn't got busy yet and the few other patrons were tables away, so their conversation was unlikely to be overheard.

'It is to this suspicious old goat, and I haven't lost my sense of expectation yet.' He grinned and sipped his whisky with relish, then waved his other hand, which was covered with liver spots. 'You know I once spent so long in hot climates these darned things used to join up to form a decent sun tan. Now it looks like I'm rotting away. Old age is shit, Brian. Don't let anyone kid you otherwise. What's the problem?'

'I have an asset,' Callahan explained, making circles on the table with the glass, 'an American who's been targeted by the opposition.'

'Targeted how?' Hoffman leaned forward in his seat. It was a tiny move and easy to miss by those who didn't know what to look for. But an easy-to-read sign of interest. Once an operative it was always there in your blood, never quite leaving you.

'Two snipers – one and a back-up. Middle-Eastern location when nobody should have known he was there. We haven't identified them yet but something tells me it wasn't a local team.'

'But you have an idea, right?' Hoffman was still sharp, able to pick up on nuance where others might miss it.

'A hint. They were carrying a photo of our man, last used by a Russian security contractor in Ukraine a while back. And one of the shooters swore at him in Russian.'

'So FSB, then.' It was a statement, not a question. 'In my experience, none of their so-called contractors ever got there without having strong connections to the KGB or their successors.'

'Would that include GRU?'

'Damn right it would. But how likely is it?'

'How do you mean?'

Hoffman shrugged. 'Well, I'm guessing if this man of yours has been targeted, he must have bumped noses with them at some stage. And they're a mean bunch. They hate losing face.'

Callahan nodded. 'He has some history there, yes. My question for you – and we don't know for sure yet – is it likely to be an individual or the state?'

Hoffman sat back as a couple of clients wandered by, his security antennae clearly still active. He waited until they were out of range without needing to check, then asked, 'Why are you asking me, Brian? Last I heard Langley is full of hot-shot analysts who can tell you everything you need to know. I'm old and tired and not a favourite of the current management. Ask anyone.'

Callahan chuckled. 'So tired you couldn't wait to come here to find out what I wanted? Right.'

'True enough. Call me curious. And bored. So?'

'So maybe I don't trust some of our hot-shot analysts as much as I should to give me an honest, unvarnished answer that hasn't been filtered through the political machine first.'

'I see. Like that, huh? You're asking me who I think in the Russian food-chain might have the hots for your man.'

'Yes.'

'Well, it could be anyone with access to the resources needed. But an assignment like this, going after one of our people? Not so many. And nobody without connections. Good connections.' His expression left no doubt where his thinking was leading.

'That's what I was afraid of.'

The older man toyed with his glass for a few moments. Then he said, 'I'm only hesitating because I don't want to set a fire under your ass merely because I'm old, cynical, experienced and wouldn't trust this current Moscow cowboy any more than I did the grey men who went before him. They're all gangsters in smart suits, in my opinion – not unlike some of our own administration, if you get my drift.'

'I'm listening.'

Hoffman nodded. 'OK. I take it your man usually has zero profile and keeps his head down?'

'He's the best I've worked with. His name is known to very few people and even I don't know where he lives.'

'Yet his photo is out there.'

Callahan winced at the thought. 'I thought that was a one-off. The man carrying it in Ukraine wasn't alive to pass it on.'

'The argument still holds, though; he's no longer covert. However, to answer your main question, whoever is after him, we have to assume they have clout and access to manpower and facilities.'

'Acting on their own initiative? That's a risky move.'

'True enough. But some risks pay off. Look at all the guys queuing up to become oligarchs. They all know their turn might come to fall under the hammer, yet they still push themselves forward. And the grey men with all the political and security connections; once they get close to the presidential office and get a taste of power, they usually want more. That includes doing what they think will be approved, even if it isn't.' He shook his head slowly. 'It's a dangerous ambition.'

'You think that's the answer?'

'It's certainly one. The only alternative is that the order might have come from the very top.'

Callahan lifted an eyebrow. 'From Putin? You think he'd really get that involved?'

'Why not? He's got the bit between his teeth right now and is riding high on a wave of popularity. The strong man of Russia who wants the position for life – and he's likely to get it. He's about as untouchable as it gets over there and he doesn't give a brass fuck about procedure.'

Callahan smiled at the unusual cuss word. Hoffman wasn't normally given to bad language. Maybe he was beyond caring.

The older man pursed his lips. 'On balance, it could be either. If it's a lone operator driving this, or someone in a small group, he's got balls, I'll say that.'

Callahan was unsure. 'But why would Putin bother? He'd be admitting that one man on our side had got to him – the leader of the Russian nation.'

'I agree. It sounds unlikely. But who the hell knows how any of them think over there? Pride is important to them and colours a lot of what we think we know. The only ones more inscrutable live in Beijing. How much has your man butted up against Moscow?'

'A bit, here and there. You know how their influence is spreading; it's not as if the globe is nicely divided up any more. We bump noses a lot more than we used to.' He thought about it and said, 'I can tell you that he pulled a State Department official out of a lock-up in Ukraine a few years ago. That probably didn't endear him much. There have been other encounters, too.'

Hoffman's eyes widened. 'I heard about that. So that was your man? Was there any collateral damage?'

Callahan hesitated before replying. He trusted Hoffman more than most former spooks, but his default position was not to give anything away. 'There was some. It got messy.'

Hoffman smiled. 'Messy. I like that. You mean he had to go active. Which I'm guessing wasn't his first time.'

'You know I can't confirm that.'

'I get it. Well, in that case I'd say he probably got picked as a target by someone with an agenda. Doesn't matter who or what he did, but if he's someone who thumbed his nose at them more than once, and they were looking to make an example of him, he'd have been up there on the list.' He sat back. 'It wouldn't be the first time they've done that. Back in the day they tried a few times to even the scores, to slow us down. It was small scale mostly, designed to unsettle us. But it never lasted long.'

'Is there any way we can stop it? If we use defensive force how do we know they won't take similar action against more of our people?'

'You don't. It could start a shooting war, and I doubt you want that.' Hoffman twirled his glass. 'To be honest I'm not sure how you can stop this particular activity short of putting a bullet in the man who issued the order. But even if you could find him and it was possible it would be counter-productive; there's always someone else ready to pick up the slack and prove himself more effective.'

'So what then?'

'The easy thing? Decommission your asset. For good. Take the knight off the table.'

Callahan shook his head. It made sense, but he wasn't about to do that without a lot of thought. 'We'd be losing a good man.'

'True. But if this is as personal as it sounds, he's become red-lined and you'll lose him eventually anyway. Get him to drop out and become invisible. That way he'll live longer and your conscience will be a lot healthier.'

'You sound as if you've been there.'

Hoffman tilted his head, indicating yes. 'It was a long time ago. One of our guys thought he'd got blown by East German counter-intelligence. He'd been in deep cover for a couple of years and was nearing the end of his tour. We wanted to extract him but the people at the top demanded one more mission.' He looked suddenly tired, the memory clearly still haunting him. 'He was ex-USAF, a farm kid from Arkansas who'd made it into intelligence work. A nice guy. I met his family. They were good people, too.'

'What happened to him?'

'He disappeared. I never did find the answer and the SSD weren't about to tell us.'

Callahan blinked. Although a former CIA field operative himself, being consigned to an office in Langley for too long tended to blur the brutal reality of what could happen out there in the shadows. But he knew Hoffman was right.

'I'm not sure our man would go for it.'

'He might not have a choice. It would be the smartest thing to do – for everyone.' He took a final sip of his whisky and put the glass down. 'That aside, you could start close to home and find out who's helping the people who're after him.'

'I'm working on that. I hope it isn't true.'

'Cautious answer.' Hoffman smiled. 'Some of the newer people seem to think that the old-world security problems we had in my day no longer exist, that all their fancy technology and analytical bullshit will take care of everything. Not true.'

'You think?'

'Sure. The answer is as old as the hills, Brian. Someone has put the finger on your man. It's as simple as that. The question is, was it someone on the outside . . . maybe someone he's worked with before? Or someone closer?' He stood up and dusted his hands off. 'Good luck.'

As Callahan walked back to his car he thought over what Hoffman had said. The man had been as direct as usual, not sugar-coating his opinions. He could have taken a purely conciliatory tone, avoiding any judgement of the situation Callahan and Portman faced. But that hadn't happened, and that reinforced just why Callahan had come here: to hear the unvarnished truth.

# TWENTY

Callahan returned to his office and got caught up in discussions on minor issues. When they were done he checked again for messages. Nothing. He sat deep in thought, trying to decide how much of what Hoffman had said was possible and untangle the lines of conflicting interest that lay in what had happened earlier in the meeting room.

Intelligence agencies were, by their construction and purpose, full of competing divisions, each attempting to keep ahead of the race for funding and prominence. A certain bear-pit mentality had always been present and even encouraged, for the most part working well enough and driving each division to do the best work possible. Such was the simple law of survival.

He picked up his phone to check progress on the search of the data files for the faces Portman had sent in when there was a knock at his door.

It opened to admit Carly Ledhoffen.

'Do you have a minute, Brian?' she asked.

He nodded, surprised by her appearance, and put the phone down. He wanted to tell her that now wasn't a good time, but couldn't think of a plausible excuse. Maybe this was a chance to sort out the reason for her confrontational attitude earlier.

She glided in and sat down, bringing a hint of expensive perfume with her. 'I got the feeling we weren't on the same page back there,' she said. 'I hope that's not the case. Perhaps we could discuss that.'

He recognized the HR negotiating tactic for what it was. Agree and control. 'Sure. But allow me to go first: are you stress-testing my operations?'

She blinked slowly twice, doll's eyes up-down, up-down. 'What makes you think we'd be doing that?'

'It's what the Support Directorate does, isn't it? Push the boundaries to see if there have been failures or weaknesses in mission objectives relating to staff?'

'We have to do that sometimes, yes. It's part of our remit of duty and care to support the use of our officers in the field.' She gave him a wide-eyed look, adding, 'Although as you yourself said, this asset is not an officer.'

'So we shouldn't look after them, too? Is that what you're saying?'

She waved a hand. 'I'm sorry, but if you have a problem I'm sure my head of department will be happy to discuss it with you.'

'I'll pass, thank you. But let me tell you, you'd get the same response from any other controller and agent runner in this building and other intel agencies. We use what resources we can for covert ops and I value each one highly, staff or not. You seemed to suggest in the meeting that my asset should have endangered himself by going deeper into the territory than he already was and finding Tango.'

She began to speak but he held up a hand.

'Forgive me interrupting but do you have the slightest idea just how dangerous it is out there? That's a rhetorical question, by the way. Also, under the circumstances, the chances of the asset getting anywhere near him, let alone getting either of them out in one piece, would have been miniscule to zero.'

She said nothing for a moment, although he noticed a slight flush had crept across her cheeks. He couldn't decide whether it was embarrassment or anger, but didn't care. Sometimes you had to play it rough to get the message across.

'I confess I don't,' she said finally, and ducked her head. 'I think I owe you an apology, Brian. These two meetings were my first at this level and I guess I'm still learning. I didn't mean to imply criticism of your asset or his methodology. I'll make sure your points are well known.' She hesitated, then added, 'For what it's worth I think the way you were treated at the end of that last one placed an unfair amount of pressure on you and your staff. I'm sure I'm not the only one who thought so. I hope it doesn't pose a threat to anyone . . . for example, Miss Citera.'

Callahan wondered what the hell she playing at. She made it sound as if she were more familiar with Lindsay than having had a had a passing chat in the cafeteria. In any case, if Broderick

wanted to ensure Callahan followed his instructions, putting a
clamp on his immediate staff was beyond his powers. He made
do with a simple, 'It won't. But thank you.'

As she left the room, Callahan's phone buzzed. It was a text
from Portman.

*On our way out following attack by armed Agusta. Seriously??*

It was followed by three words. The locator for the next
position.

He fed the words into the app and a grid-lined map of Cyprus
came up on his screen. They were heading for a spot on the
south coast. He called up another map of the island and checked
the coordinates. RAF Akrotiri.

He couldn't fault the British for their choice of safe haven.
It was as secure a place as any but only as long as Portman
stayed inside the base perimeter. Problem was, he'd have to
move sooner or later. And Portman was right to be pissed, as
the double-interrogator in his message suggested. Seriously,
what the hell was going on?

The other question was, how far would whoever was targeting
him go?

The first attempt might have been random, if you joined
Broderick's obtuse thinking and ignored the photos. But if he
and Hunt had been followed and come under fire again, it was
more than coincidence, but a concerted effort to nail him. If so,
whoever was pushing this had good resources and wasn't likely
to give up too easily.

He had to get him out of there to another safer place. And
he had to find out who was behind this. He picked up his phone
and dialled Vale's number in London. Time to ask another favour
of the MI6 officer.

As he did so a message box appeared on his PC screen.

*Urgent briefing Rm U3. 10 mins.*

There was no list of attendees attached, and no indication of
subject matter. He checked his agenda but no meeting had been
scheduled in. Coupled with Portman's problem it was unusual
enough to worry him. And room U3 was of a size to suggest
that he wasn't the only person who'd been summoned.

He continued with his call to Vale. They exchanged brief
pleasantries, then Vale listened without comment and agreed to

help without question. Thank God, Callahan thought, replacing the phone, for professionals.

As he stood up, his phone burbled. He considered ignoring it but a sense of urgency prevailed.

'Callahan.'

'Brian? Glad I caught you.' It was James Cardew of the Middle-East desk. He sounded breathless. 'I've just had a report from our guys monitoring ground movement over Syria and its border territories. They caught track of a helicopter on an early-dawn flight crossing the border at extreme low level and duck-hopping over the hills into the Baalbek area of north-eastern Lebanon. They don't have details of where it came from – it just popped up at a level to clear the peaks before dropping out of sight and continuing west.'

'Syrian or what?'

'No idea. We couldn't get any ADSB beacon or transponder signal.'

'They were flying dark.'

'Looks like it. You don't get everything going down at the same time. Shortly after that there were signs of light flashes on the Lebanon side of the hills indicating what could have been a fire-fight. Would that be anything to do with your guy?'

Callahan said, 'I don't know. Can you send me the co-ordinates?'

'Will do. If it's him I hope he's keeping his head down.' He paused then said, 'You know the Russians have a facility just across the border, don't you?'

'I heard there was one, but not the specifics.'

'No matter. It's a recent set-up. We think it's a small base for monitoring anti-government forces in Syria's northern sector, but they seem to have been scoping the border region with Lebanon a lot recently. We haven't yet worked out why.'

Callahan swore softly. It made sense. If the flight had come from a Russian base it pointed even more firmly to a sanctioned operation . . . or one with a great deal of latitude for using their facilities. 'If it was a Russian machine, why the fire-fight?'

'They might have run into trouble from a border unit who got hot to trot. Not everybody in the region is happy with the big bear being so close.'

Callahan thanked him for the information and thought it over. The idea of Russian forces crossing borders was hardly new; they had the capability and the nerve to probe borders and push boundaries wherever they could if they saw a useable advantage in doing so. They were currently doing that all over Africa. If this latest action was them rather than a rogue group pursuing Portman, then he was up against a more serious problem than they'd thought.

He jotted down the three locator words on a piece of paper and made his way to Lindsay's comms room. She was studying a map of Lebanon and the eastern Mediterranean. Already doing research, he noted approvingly, just in case.

'Another locator,' he told her, handed her the slip of paper. 'Leave it on your desk top with the other one I gave you.'

# TWENTY-ONE

After the open space in Lebanon and the air base on Cyprus the atmosphere at Frankfurt International Airport was a shocking contrast. There was too much movement, too many people and a whole lot more noise. It was like stepping from a church into a packed night-club, an assault on the ears and eyes with no way of turning it off other than by backing out.

Trouble was I couldn't back out. There was nowhere for me to go.

And it was the perfect place for an assassination. Lots of people, lots of kill-points. An open attack would cause wide panic and the attackers could slip out under cover of the mêlée and disappear.

I lingered as long as I could air-side, but my time ran out when the crowds disappeared and there was a gap before any new arrivals started flooding in. Eventually, coming under the gaze of a security cop, I'd been forced to make a move towards immigration and the arrivals hall.

I checked my phone for Callahan's instructions. They didn't amount to much.

*Terminal 1 – send locator and wait.*

It sounded very specific but I wasn't going to argue. If he wanted me to sit and wait in a particular building he must have his reasons.

I made my way to the main hall and looked around. I needed somewhere out of the crush but within sight of the main exits. I skirted the mass of travelling public, patrolling security guards, airport officials and staff, and found a coffee stall with some seating nearby. I sent Callahan a locator code as requested, then sat back and waited, eyes on the surrounding area and trying to chill when all my instincts were telling me to go dark.

Leaving Lebanon had been easier than I'd thought possible. After a brief stop at a field of new refugee tents for Max to unload his boxes, during which he'd said not to move but play dumb if asked, we'd continued on our way across-country with Max following a route which seemed to involve a lot of twists and turns. Eventually the sea had come into view and we cleared the coast and were on our way to Cyprus across a sun-sparkled water of the most amazing blue. Thankfully there was no sign of the Agusta to spoil the ride.

When we landed it was at the British RAF base at Akrotiri, where Max directed us to a jeep waiting nearby and waved us goodbye. The driver got us aboard then set out at a fast clip for a small building on the far side of the field, away from the general structures. It felt a bit like being treated as having something contagious but I didn't mind that. Even in and around military bases it was normal to be segregated from other forces to avoid being asked awkward questions.

As we got inside the building we were approached by two men. One was a uniformed officer with the rank of captain, the other a sergeant carrying a canvas bag. The officer checked our names then nodded to the sergeant and said, 'This is one of our armourers. I'll have to ask you to turn over any weapons and ammunition you might be carrying, then we can get on with processing you through to your next destination.'

The sergeant stepped forward and relieved us of the pistols and spare magazines. If he was surprised that Isobel was toting the Glock he kept his face blank. Maybe they had ladies of a certain age coming through here with guns all the time. He quickly and expertly checked that there were no shells left in the guns before thanking us and walking away. All in a day's work.

The officer directed us to a small waiting room with a phone and said, 'I'll have to ask you to stay in this room until it's time to go.' His tone of voice and the presence of two armed guards in the corridor suggested that wandering around the base would be actively discouraged. 'There's coffee and tea and toilets, so please help yourselves.'

He disappeared with a vague half-salute and while Isobel got busy talking to London, I sent a locator to Callahan, more in the hopes that he'd respond telling me what I'd be doing next. When Isobel finished the call she put the phone down and came across to me.

'This is where we part company,' she said. 'I have orders to go back to the UK, and you're booked on a military flight to Frankfurt leaving here in a few hours.'

'I wish I could say it's all been fun,' I said. 'Interesting, maybe. Are you going to be all right?'

'Me? Yes. I'll have to go through a long bitching session about why I got kicked out of the country and then I'll be off somewhere else.' She looked a little regretful. 'I enjoyed this last bit. Made a change from pretending to be an aid coordinator. What will you be doing?'

I shrugged. 'Same as you. An inquest into what happened, then a few days of down time. After that, I'm not sure.'

'I forgot, you're a free agent, aren't you? I suppose I shouldn't use the word agent around here.' She grinned like a naughty schoolgirl. 'People might get the wrong idea.'

I gave her a hug. Under any other circumstances it would have seemed odd, but after what we'd been through together it seemed a natural thing to do. 'Thank you. You saved my hide back there. I appreciate it.'

'Stop it. You'll have me in tears.' She didn't look even close to it. She turned and walked out without a backwards glance. One tough lady. I liked her.

Time passed slowly, the way it always does when you don't want to sit still. People came and went, mostly without acknowledging me, and the hours stretched out. Eventually the officer who'd greeted us on arrival came and escorted me out to an aircraft waiting on the tarmac.

A line of mixed travellers in a variety of uniforms and short haircuts was waiting patiently to get on board, with none of the eager push-and-shove of civilians. They all looked a little spaced out, with sunburned faces and varying states of body slump, and I could only guess where they'd come from and what they'd left behind. Wherever it was had to be a hot-spot somewhere to the east. I was relieved nobody tried to start a conversation and was asleep before we reached the end of the runway.

My phone buzzed. I was on my third Frankfurt-strength coffee and was beginning to feel as if I'd been plugged into the mains, with that sense of edginess that makes everything around you seem forced and induces a general body itch that won't go away. I looked at the text. It was from Callahan.

*2 gunmen accessed Akrotiri base 4 hrs ago. Both attackers shot dead and two security personnel wounded. Your photo again but no ID. Suggest extra vigilance.*

What the hell was going on? First the attack on me near Yammoune, in Lebanon, followed by the Agusta dusting down the olive grove with some serious gunfire. Now this. Launching an attack inside a British RAF base where there would have been armed security demonstrated a serious level of determination or desperation. Or maybe the attackers had had no real idea of what they were up against.

I sent a note back.

*Have you ID'd the first two?*

Not that it helped me to know much either way but it would show me they were on top of the situation.

Fifteen minutes later there was another text.

*One name possible. Checking sources.*

Well that was something. If they had a line on one of the gunmen it might lead to others and eventually give them some idea of where he'd come from . . . and maybe who was his employer. Like every other aspect of intel work it was a process: identify, confirm and connect, working along the line to check known associates, background and history to see who was pulling the strings, who had given the orders. And why.

I couldn't answer that so I focussed on watching the terminal hall around the main entrance. Passengers and greeters were hurrying by in a steady stream, each in his or her own world, pushing baggage carts, dragging kids, carrying overnight bags or clutching flight documents. A familiar sight the world over.

Then I spotted two men who'd pushed through the main entrance and stopped just inside. They were getting in the way of other arrivals but they didn't move, oblivious of everyone else. One was checking his phone while the other stood close by, scanning the hall.

On first sight they looked fairly normal: average faces, dark hair, somewhere in their late thirties or early forties. Medium height, a couple of guys on down-time, wearing jeans, windcheaters and soft boots. Not US military, though, which was common around here.

Yet there was something about them that struck me as odd. Then it hit me: where other travellers were stopping to peer up at the flight schedule boards, clutching their flight documents in the excited or edgy manner of all travellers, these two did none of that. Here to meet someone, perhaps? My gut feel said not.

Then the man with the cellphone said something to his companion and looked up.

He was looking right at the area where I was sitting.

I grabbed my backpack and slid out of my seat, moving slowly because sudden movements stood out, even here in this maelstrom of people.

I headed for the washrooms which lay at the far end of the hall. I kept my head down, walking nice and easy, not looking back and using other passengers as cover. It should have worked but didn't. As I passed a tinted window in the side of a store I caught the men's reflection.

They'd spotted me and were heading my way.

# TWENTY-TWO

T he entrance corridor to the nearest washrooms in the terminal where I was sitting was blocked by a no-entry sign and a large janitor's trolley, with two mops propped against the walls further along to reinforce the message. There was a powerful smell of bleach in the air and something else not quite nice. Vomit. The floor to one side was covered with a clutch of sodden paper towels and cleaning rags, and the air-con here didn't seem to be working, which meant the smell had got trapped in the corridor with nowhere to go.

Unfortunately the plan I had in mind to deal with this latest problem didn't allow me to go looking for another washroom. And the fact that this one was out of use served my purposes very well. I checked out the trolley. It held an array of tissues, paper towels and cleaning products, along with pale, two-litre plastic containers of what I guessed was liquid soap. Hooking my backpack over my shoulder I grabbed one of the containers and one of the mops as I passed by. I unscrewed the top of the container as I pushed through the door, hoping the cleaner was on a break.

The interior of the washroom was panelled, tiled and bright as day under the ceiling lights. It was also empty. The combined smell of vomit and bleach in here was even stronger, enough to close the throat and water the eyes. Whoever had been ill out in the corridor had continued being ill in here. I upended the container, pouring the gloop out onto the floor across the doorway a couple of paces inside, then stamped on the mop's wooden handle and broke off the head.

I'd never practiced kendo or stick-fighting but it looked as if I was about to find out if I could.

I heard the men's footsteps as they came hurrying down the corridor. They were probably intent on a quick take-down to complete their assignment and get out of here.

The door was kicked open, slamming it back on its hinges,

revealing one man. He was big across the shoulders, confident and steaming for a fight. He saw me standing halfway across the room and walked quickly forward, eyes locked on mine, an attack-dog on two feet.

He was holding something slim and dark grey in colour down by his leg, and I recognized the outline of a knife. This guy had decided not to bring a gun into a security-washed area like Frankfurt Airport and I was betting he'd settled for a ceramic blade instead. Although not guaranteed there was less chance of being pinged by metal detectors and it would be extremely sharp for maximum effect.

I glanced at his feet. He was a half-step away from the first pool of liquid soap and I wanted him to keep coming with his eyes fixed on me. I waved the mop handle in the air, swishing it around to catch and retain his attention.

Then I fumbled and dropped it. Deliberately.

His expression showed he couldn't believe his luck. As I scrabbled to pick it up again, muttering to myself, he gave a grunt of triumph and increased his pace, his knife blade now out in front, the way he'd been trained.

The second his feet hit the soap the game changed dramatically. He yelped in surprise as his boots took off and dumped him on his back with a crack. Surprisingly he didn't drop the blade and scrabbled to get to his feet. But the floor was too slick and whatever he did he couldn't get a purchase.

I swung the mop handle hard across his head, stunning him, then followed up with another strike, this time on the side of his neck. He dropped the knife and lay still. I leaned forward and grabbed his foot, dragging him clear of the soap, then frisked him for ID. Nothing doing. Some money in his pants pocket and a cellphone. But no photo. I hit the ON button and found myself looking at the same former CIA photo. He'd loaded it as his screen saver so he could check the face easily without having to find the photo gallery.

I pocketed the phone and skirted the soap. His colleague would be waiting outside. I hoped he wasn't armed with anything that went bang. But this was my only way out and I didn't have time to wait for him to come in to see where his friend had got to.

I stepped through the door. The second man was standing near the far end of the corridor, his cellphone in his hand. He looked stunned to see me and I could read the message writ clear on his face. *This wasn't how it was supposed to play out.*

I had one chance and one chance only. There was nobody else in sight and we were both partially hidden by the janitor's trolley. I took three long strides and swung the mop handle at his head. He raised a hand to block it and took the full force on his forearm. It should have put him out of the fight but he appeared not to be affected by it.

Instead he dropped his phone and reached inside his jacket. If he was crazy enough to have brought a gun inside the terminal I was in trouble.

I began to swing again but changed tack and jabbed him hard in the face with the broken end of the stick. It made a nasty liquid noise at it entered one eye and he opened his mouth to scream, so I used a round-house swing across the side of his head to knock him out.

I didn't bother searching him but scooped up his cellphone and walked away. Leaving my picture lying around would be stupid. I scrubbed at my face to give the impression of wiping away tiredness and to conceal my features from the cameras, and headed for the main exit.

As I cleared the building my phone buzzed. It was a text message from Callahan.

Stay and read it or get out of here? There was no option. If what had happened inside got classified as a terrorist incident, they'd shut the airport down tight and I'd be caught inside the cordon.

I opted to get out. Callahan's message would have to wait.

The queue for cabs outside was low and I got a ride within a couple of minutes and told him to take me to the central station. He nodded without looking at me and we were off. One hurdle cleared.

I checked we weren't being followed, aware that the two men might have had a stand-by driver in case things got messy and they had to move out fast. But traffic was heavy and I couldn't tell if any one vehicle was getting too close. In the end I gave up before the driver began to take too much interest.

With the current state of fear over terrorist attacks a call from him to the cops was the last thing I needed.

I got the driver to drop me short of the station and took a fast stroll around the block, ducking into a store and allowing a few pedestrians to go by before I exited and walked back the way I'd come.

As far as I could see I was clean.

Back at the station I bought a bus ticket for Paris. It was something like a twelve-hour trip but it meant I'd be unobserved and able to catch up on some sleep. If I was being tagged I was figuring on a team expecting me to take the quickest route possible out of here. But that meant flight schedules, passenger lists and cameras and the possibility that they would be waiting for me at the other end.

Before taking the SIM card out of my phone and going dark, I checked Callahan's latest message. It was interesting.

*One Ur Lebanon attackers Ukrainian national, former Spetsnaz. No known affils but thought contractor for Moscow. Akrotiri attackers no ID but poss same. Where you?*

I debated not telling him but thought better of it. It was obvious by now that my every move was being monitored. I had no idea how but my suspicions centred on the impossible: someone had gained access to my locator messages. Nothing else made sense. The only question was, at what point were they picking up on them? The only person who had known where I was at any one time up until we got to Cyprus was Isobel Hunt. Yet she had been in as much danger from an attack as me, so why would she risk it?

Furthermore, although she'd known I was coming to Frankfurt she wouldn't have known precisely where I would be at any one time.

That left me with the uncomfortable notion that it could only have been someone able to access my text messages to Callahan. But that was a wide field and included an outside intercept or someone on the inside close to Callahan himself. But why?

I decided to push the envelope. If I didn't take some control over events I might have to spend days, maybe weeks looking over my shoulder, all the time wondering when the next strike would take place.

I told Callahan I was taking a flight to Paris and would send a locator on arrival in the capital. Then I switched off my phone and removed the SIM. Right now I couldn't trust anyone, but maybe I could force whoever was pinpointing me to make a mistake. I focussed instead on the two cellphones I'd acquired from my attackers at the airport and opened them up.

Neither device had a security code, which told me a lot about what I could expect to find inside: no code meant nothing worth hiding. They were burners, acquired for this operation only and to be disposed of afterwards. In the event of anything going wrong and falling into the wrong hands, there would be nothing to show who the men were or what they were doing.

I deleted the photos of me and took out the Sim cards and batteries, and dropped them down a storm drain.

Then I got on board the bus and headed for the rear where I put my head down.

# TWENTY-THREE

*Moscow*

A monitor mounted on a side table in the 'dead room' was flickering, but lacked sound and image. A new meeting had been convened, but the chairman, Konstantin Basalayev, was not yet there. It was a common enough tactic used by senior officials to unsettle those beneath them, to promote anxiety and compliance. Most feigned indifference to it, even if inwardly they were not.

As the minutes ticked away, each individual battled with wondering why the meeting had been called and why the chair previously used by Anatoly Dolmatov, remained empty. All they knew was that Basalayev must have received reports from the field, which he had so far kept to himself, and Dolmatov was no longer in play.

The clues were self-evident to those who knew what to look for.

'Shot for being ugly or shot for fucking up?' murmured Sergey Grishin, the former general, eyeing the empty chair in a false attempt at bravado. 'He should have remained a chopper of wood.'

Nobody else spoke, too anxious to distance themselves from the same fate, whatever that was. Instead their attention was glued to the active monitor in the corner, itself a worrying departure from the norm in this room.

When Basalayev appeared, he did so in a rush and without a greeting, leaving one of the guards outside to pull the door firmly closed behind him. He picked up a television remote from the table and pressed a button.

The screen blossomed into life, showing a slightly grainy image but clear enough for everyone to see. It showed what appeared to be a long-range image of an airfield, with several buildings in the background bathed in sunlight. A number of emergency vehicles were moving at speed across the grass and tarmac towards a small, single-storey structure off to one side. Other transport, including an armoured vehicle, were disgorging troops around it and taking up positions.

Basalayev froze the picture and said, 'That was an attempt by Dolmatov's new team to complete the mission against Portman. They failed. I have relieved him of his duties with immediate effect.'

Nobody spoke, nobody exchanged glances, their suspicions unnervingly correct.

Basalayev pressed the remote again and the images fast-forwarded to another scene. This one had been taken inside what was clearly a busy airport terminal building. It showed two men threading their way through a crowd and approaching a corridor with signs displaying washroom facilities. A cleaner's trolley was parked across the corridor. One of the men stayed at the front of the corridor behind the trolley while the other skirted it and disappeared inside. There was no soundtrack, which lent the scene an extra sense of impending drama.

A flurry of movement came from the man near the trolley. He stepped away from it and raised one arm in a defensive stance as another figure raced towards him. It was difficult to see the detail but it was clear that he'd been attacked. He fell, clutching his face. Then the other figure stepped past him and walked away, rubbing his eyes with his hand and effectively blanketing his features from the watchful eye of the camera.

'Another failure,' Basalayev emphasized. He switched off the monitor and dropped the remote on the table with a clatter. He looked around at the faces, all of whom looked stunned by what they'd seen. He took a few more seconds to study each person, his cold gaze making them shift uncomfortably in their seats before he finally took his own seat.

'As of now,' he said, his voice barely above a whisper, 'Voronin will be running the operation.' He glanced at the former Spetsgruppa special forces officer. 'Our latest information is that Portman is flying to Paris, his location to be confirmed later. We already have a team there in readiness, do we not?'

Voronin nodded. That he didn't look too happy at being singled out for this dubious assignment was no surprise, given

Dolmatov's abrupt fall from grace. But that was the risk you took when you rose to a position where risk ran alongside honour, the former always shuffling just ahead until you took the prize . . . or did not. 'Correct. They are ready to move at a moment's notice.' He spoke with a clear voice, confidence in every word.

'Good. This time, finish it. Finish him. Do it now.'

Voronin nodded and rose from his chair.

When the door closed behind Voronin, Irina Kolodka rested both hands on the table's surface, the move capturing everyone's attention.

She said, 'You know, don't you, that another failure will end this assignment for everyone?'

'Everyone?' Basalayev stared at her. His face gave no clue to his thinking, but it was clear what he meant: everyone including who? That she spoke for someone far above them was now clear, if it hadn't been before. She who had the ear of the president now also had his voice. And the message was no less chilling.

'All of you.'

So it had finally come to this.

Basalayev's face was a mask. If the remaining members of the committee had looked more closely they might have noticed a slight tic at the corner of one eye. Had they known him better they would have recognized a burgeoning anger, even a resentful fury at the hand he'd managed so adeptly to deal himself.

As the old saying went, to run the wolf-pack you have to run with them . . . or face the risk of getting bitten.

'There will be no failures,' said Basalayev. But this time his voice sounded a little less certain.

# TWENTY-FOUR

My bolt-hole apartment in Paris was in a quiet cut-through off the Rue des Pyrenees in the 20th *arrondissement* to the east of the city centre. I hadn't used it as much as I'd have liked, as Paris was among my favourite cities for chilling out. It was located in a small block of apartments in a quiet quarter and, like many Paris streets, had plenty of local facilities which meant nobody had to go far to eat, drink or entertain. In a sense, it had a village feel about it which I'd enjoyed.

Now, however, it looked as if I was going to have to move on.

The address titles of all three of my apartments, in Paris, London and New York, were held and dealt with by Belnex, an offshore administration company based in Gibraltar. I'd acquired each property at various times, putting everything I earned into them as a hedge against the day when I might have to think about a change of profession. They were all small but in good locations, which suited me fine. If my neighbours looked on me as an absent professional I didn't mind. The cities were big enough for it to be very common and it saved having to answer awkward questions.

Disposing of the properties would be a simple matter of a written instruction to Belnex. They would deal with the paperwork and the real estate agencies and I could stay out of it. I was reluctant to sell but now wasn't the time to take risks by hanging onto them.

Life was a lot more important than property and no security could ever be absolute, especially in the financial sector where data could be hacked and sold. Whoever was after me had already demonstrated that they had the reach in spades to do that. It reminded me that I would also have to dispose of my current credit cards and open new bank accounts.

I arrived at the apartment building and took a stroll around

the block. It was late enough for the main flush of office
workers to have gone but too early for the tourists to have got
their plans going for the day. I stopped for coffee at a café on
the corner of the street from where I could watch the front
entrance of the building and picked up a copy of the sports
daily *L'Équipe*. I had no particular interest in rugby or football,
but it gave me useful cover for scanning the street.

There wasn't much to see. An elderly woman pulling a
shopping basket walked out, followed by two young girls, probably college students looking way too sophisticated for their
years. A workman picked up a pile of scaffolding clips left on
the side of the street and dumped them in the back of a pickup,
and two boys who looked as if they were goofing off from
school went by laughing.

After thirty minutes of watching and reading stuff I didn't
care about, I paid up and left the café and did another tour,
stopping to buy some fruit on the way. A plastic bag of shopping to go with my backpack and a shuffled gait was all it
needed to give the impression of being a nobody going about
their nobody daily business. It's certainly enough to make the
eyes pass over a potential target and move on. By the time
the eyes come back it's time to be gone and forgotten.

The building had no concierge and relied on a keypad entry
system for residents to come and go. I walked along the street
on the same side as the building and waited for a cab to come
along and used it as cover to dodge inside the doorway. Only
the workman saw me enter and he looked about as interested
in me as I was in him, but we both nodded and muttered
'*bonjour*' as was the custom.

I tapped in the entry code and slipped inside the building.
The foyer smelled of polish and flowers, a pleasant mix as
familiar as the last time I'd been here which was about a month
ago. I liked Paris and this place had been a haven in between
jobs; always hard to tear myself away from when the next one
came along.

I walked up the stairs to the third floor, stepping past two
bicycles and a baby stroller on the way. There were three apartments on each floor and very little noise save for a hum of
unseen activity which might have been a vacuum, a television

or a washing machine. I checked my door for signs of a forced entry but everything looked pristine.

The air inside smelled a little musty and needed a good airing. But I resisted the temptation to throw open the windows in case the place was under observation. It would be a clear tell-tale sign that I was inside and open to attack.

There was very little here that I needed to take away. But there were a couple of items I certainly couldn't leave behind. I went to a small safe I'd installed in the bedroom and tapped in the code. The door swung open. Inside was a plastic folder containing emergency cash in various currencies, two spare passports in different names, driving documents and Visa cards to match and a Beretta 92SB semi-automatic pistol with a spare magazine. As long as I didn't have to pass through any kind of scanning device I'd be fine to carry it with me.

I placed the Beretta and passports in the bottom of my backpack and pocketed the cash. From here on in I was going cash-friendly to avoid using my existing cards. I didn't want to use them unless I had to.

I checked the apartment one last time, making sure there was nothing to identify me to anyone who came looking, and cleared out some old invoices for some building work I'd had done. I'd dump those later in a skip. Then I left and walked three streets away to a general store where I bought an envelope and scribbled a note to go inside with the apartment keys.

After that I dropped the envelope through the letterbox of the lawyer I'd used to negotiate the paperwork for acquiring the place. My note told him I'd send instructions later. Until then he could set about looking for a buyer and wait to hear from Belnex who would have shared responsibility for settling any outstanding bills and approving the contracts.

I walked for twenty minutes until I found a small hotel near the Parmentier *métro* and took and paid for a room for three days. Then I left through the rear door and walked some more and took another room for the same length of time at a hotel close to the Place de la République. I was probably being over-cautious but after the events of the past few days I wasn't taking chances. As I'd learned over many years, having a plan A and a plan B and a safe place just in case, is never a waste.

In the second hotel I replaced the sim in my phone and dialled Callahan's number. Because of our past association I didn't have to go through the CIA switchboard, which would avoid any exchange of names being overheard. An additional plus point was that both our phones were encrypted. He picked up within two rings.

'Callahan.'

'It's me.' I said.

'It's good to hear from you.' He sounded as calm as always, if a little relieved. 'After Cyprus and Frankfurt I was beginning to worry. Frankfurt was you, right?'

I confirmed it was. 'They arrived right on the spot where you told me to be and spotted me immediately.'

'Yeah. They knew who to look for.'

'Obviously. In a place that big it should never have happened. And after the other team attacking the British facility in Cyprus not long after I left, how was it possible?' I wasn't angry, although I put some stick into sounding it. But I didn't think it would hurt. I had, after all, been shot at and nearly sliced open by people who should not have known where I was.

As a wise man had once said to me, it doesn't do any harm just to occasionally let the people around you know that you're royally pissed off.

'I'm sorry – truly. We're working on tracing the leak.'

So there was one. 'Any ideas?' Not that it would matter directly to me but I also wanted him to know that I was annoyed enough to ask. Callahan or the people above him had to realize, if they didn't already, that the threats against me and the attempts on my life so far were more than simply an unscheduled blip in events caused by a chain of bad luck.

'Not yet. I'm working on that. Where are you now, Marc?'

'On the move. Why?'

'That's good. In fact it's better than good because staying on the move is just what I was going to recommend. In fact, I have a job for you.'

'What – now? How does that help my present situation?'

'There's a woman journalist on our payroll in France who's being hunted by a small extreme right-wing organization. As part of her cover working for us she's been investigating their activities with a friend, compiling data on their strength and members. She got too close and a couple of days ago they killed the friend to blow her off the scent. She can't go to the French authorities as that would signal our involvement, and there's nobody else we can ask right now. You're there and I know you can handle this. But we need to keep close contact throughout. It's a sensitive issue.'

I'll bet. Spying on people in a friendly nation state doesn't go down well when the friendly nation state finds out what you've been doing. And the French could be righteously and noisily angry about such behaviour, even though they were well versed in doing a bit of snooping on their allies when the spirit moved them.

'What do you mean, close contact?'

'I'll need to know where you are so we can provide support. We can have a team standing by but we'll have to use the locator system we've been using recently. The group chasing her is particularly nasty.'

'What, worse than the group chasing me?' I didn't disbelieve he had a job for me or that it involved pulling a female asset out of a sticky situation, but the thinking behind it was devious.

'Sorry. You know what I mean.'

'You want me to be a decoy.'

'I want you on the move, is what I want. The more you move the less chance there is of the Russians being able to target you. Staying still is a guarantee that they will find you.'

He hadn't denied the decoy bit, I noticed. And he was right about them finding me. They had the resources and the manpower, and would be able to call on as much help here as they needed. If I sat and waited for them, they would eventually pin me down.

My problem was, I was now going to be threatened by two groups, not one. Part of it might reveal who the mole was, but it didn't make me feel any safer. I didn't say anything for a few moments while I thought it over.

'And the real reason?' I needed at the very least for him to admit what he wanted.

'What do you mean?'

'You said it yourself: you think you've got a leak. I'm not

even in the building but I *know* you have. There's no other explanation. It must begin with your own department.'

If he was offended by the implication he didn't say anything. But he was a professional and knew the game. 'I can't be certain of that – I wish I could. All I can say is we're narrowing down the possibilities.'

I said, 'I'll call you back,' and disconnected. I was keeping our conversation deliberately brief and wanted him to be a little off-guard. I needed time to think. Having another job to do right now had not been part of my thinking. With unknown elements after me I needed to think carefully about what I was doing. While having to worry about another person was a normal part of what I did, right now it was a distraction I could do without.

In the end, though, I had to concede that Callahan was right; moving meant staying alive. But if I did this I was going to do it my way.

I rang him back. 'All right. I'm in.'

'Good.' He sounded relieved. 'I'll text you the asset's location. The meet will be some time tomorrow, so stay in touch and let me know when you're there.'

# TWENTY-FIVE

The following day Callahan was still ruminating over the unsettling idea that the former spook, Russell Hoffman, had voiced at their meeting: that someone on the inside was fingering Portman's location trail to the people trying to kill him. A sleepless night had not filled in any blanks and he still wasn't sure what action to take next.

It might have seemed implausible had it not echoed his own fears. The CIA was not impregnable or immune to having a traitor inside the walls, as spies Aldrich Ames and Jerry Lee had proved. But a new scandal would hollow out the guts of the organization at a time when it needed to be operating at full capacity against external enemies and threats rather than beating itself to death over a possible repeat of history.

Yet he had to concede that it was more than a possibility.

How else would the Russians have been able to get so close to Portman each time? And if Hoffman was right, and they were committed to doing away with Portman, there might be no way of stopping them unless he disappeared for good.

He stood up, deciding it was about time he spoke to Sewell, when an incoming call stopped him. It was Fred Groll of the National Security Agency.

'Brian, I figure you'd want to know about some chatter we picked up that might involve your man in Lebanon.'

Callahan sat down again. 'Go ahead. I could do with some good news.'

'On the surface it's not a great deal but it sounds interesting. One of our operators picked up a transmission from a source located close to the Russian embassy in Nicosia, northern Cyprus. It said, and I quote: *Delivery location 333420 cancelled. Delivery to be re-scheduled, advise of new address.*'

'Do we know where the transmission went?'

'We're working on that but it's a slim hope. Like I said, it was a chance pick-up, so there wasn't time to run a full trace.

The thing is, that location 333420 is a basic code the Russians have used before. It refers to the British RAF base at Akrotiri. We know they keep a close eye on it for strategic reasons, and there's been a rumour that they have someone on the inside, most likely posing as a civilian contractor.'

'Akrotiri. That's where they had the recent attack.'

'Right. The "delivery cancelled" speaks for itself. Failed would have been more accurate but they don't like using that word much. It gives them a ticklish sensation across the back of their necks.'

'Thanks, Fred. Good work.'

'Glad to help. I'll keep you informed if we hear anything else.'

Callahan ended the call and sat back. Well, that confirmed who was behind the attacks on Portman. So now, if Groll was right, they had confirmation of the who and the why, no doubts about that. What they didn't have was the identity of the person pointing the finger.

He dialled a number, the decision to speak to Sewell delayed. It could wait until he'd got something moving. In any case, he'd been told to let Watchman go, so he'd best not advertise the fact that he was still helping him out.

The phone was answered immediately by David Andrews, a CIA researcher with the National Resources Division. While the CIA itself was forbidden from operating within the US mainland, the NR division was tasked with, among other things, recruiting students and other foreign nationals visiting the US, to be schooled as assets when returning to their home countries. Andrews had a specific interest in and knowledge of Russian security and intelligence operations, and had been useful in providing information to Callahan on a number of occasions before.

'Do you have a moment?' Callahan asked him. 'I could do with some help.'

'You kidding?' Andrews replied. 'I haven't been away from my desk in weeks. Is it dangerous, is it exciting, do I get to carry a gun?' There was a definite hint of boyish laughter in the young man's voice which made Callahan smile. There were times this place could do with more of that.

He said, 'None of those things, but you might have to go outside the building for a while, if the thought of daylight and vitamin D doesn't scare you.'

'Hell, no, sir. I'm on it. Be there in three.' The phone went down.

David Andrews was in his twenties, short and chunky, with a thin moustache and a sallow complexion everyone put down to spending too much time under subdued lighting crouched over his monitors. He wore a tie in name only as it rarely looked as if it belonged and was usually skewed to one side or tucked into the front of his shirt.

When he arrived he dropped into a seat opposite Callahan and looked around with ill-concealed interest.

'I haven't been up here before. Is this where you send out men to do dastardly things to our enemies?'

'That's pretty sexist,' Callahan told him mildly. 'We have female field officers, too.'

Andrews looked unabashed. 'My bad. How can I help?'

Callahan had been rehearsing just how much he could tell the researcher, and he'd decided he had to be as frank as possible, otherwise he'd be asking Andrews to operate with his hands tied. He explained what had happened to Portman, how he was being hunted by a kill team belonging to a hostile state who appeared to be operating with the guidance of someone using Portman's location tags.

Andrew dropped the boyish air and got serious. 'You mean someone in here? Jesus. Are you sure?'

'Not yet, which is why I need your help. I don't have proof other than that the opposition have now turned up three times for sure right on Watchman's last known location.'

'I get it. Too much to be a coincidence. But isn't this a job for internal security?' He added quickly, 'Don't get me wrong, I'm not looking to palm it off on some guy in uniform who knows nothing about Russian ops, but I don't want to tread on any toes.'

'I'll cover you on that, don't worry. But as of this moment, you keep this to yourself, you hear? I don't want it doing the rounds that you're working on our behalf. Should anyone ask, we'll keep it to a simple research job.'

'No problem. What do you want me to do?'

'I want you to take a close look at how these details might have got out; where there might be a weakness in the system that allows someone not in this office to have picked up data received or circulated internally. Also, who it might have been passed to on the outside, although that might be expecting too much.'

Andrews nodded. 'If they committed the details to memory and walked out the door then passed it on, there would be no trace.'

'In that case it would be the potential recipient I'd like to know about. There has to be an external contact point somewhere. I figured you might have some views on that.'

'A Russian contact? There are a few I can think of, some of them right here in DC. If you have any hints, though, it would help me narrow down the search field.'

'Such as?'

'Well, an idea of who not to look at is always good. It saves time and from what you say I'm guessing this is time sensitive, right?' When Callahan nodded, he continued. 'You mentioned that this photo has been outed once before, and has now turned up again?'

'Correct. We don't know exactly how, but we think it was acquired a few years ago from the entrance security system at one of our field offices. The person we think was responsible was using an outside source with access to the building – but they've now gone dark or are deceased.'

'I get it. In that case turn it on its head: who benefited most the first time by getting the photo out there?'

Callahan was impressed. He was no investigator himself; he kept his analytical skills for a different kind of search and detect – the kind that looked for people in foreign lands who might prove useful to the endeavours of the CIA. He'd been instinctively thinking about current events, not whether they might have some relevance to what had happened in the past. But already a fresh mind looking at the issue had come up with a new perspective, and Andrews could be right: the original theft of the photo might prove the lead they required.

He thought back to when the photo had first popped up.

Portman had been tasked with pulling a State Department official named Edwin Travis out of Ukraine, where he'd gone to conduct talks. Instead Travis had been held hostage by one of the factions in a bid to disrupt progress. It was while he'd been getting the man out of the country that he'd run into opposition from some FSB operatives, one of whom was carrying photos of both Portman and Travis.

'We were told a senator named Benson instigated Portman's photo being outed, but that was on the say-so of a man we haven't been able to trace, so it's unconfirmed. And since Benson is dead that avenue is closed, too.'

'Unless he had associates,' Andrews pointed out. 'Maybe someone who shared a grudge against your guy and is still out there.'

'That could be a broad field. Benson had been around for a long time and had a lot of supporters. As to grudges against Portman, I wouldn't know where to begin looking.'

'So we should look at who knew Benson best. He might have confided in someone he was close to, maybe someone who felt they wanted to get pay-back. If so they could have been sitting on the information ever since, biding their time.'

'Good point. How do you reckon on moving it forward?'

'Was he married? Did he have children?'

'Not as far as I know. But you can check that out, I'm sure.'

'Will do. If I can focus on a couple of people to start with, it might help me before I have to look wider at other candidates. I'll start close to home, say, associates and the people he worked with.'

'You're thinking like a cop,' Callahan said. 'Does this mean you can do it or not?'

Andrews looked pleased. 'Actually I wanted to be a cop at one time, but I got side-tracked into this job and never looked back. And yes, I can do it. You get me covered for a free rein with my supervisor and I'll see what I can turn up.'

'Good. I'll send over whatever we have on Benson and you can start from there.'

# TWENTY-SIX

I took a rental car and headed south-west out of Paris on the E5, then the A10 past Paris-Orly Airport. Hopefully if anyone was already on my tail they might conclude I was taking a flight out and set off to intercept me. Good luck with that.

I was feeling more lively after some sleep and a sandwich and ready to face whatever the day was about to throw at me. Following Callahan's last text message I was heading for Épernon, a small commuter town in the Loire region about an hour's drive from Paris. I stopped once at a pull-in service area near Janvry and took a stroll, eyes on the approach road to see if anyone came in after me.

It didn't amount to much: a Dutch-registered transporter loaded with caravans, a small Citroën with a family of five on board all shouting at each other and looking as if they'd like to indulge in group murder, and a coach from Manchester, England, full of old folk who appeared to be having an early karaoke session.

None of the above looked like the kind of cover anybody would use for tracking me. The other traffic was fairly light and kept on going by, so I gave it thirty minutes before getting back on the road. I stopped again near the forest of Rambouillet and went through the exercise once more before continuing.

The road skirted the southern quarter of the forest, and I headed north at Abli. I'd never been to Épernon before so I was stepping into the unknown. But what else was new?

Callahan's last text had stated the town as a meeting point but with no specific location. It was a wise move. If someone was tracking me it would be insane to allow the CIA's local source to be pinpointed, too. All I knew was that her name was Marie-Josée Chesnais and Callahan said she would meet me at a pre-arranged spot and time of my choosing. From there I was to get her on a flight out from the nearest big airport, which would be Orly.

As a precaution I scouted out a hotel tucked away in a quiet street and checked the keyboard behind reception. It looked like there were plenty of spare rooms but I didn't want to book one yet unless I had to.

It was an indie establishment which was a plus point. If someone with sophisticated hacking capabilities was trying to find me and knew I was in France, their first logical move would be to plug into the French chain hotels and use their corporate reservations intranet to check names, arrival times and length of stay – all details which would lead a cautious team to check out single travellers as worthy of a look. The downside of using a small private hotel was you were more easily remembered.

I went back out and scouted the town on foot to familiarize myself with the surroundings. It had a pleasant atmosphere and was built partly on the side of a hill, with narrow, twisting thoroughfares and ancient houses leaning over some of the older streets. Apart from a cluster of retail shops in the centre, the community's advertised pride and joy was a park catering for the well-being of its citizens and visitors. This facility included a fitness trail for the jog-and-exercise enthusiasts, and a park for dogs. So cool, the French.

I returned to my rental car in a quiet side street and sent a text to Callahan stating that I'd arrived in the town and was ready to go. He came back within a few minutes.

*Confirm RV.*

I still wasn't sure I trusted the system he was using, or the fact that I was being put out like a sacrificial goat to flush out a hit team. But since I'd agreed to go ahead with it, there was no point getting cold feet now.

In any case, I didn't do cold feet.

I'd already chosen a spot where we could meet, so I sent him the general locators for the park, then took my backpack and made sure the Beretta was good to go. I didn't like walking around a friendly country with a gun on me, but I'd have felt half naked going without one. Unless Mademoiselle Chesnais was going to turn out to be a secret psycho I figured I should be fine for the time being.

Callahan's response came quickly.

*RV 1 hour. Sending help.*

One hour wasn't long. It meant Chesnais must be fairly close by. But what was the help he'd mentioned? Had he got some Special Activities guys ready to swoop in on a helicopter? Somehow I doubted it.

I walked back down through the town, stopping at a bakery on the way for a baguette which I tucked under my arm. Then I took a different route to the park, taking my time and checking my back trail.

There were more trees than I would have liked, which was both good and bad. It made good cover for me and I could keep an eye out for any arrivals, but if they were a class act and came in numbers I'd have my work cut out to spot them all. I'd avoided choosing the dog park, since anyone walking there who didn't have a mutt in tow or chasing a Frisbee would stand out too much.

I circled the area slowly, giving the pretence of scrolling through messages on my cellphone while looking for cars or people who looked as if they didn't belong. People like me, essentially. Hopefully the baguette would help dispel that suspicion, and I chewed on one end, which my mother always referred to as the butt-end, because that's what you do with such an appealing piece of bread when in France.

As I chewed and strolled along a path towards a strand of trees where I'd decided to sit and wait for Chesnais, a figure in jeans and a light jacket, and carrying a shoulder bag stepped off the grass ahead of me and walked towards me. She was young and pretty, and had honey-brown hair cut in a short bob, and I was about as surprised as I could be at seeing her.

It was Lindsay Citera, and she was smiling.

# TWENTY-SEVEN

efore I could say anything Lindsay raised a hand and tapped her wrist, mime-speak for 'do you have the time?' which I took to be in case anyone was watching. I obliged and went through the motions of checking my watch and telling her, all the time wondering if the Langley-based comms operative I'd worked with before had turned into a CIA field asset without me knowing.

She thanked me with a graceful dip of her head, blushing slightly and pointing at the half-eaten end of the baguette.

'Sorry,' she said, keeping her voice down. 'Callahan sent me to help you out. He said a couple would be more of a cover than a squad of special ops types . . . even if he could send them. I hope he's right. Can I have the other end? Only that bread looks great and I haven't eaten in hours.'

I passed over the baguette and she gave a girlish laugh in a perfect imitation of being taken by surprise, and snapped off the other butt-end. She nibbled at it with grace and waved a hand around us as if discussing the area, the way you do in these awkward social situations. When in France . . .

'You're good at this,' I told her, and meant it. 'How's your field awareness?'

'Not up to yours. I just got here so everything's a bit strange, but I haven't seen anyone who doesn't appear to fit . . . apart from some strange guy chewing on a baguette. But he looks like he might be a local, so what do I know?' She grinned, her nose wrinkling, which made me feel nothing could possibly go wrong from here on in.

'When did you get here?' It had been a while since we'd last spoken and although we'd never traded personal details because you don't in our business, for all I knew she'd got herself a posting to Europe and was now a fixture working out of the US embassy in Paris. Of course I was wrong.

'Callahan got me on a red-eye from Washington. He got me

to book some down-time and said Paris would be ideal for a
short vacation.'

'Big of him. What are your instructions?' I was pretty sure
the CIA wasn't given to handing out occasional rest breaks to
its personnel, and Callahan had to have had some plan in mind
involving me and possibly Chesnais.

'To pick up a package from the airport and meet you here.
He sent me the locators a few minutes ago. He said there's
another party due here, too.' She looked at me. 'I'm not sure
how much of a help he thought I could be.'

'The cover thing is a good idea. A couple can skate by more
easily, especially when the other team is looking for a single
traveller. Would there be another reason he sent you?'

She didn't say anything for a moment, then said, 'I got the
impression he thought it would be good to get me out of the way
for a while. There's stuff going on back in Langley; he most
likely figured he could deal with it more easily if I wasn't part
of the same frame as him.'

'That's a good explanation.' I gestured openly in the direction
I was going, continuing the play-acting, and we fell in side by
side, two people who'd met, spoken and formed a sort of bond.
It happens all the time, all over the world, albeit not to me
when I'm working. I just hoped if anyone was watching it
looked innocent enough to pass off unnoticed and we could get
out of here. 'What else did he say?'

The downside to his idea was that he'd placed Lindsay in
potential danger by aligning her with me. Operational
personnel are trained for these kinds of games with plans for
routes in and out and well-rehearsed scenarios of what to do
if things should go wrong. We all know the risks and how
to respond to threats. But telling someone what they should
do if they should encounter a difficult situation and expecting
them to react positively is a million miles away from live
experience and field training. Lindsay seemed pretty relaxed,
though, and I guessed she must have undergone some training
on the quiet.

'He said you were to meet the asset here. He wanted me to
come along because she's highly nervous about meeting anyone,
so I can take point on that if you wish.' She gestured ahead of

us towards a small path veering off through some trees. 'Can we go this way? I have something to give you.'

We followed the path and after fifty yards or so Lindsay stopped in the shade of a large beech tree and opened her shoulder bag. Inside was what appeared to be a leather washbag. She unzipped it and revealed the black steel shape of a semi-automatic pistol.

'Is there any point me asking where you got this?' I said. I lifted the gun out. It was a SIG Sauer P229. I tucked it into my waistband under my jacket. Now, at least, I felt even better dressed than I already was, with two guns to choose from.

'A man from our Paris embassy met me off the plane. He handed it over and disappeared. I didn't even get to thank him; I got the impression he was actually nervous of being seen with me.'

'I'm not surprised.' I was willing to bet the man wasn't from the embassy at all. Diplomatic personnel don't get involved in passing weapons around like *petit fours* at a cocktail party. The risk of a diplomatic incident if they got caught is far too high. So-called allies and friendly countries take a dim view of that kind of stuff. He'd probably been a local contractor, the kind I'd used myself on several occasions; non-aligned, independent and trustworthy up to a point as long as they were paid well for their services.

'Callahan said he thought you'd be able to source something yourself but this is a just-in-case.'

'Yeah, Callahan would.' He'd been a field operative himself so he knew the problems of supply and demand, especially when a situation went hot.

We continued walking while I mulled over the situation and kept one eye on our back trail and the open area of the park to our right. Callahan must need his head seeing to doing this but I couldn't fault his wanting to provide support.

'What are you supposed to do after this?' It was a long way to come just to hand over a gun and provide a friendly face for a nervous asset.

'I'm to stick around and help. He said it would be good experience for me.'

'Only if you want to go out in the field, it might. I wouldn't recommend it.'

She stopped. 'Why not?' She was looking at me with a sharp glint in her eyes, which was quite nice to look at but told me I'd taken a step too far. 'Last time I looked fieldwork wasn't the exclusive preserve of men any more.' She said it with a show of heat. 'Or are you saying you wouldn't trust a female operative?'

'Last time I looked,' I said calmly, scoping the trees around us as a couple of dogs began tearing into each other, 'there are plenty of women who do the job extremely well. In fact the last one I met was in Lebanon a few days ago.'

'You mean Isobel Hunt – the MI6 officer.'

'That's the one.'

She was smiling now and I realized she'd been pushing my buttons.

'Are you saying she was a hottie in tights and jump boots . . . or have I got a skewed take on reality?'

I debated letting it go but Callahan had put her in a difficult situation. Seeing what I normally did through a long-range camera feed from a drone, or hearing what I did on the end of a comms line might have given her a whole wrong impression about what really went on out here. I couldn't let it lie and said, 'Her reality is she had to shoot a man dead to save our lives. That's what I'm saying.'

The smile vanished and her mouth dropped open. She went pale. 'Oh. God, I'm so sorry—'

I realized I'd been too harsh on her. None of this was her fault. I took her arm and steered her forward. Up close she smelled of something soapy and citrusy, and suddenly I was enjoying the closeness. It was a sensation I wasn't used to.

'Doesn't matter. It worked out fine. I didn't mean to be rough. Tell me what's been happening in Langley.'

'Like what?'

'Come on. I can read between the lines. Callahan's acting weird, I can tell. He told you I'm being targeted, right?'

'Yes.' She nodded and said, 'And apparently the State Department isn't happy with what happened in Lebanon. They're trying to forge closer relationships with Moscow and their allies, and something like the Lebanon operation blowing up gets in the way. That's their words, not ours. Callahan didn't tell me everything but I know he was ordered to drop you and that as a contractor you were on your own.'

'Just like that?'

She shook her head. 'I don't know. But Callahan's hugely upset. I get the feeling he's close to telling them what they can do with their job.'

'He shouldn't,' I said. 'There are times when tough decisions have to be made and they don't always make sense.' Especially, I thought, when they had a dimension that was driven by outside or political influences and ignored the situation of people on the ground a long way away with potentially no easy way to react quickly enough.

Quite how much of a shit-storm, to use Isobel's expression, that would kick up among other contractors when they found out remained to be seen. Nobody wants to work for an employer who drops the ball purely because politicians say their agenda trumps anything going on in the field.

Then my phone buzzed. I checked the screen. Surprise, surprise – it was Callahan.

'You've got some nerve,' I told him. 'So what now – is this the end of the road?'

'Not as far as I'm concerned,' he replied briskly. 'I take it you've met up with Lindsay?'

'I have. About what she told me, I have to admit to being a little pissed.' I leaned close to Lindsay so she could hear our conversation. If things turned bad here it was only fair that she knew what the situation was.

'I figured you should know how things stand, that's all. It's political and stupid and will cause a lot of people in your position to jump ship. Maybe even some of our own field staff, too. But there's nothing I can do about it until someone at the top sees sense.'

'Is that why you're calling?'

'I wish it was. But no. Chesnais got careless before she went to the embassy and blabbed about her situation to a friend. The friend said she wanted to cover her back and put the story out on a news website saying an unnamed French citizen "journalist" was being threatened by right-wing extremists who've already killed another journalist. It's gone viral.'

'How does that affect us?' I could think of only one answer to that and it wasn't long in coming. Trouble rarely travels alone.

'She won't be coming. She lost her nerve and bolted to our embassy in Paris where she thought she'd be safe. Luckily for us and her they called me instead of kicking her onto the street. The security guys over there put her on a flight out; she's probably midway over the Atlantic by now.'

'But that's not all?'

'I'm afraid not. She also told the friend about the plan to meet up with an American representative in your location who was going to help get her out of the country. They don't have the precise location but I'm guessing Épernon is a small place.'

'Small enough.'

'Right. In that case they'll be scouring the town for her.'

Jesus. Moscow killers and now right-wing terrorists converging on my ass. Correction: mine and Lindsay's. It was getting to be a crowded field.

'Wait one.'

Lindsay was tapping me urgently on the arm and pointing towards the open section of the park. Two men with shaved heads and neck tattoos were kicking at a bouncy Labrador that had got a little too friendly. The elderly woman owner was screaming at them in outrage and dragging the dog away as fast as she could.

The men were dressed in tight jeans with head-kicker turn-ups, jump boots and leather jackets, the go-to fashion statement for hard-nosed, right-wing street punks with a bent for aggression. Right here and now, though, after what Callahan had just told me, I knew they were worse than that; they had come looking for Marie-Josée Chesnais.

And they both had their eyes firmly on Lindsay.

'Portman, what's going on?' Callahan's voice came out of the phone.

'What does Chesnais look like?' I asked him.

He gave me a rough description. It matched Lindsay plus fifteen years or so.

'Stand here and don't move,' I told Lindsay, and pushed her against a tree with her back to the men. I gave her the cellphone with Callahan's voice still squawking out of it, then took the Sig out from my waist and held it down by my leg. The gun felt instantly comfortable, the grip almost moulding itself to my hand. I'd used Sigs a lot over the years and trusted them implicitly.

'What are you going to do?' Lindsay asked. 'There are two of them. You can't face them both down.'

'I can't walk away, either.' The men had seen Lindsay and drawn an obvious conclusion – that she must be Chesnais. Visual on target. 'Stay here until I move, then head into town. Don't look back and don't stop for anyone. I'll find you there.'

I stepped out from the trees, checking the position of other visitors to the park. The elderly woman and her dog were far enough away to be safe, helped by a couple of women who'd heard the ruckus. One was on her cellphone, no doubt calling the police. There was nobody else close by, which was a good thing.

I checked that Lindsay wasn't hanging around and placed myself between her and the men, then walked directly towards them, drawing their attention. We were about fifty feet apart and closing fast. Any second now they'd have to make a decision about who or what I was, whether to go after Lindsay or deal with me first.

I made sure that I stayed centre-point in their field of vision and kept walking.

# TWENTY-EIGHT

'*Fous le camp!*' one of the punks snarled at me and motioned for me to get out of his way. He was bean-pole thin and the ugly zig-zag tattoo on his throat was shaded red like a blood vessel about to burst. He probably thought it made him look mean and tough, but it didn't.

When I didn't move he upgraded the threat level by producing a handgun. He pushed it towards me, waving me to move to one side. I figured he'd written me off as a no-threat bystander who'd scare easy. Big mistake.

The way he was holding the gun, gangbanger-style and sideways on was a sure sign he'd been watching too many lousy gangster flicks and thought it looked cool. It was no way to get off an accurate shot but I wasn't about to tell him that.

His colleague meanwhile was moving off to one side and shouted something I didn't catch, but the meaning was clear: he was telling him to blow me the fuck away so they could get the woman and finish the job.

By now we were twenty feet apart. The man with the gun shouted something else and I could see his knuckles going white as he debated pulling the trigger. That's the trouble with extremists: they're short on limitations and high on hate. Anyone who doesn't agree with them is an enemy and therefore to be pulped.

It was about as close as I wanted to get.

I stepped two fast paces sideways and tossed the baguette in his face. He flinched and used his free hand to bat the bread away and discovered that accurate shooting, especially up close, is all about cool nerve and alignment. He had no nerve and the idiot way he was holding his gun meant he instinctively over-adjusted and the barrel wavered off-target.

Even so he got off a panic shot which went past me by about a yard and snapped harmlessly into a tree-trunk. He pulled the trigger again and scowled when nothing happened. He gave it another try.

Trigger-jam.

I didn't want to take a chance on it clearing, so I shot him in the leg. All this happened within a second or two. The shots were loud, setting off a flurry of birds from the trees above our heads. Someone screamed in the distance followed by some shouting and barking, the dogs latching on to the tension in the air.

In a hunting-happy country like France and with an armed police force, a lot of people and dogs knew what a gunshot sounded like.

The wounded skinhead squealed and dropped his gun, then fell over with his leg pumping blood. His pal swore in shock and dragged a gun from his jacket, but he was way too slow reacting. I ran at him before he could untangle the safety on his weapon and slapped him hard under the chin with the Sig. The blow knocked him backwards onto the grass, his eyes wide open with shock. Then the lights went out and he lost all further interest.

I quickly checked his pockets for ID and found a licence, a cellphone, a crumpled pack of cigarettes and some cash. Extremism on a budget. The phone was switched on but there was no photo. So, not part of the kill-me plot. I didn't have time to check the other punk so I kicked both guns away and made sure nobody else was near before turning to follow Lindsay into town.

As I filtered through the trees something made me look back. The two skinheads were still out cold and the dog-walkers had disappeared. But a movement on the far side of the park caught my eye.

A man in dark clothing was standing there looking my way. He had a cellphone to his ear and I thought for a split second that he might be a cop, in which case I definitely had to get moving.

But when he didn't move I realized I was wrong.

He was a spotter. I'd been here too long.

# TWENTY-NINE

Callahan was waiting anxiously for news from Portman or Lindsay Citera when he saw David Andrews lurking in the corridor outside. The researcher wore a grin on his face. He beckoned him in and told him to close the door.

'What have you got?' He wasn't being totally optimistic, but figured Andrews wouldn't be looking so chipper if he hadn't made some progress.

'I got lucky,' Andrews said, waving a tablet. 'I've been trawling our files for information on known or suspected Russian agents or sympathizers here in DC area, to see if any have popped up on the watch reports recently. I knew of a few from my previous work and figured it was a good place to begin. I stumbled on this.' He held out the tablet so Callahan could see it and tapped the screen. A formatted document appeared headed with the name 'Valentina J. Desayeva', followed by a list of personal details. 'This is an FBI surveillance report on this subject from a few weeks ago. Do you know her?'

Callahan racked his memory. The name was vaguely familiar but he couldn't place it. Too much was going on in his head at the moment and he needed time to think. 'Let's pretend I don't. Remind me.'

'She's long been suspected by the FBI of having close connections to people in Moscow, but nothing has ever been proved. She's a resident in DC and calls herself a businesswoman and charity fundraiser with a lot of friends in social and political circles. Before that she was a close associate of a man named Boranov.'

Callahan stared at him. 'Gus Boranov?'

'The same. He was a Russian, the US representative of—'

'BJ Security Group. Yeah, I know. They've got connections with state-run companies in Russia and the Kremlin. Boranov disappeared a few years back when things got too hot for him.

The FBI had him figured for espionage and were about to take him in for questioning. Desayeva was tied in with him in some way, but with Boranov gone they couldn't prove how deep it went.' He recalled now how Desayeva had been investigated, but had come up clean, with Walter Broderick being among her more enthusiastic supporters.

Being close to Boranov hadn't been enough to land her in court or even to have her kicked out on the next Aeroflot to Moscow. Instead someone in the State Department had suggested using her knowledge and background to provide information on current Kremlin thinking.

Beyond sounding a note of caution, which he suspected had been ignored, it hadn't been part of Callahan's or the CIA's remit to be involved so he'd got on with his job and put Desayeva out of his mind.

'Right. I followed the trail of the report back into Boranov's activities, just to see if there was anything useful like other contact names who were still around. The trail ran dry when I found that some of the reports that included Desayeva's name had been redacted. It didn't say why, though.'

'It wouldn't,' Callahan said sourly. All he knew was that Desayeva was being used by the State Department for reasons they wouldn't go into, and that made her beyond suspicion in their eyes. It hadn't made sense then and it didn't now. 'So?'

'It didn't leave much to go on, but that's where two lines intersected.' Andrews smiled, 'It's surprising how so much comes back to Washington.'

'Get on with it,' Callahan growled. 'Time's a-wasting. What lines?'

Andrews lost the smile. 'Sorry.' He flicked a finger across the screen to reveal a photo. It showed the interior of a smart looking restaurant. The room was large and airy with panoramic windows at the far side. Waiters in short white jackets were cruising in the background. 'This was taken four weeks ago at a place called the Pines View Golf Park near Charlottesville. It's an upscale country club type of place aimed at people who like a touch of class with their golf and a place to chat.' He enlarged the screen shot to show a couple sitting to one side.

'The woman is Desayeva. The man with her has been identified as a Bradley Dalkin, a Washington resident.'

'Is he anyone we should know?'

'Well, referring back to the file you sent me, he was chief of staff to a Senator Howard J. Benson – or was until Benson's death four years ago. Since then he's been scratching for work wherever he can get it.'

'Benson? Now that's a name I know.' The memories came flooding back. The senator had been a member of the powerful Intelligence Community, set up to co-ordinate and support special activities among the various US intelligence agencies with regard to US foreign policy overseas. Benson had been a rabid CIA sceptic intent on dragging the organization before an investigative committee given half a chance.

His death, while shocking, had not been universally mourned among those he had targeted. And one person he had seemed especially averse to had been Marc Portman and his assignment for the CIA.

There had been questions about Portman's possible role in Benson's murder, but concrete evidence proved he'd been in Arlington in the company of a trusted CIA staff member at the time, over sixty miles away from where Benson had died.

Callahan skim-read the details on the tablet. Desayeva's name had come up on a list of targets kept under regular review. These were mostly mid-to-low-level foreign nationals, especially Russians, who had popped up on the FBI's radar but lacked anything substantial with which to charge them. A two-man team had been put on her for a few days to scrape off whatever barnacles they could find.

Usually such reviews proved little and took up time, shoe leather and money, but were considered essential to the fight against espionage. This particular surveillance had coincided with Desayeva taking a trip out of Washington and the team had decided to follow her to see who she met with. Now it seemed that a routine and previously uneventful surveillance might have turned into something else entirely.

'Dalkin doesn't play golf,' Andrews said, filling in the next answer, 'and as far as the team could tell he wasn't there for the ambiance or the food. Same with Desayeva. They met, talked briefly, during which Dalkin passed something across the table to her. It could have been a slip of paper but it was too quick for the team to see. The team said it seemed like they'd met before; there was no shaking hands or that stuff. She left immediately afterwards and returned to her apartment in DC. Dalkin waited for a couple of minutes then also left. He didn't appear to be conscious about being followed.'

'He wouldn't – he's a bureaucrat.' What if it had been a brush-pass, Callahan wondered? It was a common piece of tradecraft for passing on information and one which worked well enough to still be in use. However, with no clear visuals on what had been passed, they were no further forward.

'Did the surveillance include audio?'

'It did but the restaurant's mood music blanked it out. They got plenty of CCTV coverage though, showing them arriving, meeting and leaving.'

Callahan sat back. It showed a connection and possible intent but it was a long way off proof that anything untoward had gone on. Desayeva was a charity fundraiser, so she could claim the meeting was all done in the name of some noble cause. And if Dalkin backed her up they'd never prove otherwise.

'That's good work.' He picked up the tablet again to give himself time to think. His big problem was how to progress this further. He couldn't ask Andrews to do field work because he wasn't trained for it. But while passing any job off to the FBI went against the grain, protocol demanded that that was exactly what he should do. There was no other option.

Andrews jumped in and solved the problem for him. 'I've done some research-liaison work for a Special Agent Bill Warner over at Pennsylvania Avenue, and I know he'd love to get his teeth into this.'

Pennsylvania Avenue was the FBI's address in Washington.

'Warner? I know him. He's a good man.'

'You want me to speak to him?'

'To do what?'

'Well, they could arrange more surveillance, wiretaps, checking out this Dalkin guy's financial status . . . that kind of thing. And I could tag along to make sure they got everything.'

'You?'

'Yes. My girlfriend says I need to get out more and this would be a good excuse.'

Callahan made a decision. Andrews was onto something, he could sense it.

'Do it. I'll leave it to you to sell it to them. If they seem unwilling let me know. Focus on Dalkin first. He's new and we still don't have anything on the Russian. Keep me informed.'

# THIRTY

The leafy streets surrounding Bradley Dalkin's Rockville apartment building were quiet when David Andrews and two FBI Special Agents arrived. Quiet was good but some traffic was useful for cover. Too many older singletons behind curtained windows and with time on their hands could easily spot a strange vehicle and take too close an interest to consider calling the cops. Result, one busted surveillance job.

Special Agent Charles Cahill, thirty-two, clean-cut and innocent-looking, made a phone call to Dalkin's apartment number, ready to slip into a call-centre script in case Dalkin should pick up. He hung on longer than eight rings in case Dalkin was busy on his cellphone. Eight was the norm for most people's annoyance limit to trip in, but it seemed like he must be out.

Special Agent Bill Warner suggested they do a sweep of the area before entering. A thickset man nearing retirement, he had a calm voice and exuded authority and experience.

'Why are we doing that?' queried David Andrews. This was his first time on a field operation and he was eager to see what they did next. Somehow this calm, low-level approach hadn't been what he was expecting. Where were the fast stops, slamming car doors and bursting into buildings he'd always imagined?

'To make sure there are no competing factors in play,' Warner explained.

'Like what?'

'If Dalkin is talking to the Russians through Desayeva, they might have put a watch on him to make sure it's not a set-up. Or there might be another agency taking an interest. We don't want to run into any traffic and tip our hand.'

'Or if he's just a traitorous weasel of a scumbag bureaucrat,' suggested Cahill sourly, 'which he probably is, he might be looking out for us to turn up and shake his tree.'

'Don't mind him,' Warner said. 'His last girlfriend got snaffled by a bureaucrat and he's never going to forget it.'

Andrews nodded. 'Are we going in?'

Warner gave him a tolerant look. 'You haven't done this before, have you, son?'

'Not a lot.' Andrews felt a flush growing on his face. 'Actually, not at all.'

Warner nodded, inscrutable. 'Just so's we know. There's a couple of rules I need you to bear in mind.'

'Oh. OK, sure. What are they?'

'Follow our lead and do not speak.'

'Right. Is that it?'

'That's all you need to know. Stick to that and everything will work out fine.' He smiled to take the sting out of the comment and explained, 'We've been trying to nail Desayeva for a long time and tying in this Dalkin guy with her could be our way in.'

'It's good you got the CCTV footage on them, though. We wouldn't have had a clue otherwise.' Andrews was referring tactfully to the video footage at the Pines View golf club, but which had not been followed up until now. He hadn't raised the issue before in case they felt insulted and told him to get lost.

Warner wasn't fooled. 'If what you're saying in that round-about superior spook-trained manner,' he growled, 'is that we missed an opportunity earlier to find out who Dalkin was, then yes, I guess we did. Our bad. I'll make sure the agents responsible are tarred and feathered and flayed at dawn. That do you?'

Andrews swallowed and nodded. 'No offence.'

Warner indicated a walkway between buildings and they all turned in. 'I hear you're some kind of Russian expert, is that right?'

'I guess. Why?'

'We could use some of that knowledge, you ever feel like a change of office scenery. The coffee's shit but it's served by a machine that knows its place.'

'I'm not sure, but thanks for the offer.' Andrews felt a warm glow at the idea that he'd been acknowledged as having something special to offer. That didn't happen every day. 'Can I quote that offer on my résumé?'

'No, you fucking cannot,' Warner muttered mildly. They turned back into the street running past Dalkin's apartment building and approached the front door. 'You ready, *tovarich*?'

'I'm ready.'

'Let's go.'

# THIRTY-ONE

I caught up with Lindsay in the town centre. She was standing outside a *crêperie* and looked nervous, which was no surprise. Going by the calm street scene the news of the action in the park hadn't caught on up here yet and people were going about their business seemingly unaware that there had been gunfire in their quiet little town.

She said, 'I wondered if you were going to come.' She held my phone up. 'Callahan rang off. I told him you'd call later when we got clear.'

'Walk casually and smile a lot,' I told her, and took the phone. I put her arm through mine, heading for the street where I'd left the car. 'We're just two normal people doing everyday normal things, taking in the sights and about to leave this place as quickly and as calmly as we can. If you feel like laughing any time soon, do so; it's a great way to dispel tension.'

'I'll try to remember that,' she said, and broke out a rough facsimile of a laugh which sounded anything but real.

I said, 'On second thoughts, best not do that again. People might think I'm taking you hostage.'

A thin wail of approaching police sirens drifted up the hill, and I guessed that they were a mile or so off, maybe less. Damn, that was a fast response time. We hadn't got long before they'd have the town closed down tight.

'Where are we going?' Lindsay asked, keeping her head down. Her nearness felt pleasantly warm, as did the touch of her hand on my arm, something I didn't usually experience on an assignment. I had to force myself to focus on the here and now and remember what we were doing.

'We have to get out of here and do it nice and easy. There's no police station in the town but it won't take them long to have units placed on all roads in and out. The French cops are very quick to respond to reports of shootings.'

'What happened back there?' she queried. Her voice held a

tremor which I put down to nerves, but it might have been the way I was hustling her along the narrow street. 'I heard shots . . . are you all right?'

We passed a church with a priest standing outside, chatting to two elderly ladies. They all turned and smiled with a traditional greeting, and I waited until we were past before replying. 'I'm fine. They were amateurs, probably local bully boys sent by their far-right bosses to deal with Chesnais because they thought she'd be easy meat. Don't worry – I didn't kill anybody.'

'I'm glad to hear it.' She stared at me as we got to the car and climbed in. 'Is this what it's always like for you in the field?'

I shook my head and drove out through the town on the opposite side to where the action had gone down. 'Not at all,' I told her. 'Most of the time life is very quiet.'

'Seriously?' She almost managed a smile. 'Not from what I've seen it isn't. Remember me – your eye in the sky watching your back?'

I had to give her that one. She was right. There had been moments while watching my every move from on high as comms support, either via a drone camera or a satellite feed, that events must have seemed chaotic and ridiculous and anything but quiet.

'It's different on the ground. Circumstances change all the time. Sometimes it gets messy.'

Like right now, I thought, and decided not to mention the spotter who was probably calling in the hit team as we spoke. Hopefully we'd get away before they arrived and slip by under cover of the cops who would be arriving any minute.

'Tell me about it,' she murmured eventually, sounding breathless. 'That just now was . . . it was scary.' She hesitated, then added, 'Sorry. This place is so peaceful and . . . serene. I guess I wasn't expecting it.'

I was glad to hear her say so. Being scared was good; it would ensure she didn't take lightly anything that happened later. Next time, if there was a next time, she'd know that this stuff could get serious in the blink of an eye, wherever she happened to be. I handed her back my cellphone. 'Can you send a report to Callahan for me? Don't give him our location just yet.'

A flicker of blue lights showed behind us but they were moving crossways to our line of travel towards the park. I tucked in between a large truck-and-trailer combination and a coach and drove nice and steady, ready to split if we had to but hoping that wasn't necessary. We wouldn't get far if they latched onto us and the countryside here was too open to drop out of sight for long. A sign told me we were heading towards the towns of Gazeran and Rambouillet.

Rambouillet was the forest of the same name. Lots of trees and quiet country roads and a chance to get lost. All we needed was time.

Lindsay said, 'I thought Callahan wanted you to keep him informed of your location.'

'Yes, he did. I'll explain why later. Before that can you check my maps app and the roads out of here. I'd like a quiet route to Paris if you can find one.'

'Not the quickest?'

'Too risky. They can close down freeways too easily and we'd be trapped. We need to drop off their radar until I can figure out what to do and where the next threat might come from.'

That threat wasn't helped by the fact that if Callahan had been told to drop me, he was limited in what resources he could provide for us in an emergency. Forget armed support or an evac flight out of here; that would only work short-term until the other side caught up with my next location. Sending Lindsay would have been taking a heck of a risk; if the people above him calling the shots ever found out that she wasn't merely on vacation but here with me and actively involved in an operation, he'd be out of a job.

The other point was, if she knew for certain the leak of locators was being used to track me across half the known universe, she would know that she was now in the same small frame and therefore as much of a target as me.

She tapped away and sent the text, then called up a maps screen on her own cellphone. 'Take the next left. It's a narrow road but connects up to others after a few miles. What did you mean, the next threat? Will those two men have colleagues?'

I took the left turn and found we were on a virtual single-track paved road through a spread of open fields, with a high centre-line and few passing places. Small farms and a few remote houses were strung out across the area in front of us, and directly ahead and over to the right was the dark stretch of the Rambouillet Forest. Until we reached the relative safety of the trees the lack of hedgerows and flat ground made us easy to spot from a long way off.

'Forget those two,' I said. 'They're not part of it.' Unlike, I thought, the team tracking me across the globe and pinning me to the board like a specimen in a butterfly collection. 'If Callahan hasn't been able to isolate who's been intercepting the references, I'm still vulnerable . . . and so are you as long as you're with me.'

She thought that over for a while, then said, 'It's that easy to do?'

'It's the same as using map references – only more specific, right down to a few feet. Even getting lost in a crowd isn't as simple any more. The only advantage of being in a city is you can use other people as cover. I don't want to do that.'

'Who would be doing that to you?'

'Somebody with know-how and resources. And a contact on the inside.'

She didn't speak for a couple of miles, and I guessed she was trying to equate the CIA she knew and worked in with this shocking new reality. I'd never been inside the Langley complex, but I'd been in similar buildings. They provided an aura of solidity, of security and indestructability. Throw in a network of electronic counter-attack measures and a small force of armed guards and you'd feel genuinely safe, regardless of what was going on elsewhere.

But we were on the outside with none of the above. It would have been scary to anyone.

'It's likely to be one person giving out the leads,' I told her. I didn't want to frighten her off completely or torpedo her trust in the organization she'd come to believe in. 'That's all it takes. But it won't last long.' I added that in the fervent hope that Callahan would get to plug the leak sooner rather than later.

She said, 'I hope that doesn't mean you're thinking of dumping me at the airport.' Her voice had lost the tremor and a quick glance across at her showed she was giving me the *don't even think about it* evil eye.

'I wouldn't dream of it. Anyway, as you said, you're the perfect cover.'

I don't think she knew what to make of that, which was good, because she didn't ask any more questions. And that gave me time to think about what to do next.

Unfortunately, that's when I took my eye off the ball. I was so busy looking ahead and strategizing that I didn't see the threat emerging behind us. The first thing I knew was when a volley of gunfire blew out the rear window and punched holes in the rear of the car.

# THIRTY-TWO

Lindsay screamed in shock and I glanced across to make sure she hadn't been hit. But she turned in her seat and looked backwards and muttered a very unladylike cuss which, in different circumstances, would have had me smiling.

'I'm fine,' she said, brushing a couple of bits of broken glass out of her hair. 'I'm fine.'

The car behind us was a chunky black SUV with a cut-down roof. It looked like a Range Rover Evoque. It had emerged from out of nowhere and must have been lying in wait for us. It was a fancy set of wheels for this kind of work but carried enough weight and punch to make life difficult for us if they chose to ram us off the road and finish the job at their leisure. And they certainly had opportunity on their side; this road wasn't the busiest I'd seen and the risk of them being interrupted if they did choose to launch an attack was minimal. But then after their tactics in Lebanon, Cyprus and Frankfurt, I guessed they were plenty ready to deal with that eventuality, too.

I risked a glance in the mirror to check the size of the threat. I counted three heads up and a hand hanging out the passenger window holding what looked like a machine pistol. Not a great weapon to use at distances, especially from a moving firing platform against another vehicle, but useful for spraying at a target on the grounds that you were bound to get a hit eventually.

And one hit in the right place was all it would take.

I put on speed, the back of my neck feeling vulnerable. The car didn't like it much, but hanging around wasn't going to end well. I was wondering how they'd managed to be waiting at the right place and time, and ran a map in my head. We'd been on the road to Rambouillet, heading north-east towards Paris, and had hooked a left almost at random. So popping out behind us the way they did was either a stellar piece of guesswork on their part or the spotter back in Épernon had seen which route we'd taken out of town and called it in.

Instinct told me that guessing didn't come into it; their insistence on trying to nail me had already shown they had reach and resources, which included man-power enough to post watchers and hitters wherever they needed them. Sending in a single man to make sure we were in place first would have been a logical move, allowing their hit team to stay back until they were needed, then move in the moment they had instructions.

Lindsay must have been having the same thoughts. 'These are the people following you, aren't they? Not the same as the other two.'

'Forget them. They were following Chesnais. They'd been given a rough description and told where to find her. It was sloppy organization.'

'So why come after me—?' Then her eyes went wide as the realization hit her. 'They thought I was Chesnais!' She uttered another oath as she realized how close she had come to being a wrong target.

'Can I have the gun?'

'To do what?' I glanced at her but she looked serious.

'Please.'

I gave in. 'In my backpack. A Beretta.'

She grabbed hold of my bag from the rear seat and hauled it over to the front. She took out the Beretta and checked the magazine. If she was frightened she did a great job of hiding it and seemed to be handling the gun with surprising ease.

'Listen to me: the people behind us are different to the other two morons. They're Russians – Moscow contractors like the men behind the previous hits. And, no I don't know why they're doing this.'

'Callahan mentioned it but I wasn't sure I really believed it . . . until now.' She glanced to the rear. The Evoque had fallen back a way after hitting a dip in the surface and nearly going off the narrow road, but I knew it wouldn't be long before they made up ground again.

'And you agreed to this . . . having your locations known? Why?'

'Because one, we need to know where the information is being intercepted, and two, I don't like being used as target practice. This has to stop. We either plug the leak or I stop them coming after me.'

'How do they manage to move so quickly?'

'They have the resources. As soon as my location is picked up and passed on, they swing a team into position. In this case they must have had people in the area ready to go. Putting a man in the town as soon as they had the location was a clever move; it meant the hit team could hold back and wait for a call telling them which way we'd gone. Then they could set up an attempt outside of the town. Safer for them and allows them a way out afterwards.'

She looked at me, her mouth open. 'You make it sound like a freaking board game. How can you be so calm?'

I couldn't help but smile at her cross face. Even under the circumstances it was endearing. 'I've tried panicking but it never works.'

We covered another mile in silence while the Evoque crept up on us. I wondered what their strategy was until I realized they were probably waiting until we got into the forest where they could take us without being seen.

'So it's really happening – there's a leak inside Langley.' She sounded shocked, as any insider would have done. A traitor inside the CIA was tantamount to sacrilege. Then she told me about someone having been at her comms desk and Callahan's instructions to leave the details in full view.

'Did they find anyone?' I asked.

'Not yet – at least, I don't think so. It's a busy place . . . people come and go all the time, and when you're on the inside of the building you don't think about CCTV apart from what's on the outside.'

I knew what she meant. It was the concept of the middle ages: the bigger the fort the safer you were. And look how that worked out. Lindsay and her colleagues were going to have to come to grips with the idea that someone inside the CIA bubble was sending out information which threatened the life of a co-worker – even a non-attached person like me. The whole concept was not easily accepted or understood, especially in an organization which saw itself as the centre of the nation's intelligence, and therefore invulnerable.

She huffed a bit and checked the position of the Evoque. It was still there but hanging back. The road stretched out for a good way in front of us but was too narrow to risk passing us. Big as it was, it still stood a chance of driving off the road by mistake.

They were waiting their chance to jump us.

'Wouldn't it have been easier for them to take us back in the park?' she said.

It was a reasonable conclusion to draw, but I was guessing they hadn't had time to get their apples in order. I had no idea where this latest crew had come from, but it was probably Paris. The Russians have people all over, small teams of men and women in place and waiting for orders. If they needed specialist work they would fly in a unit from Moscow or one of their special ops bases.

'It's a matter of logistics,' I said. 'We're mobile, they have to play catch-up.'

The whole thing about following a target constantly on the move is that the pursuer is always on the back foot. Responding to a new location or turn in the route is inevitably after the event, thus rapidly becomes old news. Whatever local resources these people had on the ground to provide intel would call it in, but the reaction team would be constantly running to make up lost ground, relying on their latest information still being relevant by the time they got geared up and arrived in place.

The Evoque dropped back again as we barrelled over a narrow, cratered stretch of road like a switchback. The centre line had a curved surface and the edges were crumpled where I guessed a succession of heavy farm vehicles over the years had chewed away at the tarmac. I didn't think the Evoque would hold off for much longer; up ahead the trees were getting closer, throwing a dark shadow across our horizon. It was an illusory suggestion of safety that could switch in a heartbeat to one of disaster if the men in the car behind saw their chance and decided to take it.

When we hit the treeline it was like entering a dark horizon, an impression of gloom suddenly closing around us as the light was filtered out by the foliage overhead and the thick growth of trees on each side. I put on speed and hoped there were no happy campers out on a field walk to get in the way. The Evoque did the same, only faster, and I gave it about ten seconds before they got close enough to open fire again. They needed this to be over and to be gone before the cops responded. Quiet as the road was right now, someone would have heard the burst of machine pistol fire and called it in, and the area couldn't stay that way for long.

Isobel, I reflected, would have reacted well to this. Maybe not accurately, but well. *Just because I don't, doesn't mean I can't.*

Then Lindsay surprised me. She lifted the Beretta, flicked off the seat belt and, twisting round, squirmed like an eel through the gap between the seats into the rear of the car.

'What are you doing?' I asked, although it was pretty obvious the moment I said it.

'They just scared the living crap out of me,' she said shortly. 'I want them to know how it feels.'

At least I think that's what she said. The wind was howling around the broken rear window and drowning out some of her words, but I got the gist. She was good and mad.

'Great. Remember to keep your mouth open when you—'

But she lifted the Beretta before I could finish and fired off three rounds at the Evoque's grill, which was now barely thirty yards away. The gunshots were very loud and bounced around the inside of the car. In spite of the noise being dampened by the absence of glass at the rear it was still painful on the ears.

In the mirror I saw the rim of one of the Evoque's headlights separate and fly off. Another round punched out part of the upper grille before carving its way up the hood. It made a spider's web of the windscreen, which held for a second or two before caving inwards under the air pressure and vibration through the suspension.

The driver nearly lost it, the wheels wobbling sharply, and they almost came off the road before falling sharply back, the screen now completely gone. I didn't see where the third shot went but slammed my foot down and opened up the gap between us as quickly as the engine would allow me.

I needed a turning, somewhere to fight back. But where? We

were in what resembled a corridor of trees with nowhere to
turn. Then I saw a gap coming up on the right. It looked like
a fire-break road if they had them here, narrow and unmade
and unlikely to be a through-route, so we'd have no way of
getting off it without turning back.

We really didn't have much choice; they would soon overhaul
us if we stayed on this road, and I figured they were mad enough
now that Lindsay had bruised them to want to take the first
chance they got to end this. They also had the firepower to
make it happen.

'Hold on tight,' I shouted, and stamped on the brakes. I
hauled on the wheel, taking a sideways drift into a ninety-degree
turn. The rental protested, a vicious banging sound coming from
underneath as the wheels bounced, but it held firm and didn't
give out on us.

By now we were on a single-track route leading away through
the trees with vegetation close in on both sides and a hammering
of twigs and stones beneath the chassis. A couple of pull-ins
flashed by, but they were only big enough for a couple of cars
at most and proved to be dead ends, great for dog walkers and
hikers but not for defending yourself against armed assault from
a bunch of assassins.

I checked the rear-view mirror. For a moment after the sudden
turn the Evoque was gone from my sight. It was all the opportunity I was going to get. I hit the brakes again, this time much
harder and bringing us to a stop. Lindsay yelped in surprise as
she was thrown against the back of my seat. I grabbed the Sig
and jumped out of the car.

'What are you doing?' she shouted, untangling herself from
the car.

'Get into the trees and stay down,' I shouted and started
running back towards the turning. I could hear the Evoque
coming up fast, its engine sounding brutally stressed as the
driver fought to catch us. Then I heard the engine note drop
sharply and the tyres protesting as he braked hard to follow us
into the turn.

By the time the busted grill and headlight came into view
round the corner I was standing just fifty feet away in the centre
of the track. I had my feet planted and both hands held out

front holding the pistol steady, waiting and breathing easy. It threw my mind back to an exercise a million years ago, just one of many battle scenarios we had to train for that were unlikely ever to happen yet still had to be practised, testing the nerves and the will.

The look of shock on the driver's face as he clocked me in the centre of the track was almost funny. Pity I didn't have time to enjoy it.

Just for a second I thought he was going to stop out of instinct. Then he hit the gas and the engine fought to gain forward traction on the soft surface, suddenly growing larger as it roared towards me.

I fired twice at the driver and twice more at a man on the passenger side who'd been waving the machine pistol. Then I stepped off the track and watched as the big car gave a frantic wobble before the front wheels turned and took it off into the trees.

There was a ripping sound of devastated vegetation as bushes and saplings were torn down by the big car, ending with a bang as it buried itself into something solid and unyielding. A long hiss of steam and the engine stalled and went dead. In the silence that followed, someone screamed once, then stopped.

I checked behind me to make sure Lindsay was out of the way, then crossed the track. The car was still upright but only just. It was tilted over towards the passenger side, and I could see an arm hanging down limply out of the remains of the window. I moved up carefully alongside the rear door and saw a body crumpled in the rear foot-well. There was a lot of blood and he'd got a visible head-wound, his neck at a crooked and impossible angle.

I placed the Sig's barrel against the front passenger's head as a precaution, but he was no threat. A thick branch had entered the front window space and pinned him to the seat. The machine pistol was lying on the floor at his feet.

The driver was still alive but only just. He was breathing with difficulty and I could see why: he hadn't been wearing a seatbelt and the air bag had only partially inflated. The air around him was a haze of white corn-starch used to keep the bag pliable while stored, and the steering wheel had done major damage to his face.

I reached in to his inside pockets and found a cellphone. The screen opened and there was my photo again. I debated going through the other men's pockets because they were sure to be carrying the same image, but we didn't have time. I had to face it that sooner or later this was going to get out if it hadn't already and I would become the mystery man everyone wanted to speak with.

I trekked back to the car and met Lindsay as she stepped out from the trees.

'Are they still alive?' she asked, as we climbed in. She dropped the Beretta in my bag almost with a gesture of relief and sat back, her face frozen.

'Mostly,' I lied, because she didn't need to know that she had killed at least one of them, the guy in the back. 'But they're pretty busted up.'

She nodded while I turned the car round and got us back on the road. She didn't look at the Evoque as we passed and I didn't blame her.

A little while later she said, 'How do you deal with this each time?'

'I push it down,' I replied. 'It's the only way.' As explanations went it wasn't deep or clever and a psych would laugh at it. But it was as near to the truth as I was ever likely to get.

'Are you all right?' I asked. 'You did brilliantly back there.'

'Thank you. It didn't feel like it.' She took a deep breath and said, 'Is this ever going to end?'

'It has to,' I said with as much optimism as I could manage. It had to end sometime; the only thing I couldn't figure out was how. Or when.

# THIRTY-THREE

The lobby of Bradley Dalkin's Rockville, Washington apartment building was neat, clean and devoid of character, a unit by appearance more suited for worker ants to live in but apparently not to socialize. Modern living for the mid-level governmentally employed. To David Andrews it had all the excitement of an office block and he half expected to have a uniformed guard pop out from a cubbyhole and ask to see some ID.

In fact getting inside had been simple; no lock-picks or forced entry, not even waiting for one of the residents to come along and provide a simple open door for them to slip through. The door opened at the first push by Agent Cahill and they were in and staring at a bank of mail lockers against one wall. Discreet LED lights in the ceiling tiles gave off a cold light reflecting from the metal boxes, lending the scene a slightly clinical air.

Warner tapped on the locker assigned to Dalkin. It didn't spring open but gave off the hollow boom of an empty space. He turned and headed for the stairs with Cahill and David Andrews close behind. They arrived on the second floor without encountering anyone and stopped at Dalkin's door. Warner motioned Andrews to stand to one side, then knocked, his big fist surprisingly gentle.

No response. Warner knocked again. Silence. Then a door to an adjacent apartment opened and an elderly lady appeared. She was tall, stick-thin and neatly dressed, with a shopping bag in one hand and purse on a long strap over one shoulder. She locked her door carefully behind her and turned to stare at the three visitors with a look of mild surprise.

'Can I help you, gentlemen? You look a little lost.' Her voice carried a hint of a snap as if they'd been caught out misbehaving by a teacher.

Cahill stepped forward and gave her his most innocent boyish smile. 'We're not lost, ma'am. We're here visiting Mr Dalkin—'

She cut him off. 'I know who and what you are, young man, so stow the ersatz charm. I was with the Bureau before you were born so I recognize the suits and the look.' She turned her eye on Andrews, adding dryly, 'Although maybe some standards have been slipping lately.' She allowed a smile to touch her lips. 'Darn, if you could see the look on your faces. Dalkin, you say?'

'Yes, ma'am. Do you know when he'll be in?'

'No, I don't, Special Agent—?'

'Cahill, ma'am.' He indicated his colleagues and said, 'Special Agent Warner and . . . Mr Andrews.'

The elderly eyes were sharp as they flicked between the two other men, resting briefly on Andrews. 'Huh. A Mister riding around with the Feds? The world has changed. If you're not Bureau, what are you?'

'He's on attachment,' Warner explained smoothly before Andrews could speak. 'Ma'am.'

'Well, good for him.' The old lady walked past them saying, 'Sorry, I don't know when Mr Dalkin will be in and nor do I care. He's never given me so much as a nod all the time he's lived here. He's one of those stuck-up little Washington staff pricks who doesn't look kindly on us lower orders. I hope you get him, whatever it is he's done, and nail his ass to the wall, or whatever the polite terminology is these days.'

They watched as she disappeared down the stairs, back ramrod straight, and turned to look at each other in amusement.

'We should re-employ her,' said Warner softly, in awe. 'She's scary.'

'What do we do now?' Andrews queried. He felt a sense of anti-climax, as if the potentially exciting day in the company of a couple of FBI agents had fizzled out to nothing.

'We're going to stay on the stuck-up little staff prick,' Warner said, testing Dalkin's door to see if it would give. It didn't and he looked disappointed. 'You're going back to Langley to do whatever it is you whizziwig computer guys do when the oversight committee isn't looking. Cahill will give you a ride. I'll stay on here in case I get lucky and fall against the door.'

'Not a problem,' Andrews concurred. 'I do have some digging to do.'

'I bet you do. Let's hope it turns up something useful.' He turned back to the door saying, 'Keep us in the loop, though, you hear? We didn't give you this exciting day out for free, us being on the same side and all.'

Andrews was relieved to get back to the familiarity of his desk. He'd enjoyed the momentary thrill of the chase with the two Special Agents, but he much preferred hunting down leads through his keyboard; specifically information on all things relating to Valentina Desayeva and her presence here in Washington, and anything else that his trawling through the archives might turn up.

On the surface, Desayeva was a very open book with no appearance of trying to hide from anyone. She penned articles for magazines and journals on life and social history in Russia, about which, of course, she knew a great deal; she spent a lot of time schmoozing the rich and easily-flattered for donations to a list of socially worthwhile charities, appearing regularly on social media sites and gossip magazine pages in designer dresses; and being escorted to artistic events at the Kennedy Center, often on the arm of some senator or other D.C. worthy.

However, anything related to her back-life was anything but open. There seemed to be no family, regular partner or significant other, and if she had a private life outside her charitable or public persona, it was well hidden. Equally, if any of the usual government agencies interested in foreign residents of Washington had anything on her, there was precious little available for him to trawl through.

No wonder Callahan was annoyed; if she was a spy she was being protected by naiveté if not plain stupidity

Which fact, in Andrews' experience, narrowed the field of research and made him focus on the people around Desayeva instead.

He decided to build up a photo montage, taking in the faces seen with her on the various social websites. He instinctively dismissed many of them as camera fodder seeking their own publicity, the familiar faces who seemed to thrive solely under the media spotlight. He dismissed, too, any expatriate Russians or members of the Russian diplomatic community who swirled in and out of her circle. Moscow, if they had any direct control over her activities, would not have been so clumsy as to make a direct personal approach to such a public figure.

Instead they would have employed cut-outs, drops and seriously encrypted means of contact to give her orders or receive information. Which meant her 'approved' use of back-channels to Moscow for communication purposes were probably sanitized and would take far too long, quite apart from ringing alarm bells in the State Department who, Callahan had cautioned him, had placed her off-limits.

And that was where he firmed up the connection with Dalkin. A case of pure luck, he admitted, along with inter-agency cooperation. But that was the way things should work. The rest was down to some electronic leg-work, at which he excelled. But Dalkin had proved to be his way in.

It was time to talk to Callahan and flip the whole off-limits command on its head.

# THIRTY-FOUR

'Dalkin's definitely got something going on here,' said Andrews on arrival in Callahan's office. He was carrying a tablet and waved it in the air. It was early in his digging assignment into Dalkin's background and he was looking energized by what he'd turned up. 'I've saved it on here to send you. You want to read this or should I summarize it?'

'Go ahead and summarize.' Callahan sat back to listen. He'd become accustomed to knowing when an agent or asset had something interesting to say rather than re-hashing old news, and recognized by Andrews' tone and nervy stance that it would be best to let him have his head.

'OK. As we know, not long after Benson's death Dalkin lost his job. Until recently he's had little money, no long-term work and existing on whatever stand-in, short-term contract contracts he can find. But even that's drying up.'

'Why?'

'A self-inflicted wound. I've spoken to a couple of co-workers who said he'd made himself such a royal pain in the ass skulking around in Benson's shadow, nobody's in a rush to trust him again.'

'Skulking? Is that a current word?'

'Apparently, he did it a lot according to my informants. You know – like the weedy pal of the playground bully? His wife must have felt the same because she left him and took a bunch of cash for a no-contest divorce. The way things look on paper, his credit's maxed out and his prospects of staying in Rockville don't look great. And get this.' He grinned. 'An old lady neighbour in his apartment building referred to him as a stuck-up little prick.'

'Good for her. Is there a "but" lurking around somewhere?'

'There is. I put a historic trace on his phone records and GPS and it shows he made a prior visit to the Pines View club three months ago. Until then he'd rarely left the city other than a couple of brief visits to Michigan where he has a sister, although they don't get on much. The visit to Pines View could be when he and Desayeva first met-and-matched. Unfortunately the Pines doesn't keep CCTV records back that far.'

'So far so what?' Callahan wasn't being picky, merely impatient. He knew there had to be more.

'Just recently he transferred in three separate sums of nine thousand dollars each to his checking account and two similar sums to a business account. There could be more but they haven't found it yet. There's no record the FBI can find immediately of where that came from, but they're working on it. Dalkin also bought a new car, a Chevy Suburban. Before that he drove a crappy Honda Accord that he'd have had trouble giving away.' He looked up and added, 'For a guy who's only five-seven, a Chevy's a big chunk of vehicle.'

'It's a big chunk of money, too.' Callahan's interest had grown. There were plenty of short guys driving big cars around DC and elsewhere; it went with the territory. Fronting up beyond your normal capacity was a local pastime, especially if you wanted to climb the greasy pole of political ambition. More interesting was where did the fifty-plus grand it would have cost Dalkin to buy the car have come from, seeing as he had no proper job?

'Warner ran a check of his phone calls and emails,' Andrews continued. 'Aside from job hunting Dalkin made a handful of calls over the past few weeks to a number assigned to a cell-phone from a few years back. It hasn't been used much recently, although the account is still open.'

'Do we have a name for the account?'

'Valentina Desayeva.'

'That's more like it.' Callahan's interest went hot. It was more than just a chance meeting.

'There's no indication why she kept the old phone going, but it could be she bought a new one and simply tossed the old one in a drawer like lots of people.'

Callahan shook his head. 'She wouldn't do that.'

'Why not?'

'Tradecraft. She'd have been trained to destroy it rather than leave it in a drawer and forgetting it. That's how sleepers get caught: they don't think about what's lying around in the ether and on phone and computer records. Anyway, the battery would have died eventually so she must have kept it charged for a reason. Did anything else show up on the phone records?'

'Not that we could find. But the earliest call Dalkin made was to her landline in D.C.'

Callahan nodded knowingly. 'That would have been the first contact. After that she'd have told him to use her old cell number instead. Simple and effective. Like I said, tradecraft.' He slapped a hand on the desk in disgust. 'Clean, my ass.' Then he smiled. 'Until now, anyway, which is when she slipped up.'

'How?'

'Her old phone. She should have ditched it or got a new Pay-as-you-go Sim card. That would have given her a new, clean number. She probably figured nobody else would have a record of it after all this time.'

'Does this mean we've got her?'

Callahan brought him down to earth. 'Not yet we don't. We're closer than we were, but no home run just yet. One question: has Dalkin put his apartment up for sale?'

'No. Why?'

'Because if he had it might be one explanation of where his sudden input of cash came from. And it isn't. What else?'

'That's it for now. But Warner and Cahill are digging deep. They seem pretty excited.'

'They would be; they're hunters and can smell a rat.' He nodded. 'Keep working on it.'

Callahan watched Andrews walk away and smiled. The young man was in the wrong agency, although he wasn't going to tell him that – at least not yet. He'd got the instincts of a hunter, just like the two Special Agents, but he didn't realize it. Give him the right tools and some FBI training at their Quantico Academy and he'd be downright dangerous to anyone on the wrong side of the law.

# THIRTY-FIVE

Exiting a hot contact area is not always as easy as it might seem; it can be filled with danger from back-up units or other emergency powers, all conspiring by chance to muddy the water. If the call has gone out that there's been a firefight, and there's no clear source of the threat, police and security lines tend to coincide in a rush to check the surrounding area to see who might be in play.

With the rash of extremist events occurring around the globe, it doesn't take much to get counter-terrorism departments involved almost as a matter of course, even if the problem turns out to be purely criminal. The anti-terrorist net spreads wide, immediately tapping into all available sources for potential names and claims. By its very nature, any reaction is a beat or two behind the clock, running down informants, seeking out local mouthpieces and finding out who might be the obvious suspects. That surge of activity often brings in whoever happens to be in the area, like stray fish in a wide net.

Like Lindsay and me.

'Where are we going?' she said, huddling against the car door. She looked pale and drawn, not surprisingly shaken by what had happened. I guessed that would last a while. Internal CIA staff are not trained to deal with armed assaults against themselves or buildings, and although she'd been quick to pick up the Beretta and loose off a few rounds, I figured she was now experiencing the residual effects of the action and not feeling too cool about it.

'Somewhere busy,' I said. We were about twenty miles out of the main Paris suburbs on a quiet section of road between villages. I was juggling ideas about where to go to ground. It was clear that whatever forces were after us were not short of daring or resources, and as we'd just witnessed, that would probably hold true just as much in a busy city like Paris as it would somewhere relatively quiet like Épernon. The main difference was, as long as we remained out of the spotlight, a big city would make it harder for them to locate us.

What I didn't know was how much more damage the opposition would take before they gave it up as a lost cause . . . or they got lucky. So far they had lost well over half a dozen people, either killed or out of action. But did that mean they would grow more or less determined to finish the job? I had no idea.

'We need to eat,' I said, easing the car between a couple of large trucks. Hunger when stressed was a fast way to have the body running down, sapping energy and focus. We also needed to get rid of the rental. With no rear window and several holes in the back, we were unlikely to get far now before someone called it in or we ran into a cop. And with the obvious bullet damage it would eventually be no ordinary traffic cop, but a no-messing unit with muscle and manpower.

I spotted a sign for a town called St-Rémy and turned towards it. We got close to the centre and I pulled into a side street, grabbing our stuff and leaving the car. If we were lucky it would be picked up by a local chop-shop, if such a thing existed around here. If not the local cops would have a field day figuring out who had been through a small shooting war. I couldn't help that my DNA and prints were all over it; some things you can't cover up. If they looked hard enough, they'd find plenty, although how far they got to finding me would depend how keen they were.

I stopped at a retro-style food van selling sandwiches, open rolls and pizzas and bought us enough to keep us going along with fruit juice and water and a bag to carry it in. It wasn't *haute cuisine* but would keep us mobile and alert for a good few hours yet.

The St-Rémy station was on the RER rapid transit or *Réseau Express Régional* commuter line which crossed Paris through to the north-east. I bought tickets and we had a short wait for the next train. We used the time to have a clean-up in the washroom and make ourselves look a little more respectable, including me cleaning out some stray bits of rear-window glass from Lindsay's hair and washing a slight cut on her cheek. I also swept the area for signs of surveillance or cops. After the shooting in Épernon it was possible the local cops would have put out a bulletin for unusual activity throughout the region, to include roads and rail stations in and out of the capital.

The train wasn't busy, with a mere handful of travellers heading towards the city. The interior smelled of stale deodorant or cleanser and the musky aroma of work clothes and seat fabric seemed to fit our mood. Neither of us felt like talking, which was fine by me, so we ate instead. Whatever we had to say would likely sound too interesting if anyone overheard us, and any good citizen would be on the phone to the police within minutes. The silence also gave me time to formulate where we were going and what we were going to do.

As we drew out of the station I felt a measure of relief that we were on the move. Having to stand still when every instinct tells you to get out of an area as quickly as possible is never good on the nerves. Our alternative would have been to keep going in the brutalized rental car, but that would have been a case of diminishing returns; sooner or later we'd have been caught in a net with no way out.

That feeling of relief didn't last long enough. After a mile or so the train slowed and inched along the track, the click-clicking of the wheels serving to taunt me with the idea that we were just pawns in a game and nothing we did was going to get us along any faster. A number of men in a work gang were standing by the side of the track, although they didn't look too unhappy at the interruption. As I turned to look at what they were working on, I caught a flash of movement out of the corner of my eye from the connecting door to the next carriage.

Lindsay, who was sitting across from me, saw it, too. 'There's a man watching us,' she said quietly, staring out of the window and yawning. 'I think he got on the train after us.'

Damn. It was either the watcher I'd spotted in Épernon or someone he'd pointed after us. I'd been so focussed on where we were heading I'd lost sight for a moment of checking the people around us.

'What's he doing?'

'Nothing. Just staring . . . oh, hang on – he's using a cellphone.'

I told myself it could be nothing. Another bored traveller eyeing up a pretty girl – Lindsay – the way guys in Latin countries do. For most it's harmless eyeballing in the hopes of getting a smile in return. But maybe not this time.

I turned my head and gave him a quick glance. An ordinary looking guy, dressed in everyday casual clothes of a windcheater and jeans, clean-shaven with short cropped hair and long sideburns.

Ordinary but not local. I'd bet my boots on it.

The way he had the cellphone clamped to his ear without talking was the giveaway. His eyes had that fixed look that told me he wasn't listening either, and had my every instinct kicking into top gear. Unless I was too keyed up and imagining things.

Then he looked across, unable to resist it any longer, and locked eyes with me before quickly turning his head away again. That was it.

We'd been tagged.

The next stop was Courcelle-sur-Yvette. If we stayed on this train and the guy was in touch with mobile reinforcements, they would eventually take us at one of the upcoming stops. They had already demonstrated the fact that they were able to bring in men wherever they were required, and I had no doubt they would want to complete their mission before we arrived in the city proper, where escape after an assault would be a lot harder and fraught with danger.

For us, whether cops or bad guys, the end would be the same.

'Don't look at or acknowledge me,' I said softly, and handed her the bag of remaining sandwiches and drinks. 'When the train stops we get off and you move ahead of me. Don't wait for me but leave the station. I'll be right behind you.'

Lindsay bent to fiddle with a shoe lace and her voice floated up to me loaded with concern. 'What are you going to do?'

'That depends on him.'

I could see the station coming up. It looked deserted and small, typical commuter-land territory, which was both good and bad. The fewer people around the better, in case we ran into trouble, but the area looked way more open and more difficult to run and hide than I'd have liked.

But hell, you can only work with what you've got.

The train stopped and the doors opened. Lindsay and I were the only ones getting off, with maybe a dozen or so climbing aboard. Unless the Russians were hiring elderly women with shopping bags and the rolling gait indicating bad knees, none of them looked like members of a hit squad.

As we headed for the exit I caught a glimpse of the man from the next carriage stepping down and following. He still had the phone to his ear but was now looking animated and doing all the talking. We'd caught him off-guard and he was either issuing instructions or asking for back-up.

As we reached the station building, which was small and brick-built, I slowed down and allowed Lindsay to move ahead of me. There was no ticket barrier and nobody asking to see proof of travel. In fact I couldn't see any staff at all. Lindsay walked straight through and disappeared outside while I loitered by a brochure stand near the door and began to count down the time to his arrival.

The train left the station and everything went quiet.

*Ten seconds.* I heard the man's footsteps approaching. I crouched to pick up a handful of local area tourist leaflets that had fallen to the floor. I had my backpack in my other hand with a firm grip on the straps.

*Seven seconds.* His feet scuffed on the ground as he hurried to catch up. Maybe he'd figured we had a car waiting and had been ordered to intercept us. If so he might be armed and ready to fight.

*Five seconds.* His shadow moved across the doorway to the platform. I could hear his breaths coming in short puffs. He was either nervous or out of condition. Hopefully the latter.

*One second.* As he came through the doorway his eyes were fixed on the exit and Lindsay's form out in the open ahead of him. He frowned momentarily and hesitated, no doubt wondering why there was only one figure, not two. It took him a moment to spot me, bent close to the floor, and his brain had to work hard to process what he'd expected to see compared with what was before him.

It was all the edge I was going to get. I tossed the bunch of leaflets hard into his face. He yelped in surprise and instinctively raised one arm as they flared around him. I followed up fast, coming off the floor and swinging my backpack like a flail. He tried to block it but was reacting way too late and thrown off-balance by the leaflets.

The weight of the two guns inside the backpack acted like a cudgel, striking him across the side of the head. As he grunted and dropped his phone, I followed up with a knuckle strike to the side of his neck. He went limp and hit the floor, out for the count.

I checked his clothing but there was no sign of a weapon. Just my photo on his cellphone and some French documentation naming him as Marcel Duplessier with an address in Paris. It put him down as a local hire and a spotter not a fighter.

I put the phone in my pocket and left the documentation where it was. Then I dragged him over to a bench and laid him out with his face against the wall and one arm bent across his head.

With luck the first person to find him would take him for a drunk recovering after an all-night bender.

Outside I found Lindsay approaching a man leaning against a grey Renault Mégane. He was tall and stick-thin, and by the fine features and high forehead I guessed his origins to be from Somalia in the Horn of Africa. He stepped away from the car, one hand behind his back, the other down by his side. Loose-limbed and relaxed, he looked harmless.

But his eyes were focussed on me like twin coals, instantly assessing and wary.

# THIRTY-SIX

C allahan called Andrews to his office and waited impatiently for the young researcher to arrive. What he was about to do would cause a furore if it got out, as he was about to by-pass internal security conventions and, essentially, spy on his colleagues. It was something he would never have countenanced before, simply because there would never have been a need for it. But to his mind this was justified. He was now fairly sure that he had details of a possible line in and out of the building, but knowing and having proof were two different things.

The downside was he also figured that he was on a short leash, timewise. Broderick would not have forgotten their acrimonious encounter in the meeting, nor the outspoken way Callahan had protested at the treatment of Marc Portman. And, as evidenced by the silence from upstairs, so far Jason Sewell had shown no signs of doing anything to calm the rough waters swirling around him.

When Andrews appeared outside his door he nodded for him to come in.

'Can you get me internal CCTV footage of a specific area of this building – specifically the area around the communications staff?'

'Sure. Is there anything in particular you're looking for?'

'Gaps in our security set-up here. But that's not for public consumption. I want you to focus on one area specifically.'

Andrews looked interested. 'Sure. I mean, yes, can do. Any dates or times? Only there's a ton of continual footage of all areas and they don't like to hold onto stuff for too long. If you can narrow it down for me it would help.'

Callahan thought it over. 'I'd like the last five days of run-time. That should be enough. Can you do it without anyone knowing?'

If Andrews sensed this was going outside normal bounds he kept the thought to himself, but grinned. 'Will do. I'll get on it. Can I have the access codes down there?'

Callahan nodded. 'I'll arrange it. But you tell anyone and I'll have to kill you. How long will it take?'

Andrews cocked his head and thought for a moment. 'Thirty minutes? I'll send you the links to the files.'

'Excellent.'

Andrews disappeared and Callahan got down to work on another projected mission plan. It was more to keep a lid on his impatience than anything, since he was fairly sure he was unlikely to see it through. But he was damned if he was going to walk out of the building without an attempt to nail whoever was leaking information and threatening an asset's life.

True to his word, a fraction over half an hour later Andrews sent through a number of links to CCTV files of footage taken over the past few days.

Callahan took just a few seconds to recognize that it would take too long for him to run through it; he wasn't sufficiently tuned in to this kind of job. Jumping through vast amounts of video footage was a specialist business and he didn't want to waste time or miss something vital.

He picked up the phone and called Andrews. 'Hey, Sparky – grab yourself a coffee and get to my office; I need your eyes on this.'

While Andrews drove the system Callahan sat at his shoulder, checking the layout of the section on-screen and spotting familiar faces. With one eye on the timer at the bottom of the screen he was able to guide Andrews in jumping large gaps when the section would have been vacant or otherwise closed to outside access. He was also using a note of the times when he and Portman had exchanged text messages including location codes, beginning with the hours before the first attack on him in Lebanon.

The screen appeared oddly unreal, with staff moving around the cubicles, some using their chairs to scoot between keyboards, screen and maps, or coming together in huddles before moving apart the way he'd seen them doing a thousand times before, a busy section doing what they were trained to do. It was like watching an ant farm, even more so when Andrews speeded up the film at Callahan's direction. All these people, he thought, engaged in vital work that would never see the light of day, nor be discussed with anyone outside.

Work that was now threatened by someone who'd been able to access information and get it out of the building.

The days of footage streamed by, with familiar faces and figures zipping beneath the cameras, changing light patterns, the daily run of a busy section in motion. He rubbed his eyes at the unusual intensity of screen focus and began to wonder if he'd chosen an impossible task that might in the long run prove utterly fruitless.

Then, on day three of the recordings, he saw a familiar figure come into view from the door to the stairway leading upstairs. A woman. He watched for a while, impatient to move on and half tempted to give the exercise a miss and ask Andrews to put it aside. But something made him wait.

The woman was clutching a sheaf of papers and moving from desk to desk, cubicle to cubicle, and either placing a sheet of paper on a desk if vacant or handing it directly to its occupant. Then she did a sharp turn and stopped outside a door in one wall. She appeared to knock, resting one hand against the wall to one side. Then she stepped closer to it before entering and disappearing from view.

It was the door to Lindsay Citera's comms room.

Callahan sat forward, eyes on the door. When the woman emerged, pulling the door closed again, he found he'd been subconsciously counting off the seconds while they had been inside. Thirty-five. Half a minute to do . . . what? Drop a slip of paper onto a desk and leave?

He got Andrews to go back to the earlier footage, counting off how long it had taken to pass out the papers to others. Some had been handed over directly if the occupant was there, others were placed on the vacant desks. Each delivery took somewhere between three to five seconds. Normal internal mail delivery speed, he realized . . . except that in this building most deliveries came via internal mail-messaging. The longest was six seconds and that was when someone by the tilt of their head posed a question. Mostly, though, the occupant looked up, nodded and went back to their work, too busy or disinclined to chit-chat.

Eventually the woman walked back towards the stairs and disappeared off-camera.

'Is that it?' said Andrews, picking up by the subtle shift of

Callahan's body language that something on-screen had caught his attention.

Callahan checked himself. He couldn't risk saying anything yet in case he was way off target and allowing things to add up which actually did not. The woman had been handing out an information bulletin of some kind, but so what? What was there to be suspicious about?

'Keep going,' he said, and sat back while Andrews ran more footage.

Thirty minutes later he'd seen enough. He thanked Andrews for his help then went down to the comms area and spoke to several staff members and scoured vacant desks, some of which had a collection of papers amassed over several days. Most of it consisted of updates related to current issues, country-specific news items or maps, training notes and reminders, staff-related matters and reminders about the need to remember security in and out of the building.

It was this last one that caught his attention. With one in his hand he walked along to Lindsay's office and opened the door. He looked around for a moment, taking in her in-tray. It held very little that hadn't been left there by her. It included the note he'd given her showing Portman's locators in France. That now lay to one side of her desk, with three copies of the security reminder lying in the centre.

Dumped because they were no longer needed?

He went outside and showed the reminder to a section supervisor. 'Do you get much of this stuff from the Support Directorate?' he asked.

She glanced at the paper and shook her head. 'Not usually. The internal email system deals with security issues. And there's already a copy on every bulletin board in the building. In fact I don't think it's changed in a week or more. It's like they think we're kids in the schoolroom, constantly needing telling more than once.'

Interesting, thought Callahan. Why distribute a security notice around the building that was already posted on the bulletin boards?

More importantly, why would a person on Carly Ledhoffen's pay grade be chosen to do it?

# THIRTY-SEVEN

S eeing the man standing there gave me a chill deep in my gut. I'd seen the look many times before, and on faces exactly like this one.

I'd been on a mission in and around the Somali capital, Mogadishu, on behalf of the French General Directorate of External Security or DGSE. The city was probably one of the most dangerous places on the planet and the memory of being hunted there was still vivid. This man's stance and look was familiar; fight or flight, it said, but more than likely the former because that was the way of things in that troubled part of the world.

I opened my mouth to call for Lindsay to step aside, and reached into my backpack for one of the guns. I sure as hell didn't want a confrontation here and now, but I might not have a choice. If he was on the side of the ungodly he wasn't going to let us go without trying to stop us.

Then he looked back at Lindsay and smiled, a genuine look of pleasure, and revealed his hand to be empty. I figured he'd just dismissed me as a potential client in favour of her.

I can't say I blamed him.

I looked at the Mégane. It was tired looking, with a few dings in the bodywork here and there, but was spotlessly clean. A *Libre* sign was propped up in the front window. A freelance cab operator hoping for a fare. The driver stopped smiling when I moved up alongside Lindsay, his look of disappointment palpable. Even so he recovered quickly and nodded at me.

He spoke good if heavily-accented English in a soft voice, and informed us that his name was Djamel and he would be happy to escort us wherever we wished to go. As he spoke I saw his eyes flicking over my shoulder towards the station building, and I wondered how much he had seen. If he was about to shout for help it could be a problem.

'It's nice to meet you, Djamel,' Lindsay said, giving him her most winning smile. 'Is there a car rental place in town?'

Djamel looked as if he was about to melt on the spot and nodded enthusiastically. He told us he had a cousin nearby who would be happy to rent us a car, no questions asked. I didn't know if that was his usual line, and we'd end up with a wreck that would let us down after a few miles, but we were short of options and the risk was worthwhile.

He ushered us urgently into the car as if we might vanish in a puff of smoke, then drove out of the station. It was a small town and the journey took all of five minutes, with Djamel pointing out a few landmarks on the way such as a lycée, a few shops, a supermarket and a burger bar. I think he'd slipped into tourist-guide role out of habit and was giving us the benefit of his knowledge just in case, you know, we wanted to stay a while.

The garage was located on the edge of a small industrial park consisting of half a dozen large metal-clad units and one smaller one, all surrounded by a chain-link fence. Djamel stopped just inside the entrance to the park and turned in his seat with the engine still running. His eyes looked grave, like large black pebbles, and there was something very knowing in his gaze. I had my hand resting on the backpack, wondering if I hadn't made a huge mistake.

'You have no cause to be concerned,' he said seriously, interpreting my thoughts. 'Where I come from I have seen many people like you.'

'What do you mean,' Lindsay asked. 'Like us?'

'People being . . . pursued. There is a look in the eyes . . . and the way they move. I am willing to help if I can because I have been there also. And one day it could be me again. Only God can tell.' He looked saddened by the thought and looked at me, lifting his chin. 'You know Somalia.' It wasn't a question.

'I do. It was a while ago, though.' There really wasn't much more I could say. There were too many factions over there and I had no idea to which one Djamel might have been allied, if at all.

He nodded. 'I have been here two years. I have a good life now. I am safe. But the shadows of my memories follow me wherever I go.' Then he turned and drove us up to the smallest unit and stopped outside. The roller shutter was down and there were no signs indicating what lay inside. He asked us to wait then hopped out and banged on a side door.

I was already reaching inside my backpack and fingering one of the guns. If this was a set-up by an entrepreneurial man with a good line of patter, I wanted to be prepared.

The door opened and there was a brief discussion, followed by a man in soiled overalls and a vest coming out to give us the once-over. He had welding goggles perched on his head and hands like claws. He was overweight, unshaven and very white, and came over for a closer look.

'I am Rémi,' he said in French, politely extending his two cleanest fingers to greet us.

'My cousin,' said Djamel, and smiled broadly.

I said hello back, even though thinking if he was Djamel's cousin I was Santa Claus. But he seemed happy enough to meet us and beckoned us inside, closing the door behind us.

The interior was surprisingly clean and efficiently racked out with all manner of tools and a lift . . . and no suspicious heavyweights ready to jump us. The air smelled of burned metal and oil. Most of the space was taken up by three vehicles, one of which was basically a chassis on wheels surrounded by equipment and car parts which had either been cut off or were in the process of being welded on, I couldn't tell which.

Rémi muttered something dismissive about that one and showed us over to the other two. They were an old Renault 19 and a white Citroën van, both of which had seen better days.

He climbed into each one in turn and turned over the engines, which sounded a little clacky but worked readily enough. Then he rummaged in a tray on a workbench and produced papers for both cars, followed by a brief conversation with Djamel who shook his head a couple of times in a mildly disapproving manner.

That's when I discovered Rémi must have been distantly related to the guy in Tripoli who'd sold me the Land Cruiser. It turned out he didn't do rentals either. It was buy or no deal. He shrugged and scribbled down a price on a piece of cardboard, which Djamel checked and seemed to think was acceptable. It was slightly eye-watering but I had no desire or room to argue. Three minutes later we were driving away in the Citroën van leaving Djamel and Rémi waving us off, deal done and all parties satisfied.

'I bet he's got some history,' Lindsay commented, as we headed out of town. It was a keen observation and one I'd made myself many times in the past. We can never know everyone's past, but nor should we enquire; their past belongs uniquely to them. But if you had any kind of imagination and human interest, you couldn't help wondering.

'Everyone has, over there,' I said. 'But you know a little of that.' Lindsay had been my back-up and eye-in-the-sky a few years back, and I knew she had got to know the dangers of the country through our shared comms experience.

# THIRTY-EIGHT

'Where are we going?' Lindsay asked, as we headed away from Courcelle on a quiet back road. I was avoiding hooking up with any of the motorways leading to Paris, but cutting straight across-country on a north-westerly heading. I was still formulating a plan but one that did not include any danger for Lindsay. That said, I was pretty sure she wouldn't accept the plan without argument.

As I'd learned very quickly, she had courage enough and more, but there comes a point at which courage leads to one too many risks and you have to use the basic practicality of staying away from anything that might get you killed because it doesn't help the overall plan.

'I need you to stay in Paris,' I said, and reached into my pocket for two cards. 'These are hotels where I booked a room. One is near the Parmentier *métro* and other near the Place de la République.' I handed them over and said, 'Choose whichever one you like and text me when you get there. They're both paid up for three days, although I doubt it'll take me that long.'

'Forget it. I'm staying with you.' She sounded mad, which I'd kind of expected. But mad didn't make it sensible. I needed to be by myself for the next phase if I was to get anywhere, and having to worry about Lindsay at the same time was likely to get us both killed.

I explained what I was going to do. 'I have to get this over and done with. To do that I've got to have a free hand to draw the opposition to an area where I have some kind of advantage.'

'You're going to fight them?'

'It's what I do. If I don't they won't stop.'

'But surely Paris would be somewhere we could hide until we can get out of the country.'

'That's just the point,' I countered. 'Getting out is the hardest thing to do. They'll be watching every port and airport, every route out of France that we could possibly take. Even if we got out they'd wait for one of us to surface in the US.'

She looked at me. 'You mean me, don't you? They'll get to you through me.'

'Yes. I can't risk that.' A big city like Paris was the logical choice but logic wasn't going to cut it this time. I had a feeling the opposition might be running short of people or patience, and either way it was time for me to take control – or, at least as much control as they would allow me. I also didn't want Lindsay to get hurt because I'd never forgive myself. That would be a burden I simply could not carry.

'What about the embassy – can't they help?'

'It's not an option. It has to be this way.'

She didn't say anything for a long while and I let her think it through. Whatever else she had learned working in the CIA, she knew that there was a way of doing things that might seem counter-intuitive to all normal folk, but which worked for the operative on the ground.

'All right,' she said at last. 'Get me on a train . . . but you'd better make sure you join me in Paris or I'll never forgive you.'

That threw me for reasons I couldn't explain, but I recovered and said, 'Agreed. I suppose there's no point me asking you to get on a flight to Washington? They don't know your name and I doubt the spotter back in Épernon got a good look at you.'

'I think I've conceded enough. Don't push it.'

When I glanced across at her she had a faint smile on her face.

I turned off the road into the town of Meulan and followed directions to the local train station. I pulled up in front of the red and cream painted building and noticed signs for a bus service to the city. I pointed it out to her. 'Whichever leaves first,' I said, 'take it. The sooner you're on your way the better. Have you ever been to Paris?'

'No. I've always wanted to. I just never expected to do it this way.' She smiled. 'It kind of takes the edge off it, somewhat, although it's exciting at the same time.' She picked up her bag and said, 'Don't worry, I'm a big girl. I can handle this.' Then she surprised me by leaning forward and brushing my ear with a kiss. 'Please be careful.'

A second later she was out of the car and walking away fast.

I continued driving north, winding my way into the rural region of Hauts-de-France. I had no specific plan or destination, but I'd know it when I saw it. First I had to make a couple of calls. As soon as I spotted a roadside café I parked nearby and headed inside, where I ordered a coffee and a *ficelle jambon-beurre*, or ham sandwich, from the lady behind the bar. I hadn't given much thought about eating but when I saw the size of the sandwich I realized how hungry I was.

There were only two other customers, which was good. They were middle-aged and dressed identically in blue overalls and boots, with an official-looking logo on the breast pocket. Other than a polite nod of greeting, they barely gave me a look. Also good. I took a table at the back of the room and ate, drank my coffee, then ordered a refill. I was going to have to be on full alert for the next twenty-four hours at least and a caffeine boost would do that just fine. While the lady was doing her thing with the coffee machine I looked for a phone and saw a blue plastic head-booth down the corridor to the rear.

I ducked inside and checked my cellphone, then dialled a number I hadn't used in a while. It rang five times before being picked up. I recognized the gravelly tones immediately.

'Fabien,' I said. 'You got time for a chat?'

There was a pause, then he chuckled and said, 'Marc? It's been a long time.' Cool as always, but friendly.

'Yeah, sorry about that. I've been busy. I need some stuff.'

He laughed. 'Of course you do. Where are you?'

I told him and he said, 'Get your ass to Beauvais and I'll be waiting.' He gave me an address on the outskirts of the town, then rang off. Cool and cautious.

I'd met Fabien in the Foreign Legion, and we'd hit it off pretty quickly. He wasn't on the run or any of that romantic nonsense, but simply had a thirst for adventure. He was a few years older than me and had already served ten years in the French military by then but had found civilian life too dull.

He'd done a stint as an armourer in the Legion, learning the skills in one of the toughest, most demanding businesses going. If a military unit can't get weapons as and when it wants them, serviced and fully reliable for battlefield conditions, an armourer doesn't last long. And Fabien had done the job for five years.

I'd used him a couple of times since then, when he'd retired to give civilian life another go, running an engineering workshop on a remote farm which served as a front for a below-the-counter gunsmith's business. I never asked who he supplied and never would. He didn't have much respect for authority, so I guess he got his trade wherever he could. All I knew was, he was reliable, secure and would never give away client names no matter who asked.

By the time I rolled up to the farm where he lived it was early evening and the light was taking on a soft hue. I climbed out of the van with my backpack and Fabien met me at the door with a wide grin.

'Marc,' he said, giving my hand a fierce tug before grabbing me round the shoulders, then threw a squinty look at my wheels. 'Have you gone all native on me? I expected something a bit more classy.'

'I'm keeping a low profile,' I explained. 'The van does that in spades.'

He led me inside and produced two beers, and we sat down. 'Like that, *hein*?' We chinked bottles. 'Are you in trouble?'

'No. Well, a little bit – but nothing official, I promise. I need some protection.' I opened the backpacks and showed him the Beretta and the Sig. 'These are fine for close work, but I need something longer.'

He took both guns from me, checking the actions and peering closely at the mechanisms for dirt and damage. 'They're good. Serviceable, anyway.' He returned the guns and finished his beer in a couple of swallows. 'What do you want, an automatic or something with spread?'

He meant did I need something for general distance work or a shotgun for close-up protection, the kind useful for clearing buildings. Since I didn't expect to be doing any of the latter, I opted for an assault rifle, which gave me distance and a decent rate of fire.

'I've got a couple of FAMAS F1 in stock. We can test-fire

them and you can choose which one. They're both good, standard French military models. I can fit an optical sight if you like, no extra charge. Where are you staying?'

I told him I'd planned on using the van but he wouldn't hear of it. 'Stay here. I have plenty of room and nobody will bother you.' He gave me a look and said, 'Where are you thinking of using this?'

'Somewhere away from housing, like a wooded area where I can watch my perimeter and have a fast exit route.'

'How many chasing you?'

'So far there have been teams of two or three.'

'So far?' He looked surprised. 'Is this an on-going thing?' He waved his forefinger in a rolling motion.

'You could say that. But I'm hoping to put a stop to it.'

'What the hell have you got yourself into? That's heavy duty.'

I didn't want to burden him with details so I gave him the basics; that my position was now pretty much blown and I was on my own. He listened without interrupting, and I guessed it was a story he'd heard before. We both knew guys who'd left the forces and moved into the private sector or become contracted to work with government departments. Guys like me. It didn't always end well because that was the nature of the work; it might be good for a while but not many contractors retired rich.

'You really think you can get them to leave you alone?' he asked, when I finished.

'I have to.' At least I had to give myself time to disappear, but I didn't tell him that. Whatever happened from here on in had to be done with as few outsiders knowing about it as possible. I trusted Fabien more than most, but he could also come under intense pressure if the wrong people became aware that we'd spoken.

'You know you can stay here tonight. I'll get the stuff ready for you for an early start.'

I thanked him and took out my cellphone. The second call I had to make was overdue.

# THIRTY-NINE

B rian Callahan was just completing a comms meeting when his cellphone buzzed. He glanced at the screen. There was no caller ID but he knew it had to be Portman. His sense of relief was tinged with irritation at not hearing from him sooner.

'Marc, are you all right?' he said, closing his office door behind him and waving away one of the admin staff carrying a batch of files. 'In case you haven't noticed, you do not have nine lives. What are you doing?'

Portman said, 'I'm trying to ignore the fact that you've been told to dump me as an inconvenience. How's that working for you, by the way?'

Callahan winced at the cool tone of Portman's voice. 'It's not, as you probably know. I wish I could say and do more, I really do.'

'I believe you. You work for some nice people up there.'

'Tell me about it. How's Lindsay holding up – is she OK?'

'Better than the people above you deserve. She's tough, but I sent her away to get her clear of whatever's going to happen.'

'Yeah – sorry. I should have explained. I didn't want her to become collateral damage because of my position.'

'Which is what?'

'A little restricted, truth be known. But I'll survive. It was the best way of doing it and helping you out that I could think of.' Even as he said it, it sounded lame, but he figured Portman would understand. 'I knew you might need some back-up cover and she'd be able to move without anyone watching her. I also knew you'd look after her. There's nobody else I'd trust to do that.'

'She'll be safe as long as she stays off the radar.'

Callahan sighed. He didn't bother asking where Lindsay was because he doubted Portman would tell him. Not that it would matter. Mixed with his concern was the knowledge that there

was little more he could do to help Portman, and that in all
likelihood he himself was being watched on orders of Broderick
at the State Department to make sure he obeyed instructions to
break off all contact with his man. But he was way past
that and hoped to prolong it for as long as he could.

'Is there anything I can do?'

Portman's voice was calm. 'You're in a bind, I know that.
But there is one thing.'

'Shoot.'

'It's time to end this. It's gone on too long.' There was a
pause and Portman said, 'Is the leak still active?'

'I think so. Why?'

'I'll be sending you a new locator. Make sure it gets known.
I'll do the rest.'

Callahan didn't like the sound of that. But trying to stop a
field operator like Portman would be like throwing stones at
a runaway tank. And deep down, he sympathized; being a
moving target was no fun and Portman sounded as if he'd
reached the end of the wire. 'You're going to draw them out?
How will that work?'

'It might not, but it's worth a try. If they lose enough people
they might decide to cut their losses.'

Callahan had heard that argument before. He just didn't
know in this instance how much was enough. 'Sounds like a
major piece of action. How many is it so far?'

'I haven't been counting. But with the two far-right bangers
who came after Chesnais it's getting close to two figures, mostly
walking wounded but some not.'

Callahan winced in spite of himself at the cold summary. He
hoped to God that no such statistics became known around
Washington; people like Broderick at the State Department
would throw up their hands and have a hissy fit, ignoring the
fact that espionage and intelligence-led operations were a kind
of war, and in war there were always casualties. He was pretty
sure, though, that nothing would ever come from the Moscow
end, that at some point their involvement would sink into
obscurity, the details wiped from the record as a face-saving
exercise.

'What's next?' he asked.

'You probably shouldn't know. Look out for the locators and feed them down the line. I'll do the rest.'

The connection was cut and Callahan put down the phone with a feeling of helplessness, all too cruelly aware that he was no longer running his asset, and that all he could do was sit out the next phase of whatever Portman was planning.

# FORTY

The following morning I was up early and on the road. Fabien had given me a couple of suggestions for places where I could hunker down, both of them well away from people but with good routes in and out. He'd even offered to come with me as a second gun but I'd clamped down hard on that one. It had been a long while since he'd been hunter or hunted, and those skills, no matter how well-learned and put into practice, diminish over time. The mental reactions to a threat slow down and the body doesn't retain the muscle memory needed to move instantly when danger presents itself. In any case I didn't want to put his life in danger any more than I had Lindsay's.

This was my fight and I had to finish it.

On the way out to the car Fabien handed me a large tactical bag. It was made of canvas and too heavy to be a sandwich and coffee. But I didn't need to look inside. It carried the familiar gun-oil aroma of an armoury, along with the smell and feel of something like a rolled-up groundsheet, military grade. Old smells, old memories.

'It's not much,' he said apologetically. 'I hope it helps.' He slapped me on the shoulder. 'It's all clean so use it then lose it.'

'Thank you,' I told him. 'I appreciate it.'

He gave me the sign of the gun with his forefinger and thumb for luck, then turned and walked back inside.

My phone beeped into life after a couple of miles and I stopped to see who was calling. It was a text from Lindsay. She said she was at the hotel near the Parmentier *métro* and told me to be careful. I told her I would and she should see some of the sights. I wasn't being over-casual, but wanted to take her mind off what was happening.

The area I'd finally chosen to use was centred on a stretch of marshland, with plenty of trees intersected by a small, meandering river. Fabien had described it in some detail, his knowledge gained from down-time visits to do some solitary fishing and hunting. It was currently a private reserve, he'd told me, but unused. He'd also warned me to be careful where I put my feet, a familiar warning when operating in enemy territory and traps were waiting for the unwary.

The approach roads were gated and locked, and Fabien had provided me a key which he said would get me through and into good cover for the car.

Marshes, trees, reeds and water – and no people. It looked like typical guerrilla or *maquis* country. But that suited me fine. Once in there I would be in control. I hadn't felt much of that in the past few days and I felt relieved that things may be swinging my way for a change. I didn't know what the skillsets of the people chasing me might be beyond the standard military gun and close-in knife work which they'd exhibited so far, but I guessed I'd soon find out.

I stopped a few miles later on the brow of a hill to make sure I hadn't picked up a tail. The road both ways was clear to the horizon and there was nothing in the sky tracking my progress as far as I could see. But who knew? Small drones are tough to locate, able to fly high to avoid being detected, using whisper-mode motors and mounted with high-resolution cameras capable of picking up amazing detail on the ground below.

This game was getting way too complicated.

I checked the bag Fabien had given me. On the very top was a wrap of cheese sandwiches and a couple of apples with two bottles of water tucked down the side. Field rations. Underneath was a FAMAS F1 assault rifle and three spare clips, a ground-sheet, binoculars, a sleeping bag, a survival knife, a coil of tripwire and four stun grenades, aka flashbangs in a canvas bag. I saw the way Fabien's mind was working. Every convenience required for a fun day in the country.

And he'd thrown in a military crossbow.

I eased it out of the bag. It was small, lightweight, made of a composite injection-moulded body and fibreglass limbs. I'd used one a few times on practice ranges as part of a general weapons-training programme, but never for real. Picture a skeletal rifle stock with a small bow perched across the top and you have a virtually silent and deadly assault weapon. Where they were known to be used they carried a powerful psychological aura unmatched by any gun. Nobody likes the idea of being pierced by something they can't hear coming and can't extract.

I replaced everything in the bag and continued driving until I reached the area I'd chosen. It lay in a shallow dip in the ground, with rolling hills running away either side. The trees were extensive, running from halfway down the slope on one side and merging into a stretch of marshland a good mile long and half a mile wide. Glints of water showed a number of ponds dotted here and there, each surrounded by reeds and tall grasses with a winding river bisecting the area and running east to west.

I checked out the approach road carefully through the binoculars. A turning off the road led onto a track which fed down into the trees and marshland, with another line which had to be a track leading up on the far side to the north.

One way in, one out. It wasn't perfect but for my purposes would do me fine.

I turned onto the track, which looked and felt little-used, with weed-filled ruts in the dried earth on each side and a high line of grass running down the centre which whispered on the underneath of the van like a voice telling me stuff I couldn't understand. The fields on either side were planted with what looked like sugar beet, leaving a nice open view across the land for some distance. A cloud of dust was billowing up behind me, which was a useful sign. Anyone approaching down here or down the far side would throw up a similar warning visible for some way, hopefully with time enough for me to get ready.

The track took me down to a weathered wooden gate about a hundred yards short of the trees. I got out and checked the lock and chain. The key fitted, although I had to work it a little to get it to turn. It was another indication that nobody had been down here in a while. High above me a couple of skylarks did their musical thing, and a flock of pigeons were poking about in the soil of the fields, too busy to bother looking at this stranger turning up nearby. It was like being in a different world, one I hadn't experienced enough of.

I got back in the van and drove through the gate, getting out and locking it behind me. There was no sense in making things easy for them. Then I drove down into the trees, the overhead canopy dimming the light and casting a soft shadow over the undergrowth on either side.

The track wound between ponds, each roughly half the size of a football pitch, and reached the river. It was little more than fifteen feet wide and maybe ten deep, the water running clear and smooth with long lines of weeds twisting in the current like ladies' hair.

A bridge made of weathered railway sleepers provided the only crossing, and I checked it out on foot before driving over. It seemed robust enough, each sleeper bedded down into the soil on either side and held in place by large rust-brown metal spikes. I got back in the van and lowered the windows. If anyone was around I wanted to hear them. I drove across the bridge, the tyres rumbling over the ridges and gaps between the sleepers and making the steering judder.

The trees on the other side of the river were thicker, the undergrowth tangled and untended for probably decades and forming a dense wall of vegetation that blocked out everything on all sides. It was like entering a mini-jungle, the atmosphere at once oppressive because of the absence of air and the high degree of constant humidity from the soil.

There were flies, too, and tiny midges forming clouds in every clearing. With them came the sickly smell of old mud tainted by rotting vegetation. I'd been in places just like it before and felt a shiver across my shoulders in spite of the warmth hanging over me like a cloak. Jungle fighting was a special art, and one I doubted I would ever come to enjoy.

When I reached the far edge of the trees I stopped. A padlocked gate was in front of me, the double of the one I'd just come through. This one opened onto a track continuing up the slope and disappearing at the top. I checked the padlock. Same key.

I drove back into the trees and found an area which formed a natural hideaway. It was big enough for the van to be hidden unless someone stumbled on it by accident. If they did I wouldn't be in it. Then I spent more than an hour scouting the whole area on foot.

The recce was essential. I needed to familiarize myself with the layout, noting possible choke points around the ponds and old fishing platforms with rotting planks long unused. An ancient wooden dinghy lay upturned in the shallows of one pond, but I decided against that as a hide. Once in I'd be trapped with no quick way out and no cover. I checked points where I could cross the river if I didn't mind getting wet, and potential hides where I could slip in with minimum effort and maximum effect.

All the while I was accompanied by birdsong high in the trees. They had gone quiet when I'd first climbed out of the van, no doubt unaccustomed to visitors in the backwater retreat. But after a while they'd resumed their chatter. It sounded to me as if they might be laughing, but I'm no expert on bird-talk. It seemed incongruous to think about what might happen here shortly, but I'd witnessed the stark contrast between nature and what man's presence can do to it too many times to be surprised.

With my recce over I stopped and took out my cellphone. I'd done everything I could think of to make this as defensive a position as I could. I was going to send Callahan my locators based on the wooden bridge over the river. Whichever way the opposition approached, from north or south, they would mentally pin the target area as being in the centre of the trees.

They wouldn't know about the fine detail, of the bridge, the river or the ponds until they got down here on the ground. It would leave them no time to do a complete recce of the area before they had to begin looking for me. That would work to my advantage because anything they wanted to do would have to be on a first-visit-as-seen basis, with no opportunity for preparation or practice.

I sent Callahan the locators. He would know what to do with them. If the leak was still working, the words would quickly find their way out and along the line. If the opposition were anywhere in the region, which I guessed they were, they'd be here within an hour or two max.

Then I settled down to wait and listen to the birds. If I didn't hear anyone coming, they would.

# FORTY-ONE

C allahan's phone buzzed. He checked the screen and saw three random words but no message. He wrote them down on a slip of paper and walked down to Lindsay's room. He was as certain as he could be now that this was where the leak occurred. But this would be the acid test, as much for Portman as it would be for himself.

He entered the room and placed the slip of paper on Lindsay's desk, pinning it in place with the corner of her in-tray. He made a small detour on the way back to his own office past the room where Andrews worked and gave the researcher a nod in passing. Andrews acknowledged it and turned to a second monitor on his desk showing a CCTV feed.

As Callahan sat down his feelings were mostly of unease at what was playing out. There was no going back from this, for him, for Portman and for others in the building, all in different ways. And the shockwaves wouldn't stop here; the State Department would also reverberate with accusations of deceit, gullibility and even negligence while those with most to lose would seek to step quickly away from any political fall-out for ignoring warnings and placing their trust in a Moscow sleeper.

His desk phone rang. He half expected it to be Sewell calling another meeting. Instead it was a familiar voice with a British accent. Tom Vale.

'Brian? I'm on a flying visit. Can you spare five minutes? It would be worth your while, I promise.'

The operations director for Britain's Secret Intelligence Service rarely had reason to call in person. Callahan was surprised but not displeased. The two men had had communications before and the two shared agreements on many issues. Portman had worked as a contractor for SIS on occasion and both agencies had cause to have been impressed with his work. In fact Vale had long been a supporter after Portman had saved the lives of two of his people in insurgent-riven Somalia.

'Of course, Tom. I'll have someone bring you up.'

While he waited for Vale to be escorted to his office, he wondered at the reason for the rush visit. Vale would normally have made an appointment, but clearly this hadn't been possible. Something was in the wind.

Vale entered the office and they shook hands. Callahan noted how tired the Englishman looked and said, 'Would you like coffee or tea?'

Vale shook his head. 'Thank you, Brian, but no. I can't stay long. I have a flight back to Northolt waiting.' He took a seat and launched right in. 'Are we all right to talk?'

'Of course. It's not bugged, if that's what you're asking.' He grinned. 'What's the problem?'

'It's about Marc Portman. I know all about his situation, of course – and we're grateful for him helping Isobel Hunt on their way out of Lebanon – but a few things have surfaced which I think you need you to know.'

'Do I need to be concerned?'

'For Portman, possibly. As you know it's not often our people get targeted on an operation the way he has over the past few days. Fortunately the interest is usually short-lived and doesn't get physical bar a bit of protesting and wailing. But this time has been different.'

Callahan said nothing, although he marvelled at Vale's degree of understatement; the level of violence aimed at Portman and Vale's officer, Hunt, had been off-the-scale lethal. And thus far it hadn't shown any signs of ending.

'We've picked up a whisper,' Vale continued, 'about the people responsible for the operation against him. On the surface it appears to be a select, unattributed group based in Moscow, all with previous ties to their security or intelligence community.'

'Had to be,' Callahan muttered. 'Do we know who's running the operation?'

'Yes, we do. Or did. But that's changed. And before you ask, yes, it's a reliable source.'

Callahan said, 'And you're going to share that with me?'

'Of course. I'll send you a report.'

'Thank you. Hang on – you said there's been a change.'

'That's right. The group responsible for hunting Portman is or was based in the Khoroshyovsky District of Moscow.'

'Isn't that GRU Headquarters territory?'

'Pretty much. You could throw a samovar and hit their front door. The group are not officially connected in any way as far as we can tell, but I'd be surprised if Putin's fingerprints weren't all over it.'

Callahan was inclined to agree. He didn't doubt the Russian president's willingness to set off a fire-cracker in the intelligence world if he felt the desire. Anything that would portray him in a good light would always be appealing.

Vale continued, 'I doubt we'll ever see his signature on an order, but I think we can accept that it was only going to be official if it was successful. In any case the group has been disbanded.' He gave a thin smile. 'I use that term with caution, since none of us knows what has happened to them, save that the group's leader has dropped out of sight and their office is now closed and sealed.'

'That sounds promising.'

'I believe it is.' He shrugged. 'Either way, the operation against Portman has been terminated. How is he, by the way? Sorry – I should have asked earlier.'

'He's fine at the moment and keeping his head down. But Christ, Tom, how do you know all this? Have you got a bug up Putin's ass or something?'

Vale laughed. 'Not quite – and that's definitely not for sharing. All I can say is one of the group members has been reporting back to Putin's office about the operation, and we were able to tap into the flow. They say the great man himself was kept informed of each stage in the operation but offered no specific input save for using a proxy voice.'

'What the hell does that mean?'

'The old clean hands methodology: Putin was aware of what was happening but nobody was going to be able to pin it on him if it all went wrong – which it has. That means anyone who thought he had issued an order was wrong . . . it was merely a talking point. Our information is that he became displeased with the poor return on investment of the venture and called a halt to further action. He has a notably short fuse regarding failure.'

Callahan waited but Vale didn't say any more. Instead he looked quietly pleased.

'You've got someone on the inside,' Callahan said with a mix of accusation and admiration.

'You know I can't confirm or deny that, Brian,' Vale murmured blandly. 'All I can say is our source is well placed.'

'So this is not a piece of fancy Moscow misinformation.'

'Absolutely not. In fact the source suggested we tell you as a matter of urgency, to save any further "unnecessary repercussions". I think that makes it as pretty near official as we can get.'

'And Portman's in the clear?'

Vale winced. 'As far as any future instructions go, yes . . . but I think you'll find it's too late to stop this operation. I'm told they can't call back any operatives in the field as they're observing strict radio silence. Whether he likes it or not, Portman's now a known face – and a target for anyone seeking to make a name for themselves. It's a pity because he has been a great asset for both of us. But all good things come to an end.' He stood up and added, 'By the way, I know foreign agents operating here are not your main concern, but you'll have heard of a Russian sleeper named Seraphim?'

Callahan nodded, struggling to get to grips with what to do for Marc Portman. 'Sure, vaguely. Heard mention of him a few times through inter-agency briefings. But that was a while back. The general view is he was a bogeyman – a bit of Kremlin play-acting to fool us western imperialists into wasting time and energy looking up our own exhausts. The FBI will know more than me. Why do you ask?'

'We thought the same. All we'd ever picked up was that there was a Moscow sleeper known as Seraphim based in the States but nobody had been able to verify the fact.'

'And now you have?'

'We've had confirmation that Seraphim is a she, not a he, and goes under the name of someone I think you might have heard of.'

Callahan suddenly knew what was coming. 'Christ, go on.'

'Valentina Desayeva.'

'Jesus.' Callahan didn't bother hiding his disgust.

Vale smiled at his reaction. 'Our source tells us Desayeva's been playing the double, supposedly running information both ways between here and Moscow, but with her sole focus on pleasing her bosses in Moscow Centre – namely the SVR.' He studied Callahan's face before saying, 'Something tells me this isn't entirely news to you.'

'Let's say I had my suspicions,' Callahan confirmed sourly. 'Unfortunately I haven't been in a position to do much about it. Until now, anyway.'

'I don't think you should get your hopes up.'

'What do you mean?'

'Ask your friends at the FBI to check. I think they'll find she's gone on a long holiday and won't be coming back.'

After Vale had left, Callahan reflected on what he'd just been told. If it was true – and he'd no reason to doubt Vale's sources – it meant his early instincts about Desayeva had been right; the State Department had somehow got themselves into bed with a Moscow double, and they hadn't seen it coming. Or maybe they hadn't wanted to, being too keen to have a pipeline to and from the Russians to drop information of dubious quality. No matter what value they thought she had provided on Russian thinking and strategy, if Desayeva really had been working for the SVR, Russia's Foreign Intelligence Service, she would have been intent on passing back to Moscow only hard-core intelligence culled through her many ingenuous contacts in and around Washington. In return the goofs in the State Department had sent whatever they thought was useful down the wire, congratulating themselves on doing a grand job.

What he wouldn't have given, he thought idly, to be a fly on the wall when Jason Sewell threw that bit of embarrassing information back at Walter M. Broderick, the Deputy Assistant Secretary at the State Department.

# FORTY-TWO

J ust under three hours after my text to Callahan I saw a vehicle top the rise on the road running past the marshlands. There had been a few since I'd been here but they'd continued on by, a mix of the everyday country traffic you'd expect in this part of the world. It wasn't the busiest road I'd ever seen and I couldn't imagine anyone coming after me in a truck or a John Deere tractor.

This latest arrival was a SUV. I couldn't tell the colour because it was profiled against the horizon, but it looked dark and bulky, the kind capable of carrying men and equipment while being common enough to pass without comment save an occasional glance of envy.

The engine sounded smooth, the hum floating down the hill to where I was standing in the treeline. The vehicle was moving along the road at a steady clip, and for a second I thought I was mistaken and that it was going to drive on by and disappear like all the others. But at the last moment it slowed and turned onto the track. Then stopped.

I knew what they were doing: they were checking the location on their digital map, the little square locator telling them where I should be found right down to a three-metre square.

They began the descent of the track, a plume of dust whirling in their wake. One look through the binoculars and I needed no further confirmation. I saw three heads up, the driver and two, and what looked like assault rifles carried at the ready.

I dialled Callahan. He answered as if he'd been crouched over his phone.

'They're here,' I confirmed.

'Shit.' He sounded weary, that one word carrying a world of meaning, as if too much bad news had arrived all in one hit. I knew how he felt.

I cut the connection; talking about it further wouldn't solve the problem and Callahan had to get on with whatever he was doing at his end to plug the leak for good.

The SUV was coming closer. I wasn't concerned they could see me, because where I was standing was too dense, too well concealed against the greens and browns of the trees and vegetation around me. I was hoping they weren't as well versed in this kind of environment as me, but I wasn't taking anything for granted; anyone the Russians sent after me would not be a boy scout with no experience of urban or rural conflict. They had that built into their DNA but, like all contractors, it could fade a little if not used regularly.

The SUV stopped a little way short of the gate, leaving enough room to turn on a dime if needed and head on back up the hill. They sat there for a while, the engine running, and I knew they were studying the area carefully, deciding what to do. They were probably puzzled by the gate being locked and chained, and were figuring I might have found my way inside from another direction.

Then one of the passengers stepped out and approached the gate. He looked to be in his mid-thirties, dressed in a plain shirt and combat pants. He was staring down at a cellphone in one hand and carrying an assault rifle in the other. I couldn't tell from this distance but it looked like an AK variant with a twenty-round magazine. Serious stuff.

He tried the lock and chain without luck, and gave the gate a kick to test the wood. It rattled but held fast. He shook his head and waved impatiently at the driver before standing to one side. He wanted to get on with the job.

Seconds later the SUV kicked forward and hit the gate head-on, ripping it apart and carrying the torn and broken woodwork away on the hood. The passenger gave a whoop of laughter and jogged after it to clear the debris away before jumping back inside and making a forward motion with his phone hand.

I watched them go by and set off after them. Instead of going further into the trees I moved round towards the track to come up behind the vehicle. I wasn't sure what kind of plan they had in mind, but if they were counting on me being here and to be standing in the middle of the locator square waiting for them like a good boy, they were going to be disappointed.

I followed a parallel line to the track a few steps into the trees, keeping a screen of vegetation between me and them.

The fact that the passenger had jumped back in the vehicle was a good sign. Had it been me I'd have ducked out and stayed low, checking for movement in the trees, which was far more effective than doing it from a moving vehicle. You might not be able to see a target among trees but you can hear them move. All you need is patience and focus. And concentrating all three men in the vehicle was a risky move rather than spreading them out because they'd all be vulnerable if they came up against a concerted attack.

I stopped every few yards in case one of them had got cute and bailed out to watch and wait. The engine noise was still floating back to me through the trees, muted now but clear enough in this quiet place and undisturbed by outside influences. The big difference was that the birdsong I'd enjoyed earlier had fallen silent as if nature had thrown a giant switch.

Then the engine noise ceased.

I moved slower, wary of branches and brambles, anything that would betray my presence. The muffled sounds of three doors closing gave me a fix on their position. If they were close enough to the river to have spotted the bridge they were probably wary of putting the SUV's considerable weight on the wooden sleepers, and would go for a look first.

*What the hell?* A movement from the corner of my eye. But instead of being anywhere near the bridge and the SUV, it was way off to one side, in the wrong place. I froze, hardly daring to breathe, and waited to see if the figure would notice me. I had no idea where he had come from, as if he'd materialized out of the earth.

He moved again and I saw him clearly this time. He was about fifty yards away from me and dressed in old camo clothing and a woolly cap. He moved slowly, with the gait of someone old rather than with deliberate caution, and I guessed he was in his sixties at least. He had a greasy looking canvas bag hanging from one skinny shoulder and carried an old-style military water bottle in one hand. He was heavily bearded and what little skin I could see was deeply tanned. But there was no sign of a weapon.

A homeless guy.

He must have heard the SUV and was following it to take a closer look, hoping for a handout. I was guessing he'd come into the trees across the fields after I'd done my recce, otherwise I would have seen him.

I went to move towards him, to intercept him and warn him off. But I was too late. There was a crack as he stepped on a branch, and he went still.

I heard a shout from over by the bridge and hit the ground, sensing what was coming next. The silence was shattered by a sustained volley of gunfire, ripping apart tree trunks and foliage, each contact between lead and wood a relentless snapping noise as the men from the SUV hosed down the area with no target in sight.

I dropped to the ground and waited. When it came, the silence was complete. And there was no sign of the homeless guy.

I waited, the Famas at the ready. The three men were jumpy. I guess they'd heard what had happened to the previous teams and weren't taking any chances. Better to use a heavy-duty approach on a target than taking the trouble to use tactics to flush it out.

More shouts and a whistle, followed by a rustle of under-growth, then all went quiet. I slid forward towards the fallen man, barely moving the grass around me and ready to open fire at the first sign of a threat.

Then I saw him.

He was dead. He lay on his side, his head thrown back and his throat bare, the skin beneath his chin starkly pale in contrast to the rest of his face. There was blood on his chest and more had seeped out from the ancient combat jacket bearing badges from an unknown regiment in a forgotten war. His shoulder bag had taken hits, too, the fabric torn apart revealing an old aluminium flask with a plastic screw-top, a fold of faded blue cloth that might have been a shirt, and a red toothbrush, the bristles soft and worn down with use.

I moved away. There was nothing I could do for him and if I stayed here the men would eventually come looking to see if they had bagged their intended target.

I stayed low, my thigh muscles protesting at the unaccustomed effort, and came to a long dip in the ground between three large trees. I eased into it, feeling the give of soft earth beneath me and the cool kiss of moisture seeping into my clothing. I ignored it. This was a deadly game of hide-and-seek and a bit of wet was the least of my worries.

Then, as I rolled to get a better view of the area I'd just left, I felt something hard and sharp dig into my ribs.

# FORTY-THREE

The last thing I needed right now was a distraction; checking the trees surrounding me was essential for survival. If the men made a concerted effort to scour the area they'd be certain to spot me in the end. But I had to see what was digging into me. I turned my head and looked down.

And stopped breathing.

I was lying on top of a large artillery shell. Undoubtedly a relic of the First World War that had ravaged this area of France over a hundred years ago, it was now only half-buried in the grass and damp soil of the marsh. It must have worked its way to the surface as the layers of mud and rotting vegetation had shifted over the years. The locals, who regularly came across many such dangers in the fields, referred to them as 'the deadly harvest' and the description couldn't have been more apt.

I started breathing again and studied the ground around me, not daring to move. Most of what I could see was short, coarse grass and moss, interspersed with dark soil verging on mud. It was the soil I was looking at.

That was when I saw another shape a couple of feet away. Covered in a skin of dirt and rust it was too regular and smooth to be a log. Smaller than the one beneath me it looked just as sinister, every bit as lethal. Alongside it lay a clutch of smaller shells barely held together by the remains of a belt-feed from a heavy machine-gun.

Suddenly the three men looking for me were no longer the only danger I was facing. The more I saw the more I realized that I was lying on the site of an old ammunition dump. A nest of discarded explosives, probably unmapped and now overgrown by nature, known if at all by only a handful of people in the area but with no way of doing anything about it.

No wonder this place was unused and fenced off. What lay in the ground beneath me was a cocktail of death that even after all this time was likely to explode if moved. And any one item could easily set off any other ordnance around it like giant firecrackers, razing this wood to the ground with every living being inside it.

I eased my weight off the shell, gently feeling my way across a surface soil I couldn't see clearly, and over a subsoil harbouring who knew how many similar deadly objects. In the clammy heat among the trees, where no trace of fresh air was able to penetrate, I found a sheen of perspiration on my skin, running into my eyes and making them sting and causing my clothes to stick to my body.

I'd gone perhaps no more than fifty feet, confident that I was clear of the worst of the ammunition dump when I saw a shape moving among the trees ahead of me. A man with a rifle.

I thought I'd got away without being seen but something about me must have jarred with the vegetation around me. Swinging his weapon towards me he opened fire on full auto.

The sound of the volley echoed over the marsh, snapping through the branches of the trees above my head like spiteful hornets. Luckily for me he'd been in too much of a hurry and the shots went wide. But he'd effectively nailed my position to his colleagues and more shots came my way from other directions.

I rolled to my knees behind a tree and saw another man off to my side moving in my direction, eager to come in for the kill. I fired two shots from the Famas before ducking down again and rolling.

This time I felt a sucking sensation beneath me and realized I'd moved too close to a stretch of boggy ground bordering a small pond. The dark mud was interspersed with the silvery-copper glint of stale surface water, its smell rising around me like an invisible mist.

A whistle came from my left, and I backed away in the direction of the bridge. So far these men hadn't shown much evidence of working as a team, but as three individuals. Maybe they were finally getting it together. If I allowed them to coordinate their moves I'd be sunk. In their thinking the centre of the mission was located at the bridge itself, so I was counting on them assuming I'd be moving in the opposite direction, away from their guns.

I wasn't going to do that.

I saw a glint of light reflecting off the SUV's bodywork and ducked. The bridge itself was a no-go area; it was too open, an obvious focal point which they would be sure to be watching, even if one man stayed close by while the others scouted the woods. But there was nothing to stop me fording the river further along. I slipped across the track and into the denser undergrowth, the back of my neck itching from the imagined dangers I could not see.

I counted to twenty to see if anything moved, then crept over to the river and waited again.

Nothing moving, nobody waiting. Holding the rifle and the Sig in the air I eased down the bank, watching the trees on the opposite side. Sliding my feet into the water and feeling its cool grip on my skin, I pushed down and adjusted by balance until I was able to stand up.

As I'd seen during my recce earlier, the water was only a few feet deep here, with an accumulation of silt, rotten vegetation and weeds forming a high point on the river bed.

I didn't dare splash because it was a sound that would carry a long way in this silence. The current, steady and insistent, drew the hair-like strands of weed around my legs in a caress, and I kept moving, wary of getting tangled in their grip. My shoes were sinking into the soft mud with every step, but I'd done this kind of thing before and kept going, taking step after step before the mud could increase its grip on me.

On the other side I dragged myself up the bank and eased over the top into a tangle of low-lying bushes, then held my position while I scanned the area around me. Getting my bearings I saw a familiar fallen tree trunk and moved towards it. In a hollow beneath the trunk was the crossbow wrapped in a blanket I'd found in the back of the van and placed there earlier.

I set one of the six bolts Fabien had provided in the bed of the bow and placed it to one side on a bed of leaves. Each bolt was about a foot long. I also made sure the Famas was good and ready and checked the Sig.

A voice close by made me freeze.

A man was walking along the track from the north. He was carrying an assault rifle and using a cellphone held across his mouth. I couldn't hear or understand what he was saying but he had the sound of a man in charge who was fast losing patience. That was good for me; if they were on a clock that was running down fast it would make them all the more careless and rushed to get things done. A crackly voice came back in reply and he barked an order and clicked off. He sounded testy.

He was also careless. The one thing you don't do in a close combat situation like this is give away your position by leaving your comms open. It's the kind of thing that can get you killed.

I felt around for a large stone and turned to face the river, which was about twenty yards away. Lying on my side I did an overhand grenade lob, and saw the stone curve through the air before dropping to the water. My instructor from years ago would have been proud of me.

As it hit the water with a healthy splash, I was rolling to give myself room to manoeuvre. I picked up the crossbow and waited.

A shout came immediately after the splash and three shots echoed close together, followed by footsteps pounding along the track from the direction of the bridge. I guessed it was whoever had been on the other end of the short conversation moments ago. He'd opened fire without having a sighted target, and was now coming to investigate. And that brought him across a clearing right in front of me.

I couldn't see where the boss man had got to but I couldn't wait; I had to take advantage of the situation while it presented itself.

It was time to mess with their heads.

As the second man stared down into the water and saw no sign of me, he must have realized he'd been set up. He spun round, his mouth open and dragging the assault rifle up to open fire again. I breathed out and pressed the trigger.

There was very little recoil and hardly a sound from the elastic firing mechanism, and the bolt snapped across the yards separating us. I only saw it again when it hit him, spinning him around. He dropped the rifle and screamed, clutching at the shaft protruding from high in his shoulder.

A shout came from nearby and more footsteps crashed

through the undergrowth between the trees. The voice had sounded like the boss man. I couldn't count on being lucky twice in one go, and if the man I'd shot was able to communicate with his colleague, they'd have a reasonably good idea where I was hiding if I stayed here.

I slid back out of my makeshift hide, leaving the crossbow which was too awkward to drag through the vegetation if I had to go to ground in a hurry.

For now, though, I'd sown a seed of doubt in their minds and taken out one of their team. Nobody with a crossbow bolt in their shoulder is going to be able to do much in the way of fighting. And when the others saw it they'd be inhuman if they didn't freak out just a little.

Two to go.

I followed the line of the river, moving away from the men and the bridge towards the edge of the marsh. I intended circling around and coming up behind them from the direction I'd used coming into the area. I was also keeping my eyes open for traces of the third man, who'd shown no signs of appearing yet. As I kept the water to my right I was also checking the ground in front of me in case the ammo dump was more extensive than I'd thought, and thought how odd it was that I hadn't considered the boat on my earlier recce.

*A boat?* I stopped dead.

The only boat I'd seen then had been upside down and lying in a pond, rotten beyond use. Yet here was a dinghy in good condition, sitting by the bank of the river, a mooring rope hanging in the water and two paddles on the bottom. And two backpacks.

Next thing I heard was the click of a gun being cocked.

# FORTY-FOUR

David Andrews appeared in the outer office and Callahan beckoned him straight in. He was due at another meeting upstairs but if he had any really hot news he might be able to call it off on the grounds of a greater priority.

He pointed to a chair. 'You've got three minutes. Make it worthwhile.'

Andrews sat and said, 'We might need more time than that. Ledhoffen did what you expected: she walked into Lindsay's room, lifted the bait and left. I couldn't track her phone but I'm guessing you'll know pretty soon if it worked or not.'

Callahan nodded just as his phone buzzed. He said, 'Wait one,' and snatched it up.

It was Portman.

He listened for a moment, then swore before putting the phone down. Portman had sounded almost relieved at the prospect of dealing with this latest threat. And there was nothing Callahan could do to help him.

'Bad news?' said Andrews.

'Bad for someone.' Callahan scowled and brought himself back on track. 'How do you know Ledhoffen lifted the bait? The CCTV footage doesn't show the inside of the office. Couldn't someone else have gone in there?'

'I covered that.'

Callahan had a sudden sense of alarm. 'How?'

'I figured we'd need some close-up action inside the room. That way we'd know for sure.'

'Close-up? How close?'

'I placed a small camera in a bookcase. It only covers the last twenty-four hours but it was enough—'

Callahan nearly choked. 'You did *what*?' Christ, there would be a riot if anyone upstairs learned of this. They'd have his and Andrews' heads on a spike . . . or whatever the current indignity was likely to be. 'And how did you get in there?'

Andrews looked mildly alarmed. 'I remember the keypad code from a while back. I know that was pushing it but I think you'll be pleased I did.' He placed his tablet on the desk before Callahan could say anything and pressed a button.

The screen showed Carly Ledhoffen entering Lindsay's room and moving towards the camera. She glanced at the desk before bending to pull the slip of paper Callahan had placed there towards her. Then she scribbled something on one of the bulletins and dumped the rest.

There it was, thought Callahan, ignoring for a moment that he and Andrews had stepped way over the line of what was permissible or acceptable in this building unless officially authorized. All the proof he needed. But could he tie it together?

He watched the screen as Ledhoffen left the room. Then something caught his attention.

'Show me the footage of her outside the room,' he said, 'before going in.'

Andrews did. Re-running the film when Callahan asked him and slowing it down.

'She used the access code,' he said softly. 'Jesus. She used the fucking code!'

Andrews looked at him. 'Doesn't her section have access to all doors?'

'No. Not all of them. And not that one.' He stood away from the desk and growled, 'And nor do you. Remember that if they ever strap you to a polygraph.'

'Absolutely. Already forgotten.' He crossed himself. 'Scout's honour.'

'Balls. You were never in the Scouts. I checked. And you'd better never tell a living soul about that camera. Understand me?'

'Got it. It's already gone – I promise.'

'Good. What else have you got?'

'A couple of things. I've been looking into Dalkin's background, hoping to find a link to his recent acquisition of money, like a family bequest or an old insurance policy we didn't know about.'

'Good thinking. And?'

'There's nothing like that. I got as far as a transfer account but it was blocked. Some kind of offshore fund thing which I thought might be a family trust fund arrangement. I trawled his family records but it wasn't heavy on numbers; a sister he rarely sees who's been in intensive care with cancer; no brothers, uncles or aunts still alive . . . and no associated funds. But I did come across a cousin with an interesting name.' He smirked. 'You'd never guess—'

'Surprise me.' Callahan stole a glance at his watch and got ready to stand.

'Carly Ledhoffen.'

Callahan froze, his jaw dropping. 'Say what?'

'She and Dalkin are first cousins. I took a squint at both their records and neither mentions having a cousin anywhere, least of all here in DC.'

'I guess if they didn't know the other was here they wouldn't have to mention it. I have cousins I've never met nor would I want to. Do they have any contact?'

'They exchanged a couple of calls recently. Prior to that almost never. They're not Facebook or social media buddies either.'

'Yeah, well they wouldn't be, would they? If what people say is correct, Ledhoffen's a social climber and I doubt Dalkin inhabits any kind of rung on her ladder, especially now he's out of a regular job.' He chewed his lip. 'What about their phones?'

'I had a quick look, but the recent calls lasted less than a minute, max. It was like they were saying hi and goodbye. They both have WhatsApp accounts, but we can't access those.'

'Hi and goodbye after a long period of no-contact?' Callahan looked sour at the idea of encountering a dead end. 'That doesn't sound likely. What does your wannabe cop instinct tell you?'

Andrews shrugged. 'It set me thinking: cousins or not, would she help him for free?'

'What do you mean?'

'Right, please bear with me here; this is cafeteria scuttlebutt so has to be taken with a bucket of salt, as my mom always says. Ledhoffen name-drops a lot, about who she knows, the people she parties with and so forth. Most are high on the DC totem pole, a lot in politics and a fair few celebrities. She's got a nice apartment in Mount Vernon and she hobnobs with people upstairs more than she does general staff, which has earned her a nickname—'

Callahan scowled. 'I know what they call her. It's unpleasant. But hobnob? Do you have any more of these quaint words, only I'm growing older and greyer by the minute?'

'It's Shakespeare,' Andrews replied. 'Allegedly.'

'Thank you.' Callahan's face was deadpan. 'It was a rhetorical question.'

'Oh. Sorry. Well, she's dropped hints in the past that she has family money, but there's no evidence of it.'

'So maybe they're good at hiding their cash. That's not a crime; my wife does it all the time. What about a secondary bank account?'

'I was going to ask if I should try that . . . or let Warner and Cahill take the lead. Only I'm not sure how much more we can do.'

Callahan considered it. 'Good point. We're already beyond our remit on this thing. If this business involves some kind of money transactions that contravenes a host of regulations, it'll be something the FBI can get their teeth into.' He gave a thin smile. 'It'll probably make their day.'

'There's another point I found – well, two, in fact; one about Ledhoffen's skill-set, the other I'm not so sure about. It could be a coincidence.'

'Go on.'

'She's smart. And I mean *very* smart. She's got degrees like some people pick up groceries at the supermarket. Mathematics and economics are the main ones. But I got chatting to one of the gals in IT. They had a clash just recently and she was happy to dish the dirt. She told me Ledhoffen let slip once that she took a combined course in information technology and software engineering, although she dropped it after a couple of years because she didn't want to spend her life below-stairs with a bunch of geeks.'

Callahan was impressed, although not surprised. Langley had more geeks than most places had windows. 'They fell out over a minor slur?'

'Ledhoffen made a remark about geeks not having any fashion sense.'

'Jesus. That probably hurt. OK, so how much could a smart person learn in a couple of years?'

'A lot. Ledhoffen's obviously got a talent for learning. I've known people like her who absorb stuff without even trying. I wish I'd got it but I had to put in the hard work.'

'But why would she go to the Support Directorate? It's kind of limiting, isn't it, with those skills? She could have gone anywhere inside the building or out.'

Andrews shrugged. 'She gets to mix with some powerful names. And it's the world's best known intelligence agency. For some people that's enough. Anyway, if she transfers across departments, who knows where she could end up in a year or two?'

That was a thought Callahan didn't want to entertain; if she was involved in supplying information from the comms section to her cousin and, by association a Moscow sleeper agent, how much more damage could she do if she was allowed to continue?

'You said there were two things. What else, only I'm out of time.'

Andrews referred to his tablet again. The screen showed a series of media photos taken at functions and events, some black tie and gowns, others less formal. In each one a familiar face showed centre-page.

'Desayeva,' said Callahan. 'So what? She's like a honeybee on steroids – she gets around a lot.'

'But look who else is there.' Andrews pointed at several specific photos in turn. In each one another familiar figure appeared, each time in close conversation with the Russian woman and clearly on very familiar terms with her, judging by the way she was hanging on her arm.

It was Carly Ledhoffen.

Callahan frowned. 'I'm going to play devil's advocate here: Ledhoffen's a fashion and social freak, we all know that. She's also keen to let people know she's from a wealthy background. Desayeva collects rich people like I collect parking tickets. Why wouldn't they meet?'

He shrugged. 'I thought that, too. But it gave me an idea.'

Callahan scowled. 'Don't tell you got creative with another camera. I don't think my heart will take much more.'

'No. I promise. What if there was more to these photos? What if Desayeva and Ledhoffen weren't merely fashion show buddies? What if Dalkin's no more than a convenient point of contact for Desayeva, and the real connection is Desayeva . . . and Ledhoffen?'

Callahan blinked. 'What – Ledhoffen supplying the information directly?' He stared at his desk, trying to see a negative. He couldn't. Or maybe he didn't want to. 'That's a jump. A fucking big one if you don't mind my French.'

'True. But we know there's a line of connections, right? Ledhoffen to Dalkin and Dalkin to Desayeva. Links in the chain. We might have jumped to the wrong conclusion about which way the links ran, that's all.'

Callahan wanted to believe it but was still unsure. Andrews had a useful way of talking things out; the young man had none of the interference of long-held field experience or cherished ideas blinding him to finding conclusions even if they were unacceptable. Even so, it was tenuous. A court of law would rip the chain apart like tissue paper.

'I met Muhammed Ali once,' he said. 'It was at an airport and our flights had been grounded due to snow. That doesn't make me a fight fan. See where I'm going?' He glanced at his watch and made a decision. 'I have a meeting to go to. In the meantime, get me a meeting with Bill Warner and his team. I'd like to get inside his mind.'

'About what?'

'Get him to run a deep check on Ledhoffen's phone calls and accounts. There has to be a hook we can use. We need to bring this thing to an end.'

# FORTY-FIVE

It wasn't the time for heroics. Whoever it was had the drop on me and was lying somewhere in the reeds on the river bank, way off-centre of where I was pointing my rifle. By the time I dragged it into position he'd have blown me off my feet.

A soft laugh came from low down, then the man moved and got to his feet, rattling the reeds where he'd been hiding. He wore hunting gear with a cellphone clipped to the front of his jacket. He was short and squat, with the high cheekbones of a Slav and crooked teeth, strong looking and somewhere in his forties, probably a contract man. He was grinning at his good fortune like he'd won first prize in a pig-sticking contest.

And I was the pig.

I shrugged, wondering where the second man had got to. I lifted both arms out from my body, demonstrating that I wasn't a threat. I dropped my shoulders in a slump to signify defeat, and swore. It was the kind of thing he'd be expecting. Defeat, then submission.

He motioned for me to drop my rifle, using the business end of his AK-47. It looked clean, if a little battered around the woodwork, but these things are readily available for a song all over the world, and I figured this team, like the others, would have got their weapons from local sources. Easy come, easy go, and no trace back to the organizers of their mission.

I dropped the rifle and held my palms out, then sank to a sitting position on the ground, crossing my ankles. He lost the grin in favour of a suspicious scowl, as if this had been too easy. Then he tilted his head towards the phone on his jacket and said something short and sharp which I couldn't hear.

It was probably something along the lines of '*Got him*'.

Shouting came from deep in the trees. I hadn't got long. The others would be here soon and it didn't take rocket science to know that when they arrived they wouldn't be looking to take me away in one piece. That wasn't their mission. All this guy had done was merely delay the inevitable.

He motioned for me to move away from the rifle, which I did, in case he suddenly recalled his orders, which were probably to shoot me on sight. I used my hands to propel myself across the grass in an awkward hopping motion, grunting and making a meal of it. When he told me to stop, I stopped.

Which was about the same moment he must have realized that each time I'd moved, my hands were closer to my body . . . and closer to anything I might have concealed in my waistband.

The Sig.

Then my cellphone vibrated in my pocket. Great timing. 'Jesus – look at that!' I stared past him at the other side of the river, my eyes wide open as if I'd seen the ghost of my long-dead grandmother.

It would have taken any man a massive effort to have avoided turning his head out of instinct. But all I needed was a fraction of movement. When he turned to look, the rifle barrel dropped away a few inches, and I rolled sideways, lifting the Sig out of my waistband. I shot him once, mid-section. When in doubt, aim for the body mass.

He fumbled with the rifle, at the same time looking down disbelievingly at the hole in his jacket, before tumbling sideways and rolling down the river bank into the water.

By the time the first ripples got halfway across the river I was scooping up the Famas and moving fast, keeping low and checking the trees for signs of the company I knew was on its way in.

I made it back to the area where I'd left the crossbow, hearing voices filtering through the marsh. It sounded a lot like the man in charge demanding an inquest and promising hell and damnation on whoever had messed up this time. That suited me; I needed all the help I could get and the more he yelled at his men the better. I located his voice somewhere ahead of me, with other voices coming closer to the spot where I'd just shot their colleague.

I ran past the hide, snatching up the crossbow on the way, then moved over to the river. There was no sign of the man with a bolt in his shoulder so I figured he was in the SUV and out of action. I slid down the bank and into the water, dragging my legs against the current and pushing up the other side.

It was awkward going with the rifle, the Sig and the crossbow, but I couldn't afford to leave any weapons behind. I took a second to check I wasn't about to run into trouble before ducking into a mess of brambles and bushes clumped around a large tree trunk that had seen better days.

It put me back near the ammunition dump and as close as I wanted to be. I dragged some leaves away and pulled out the canvas bag and tripwire Fabien had given me.

This wasn't going to be sophisticated; I'd done this kind of thing before and not always using flashbangs. But these would serve a purpose. It took me five minutes and then I was ready.

I fired the Sig twice into the air, then screamed and sat back to wait for the reaction.

It came good and fast. The boss man was in the area to my rear and the other two were somewhere deep in the trees. Three on the move with two down made five. I hoped that was all they had and that someone I hadn't seen yet had got cute and was waiting to ambush me.

The boss man came charging through the undergrowth behind me like a tornado, breathing heavily and clearly pissed, ready for a fight to make up for his losses. I waited until he was close enough before pulling the length of tripwire by my right hand. There was metallic *ping* of the pin coming out and I counted to three before ducking my head and covering my ears.

The blast came good and loud, shaking whatever else in the way of wildlife that hadn't already moved out to scatter far and wide. Even with my eyes closed I caught a sense of the flash that came with it lighting up the gloom among the trees like an exploding movie studio arc lamp.

If the running man had heard the warning ping he hadn't paid it much attention, but the blast would have certainly been enough to deafen him. The following eyeball-searing flash of light would have made him think the sky had fallen in.

He kept on running but he was moving on a dry tank. His eyes would have been hurting like hell and his balance shot to ribbons. He also wouldn't have been able to hear a thing, so the fact that I was standing up as he came close simply didn't register.

I shot him once centre-frame, then stepped forward and kicked the AK out of his hand. I bent and ripped his cellphone off his shirt front and frisked him, retrieving a Makarov nine-millimetre pistol. All three items went into the river.

Then I got away from there.

There was a lot of shouting, none of it controlled, and I heard the man I'd just shot yelling into the air. I guessed he was telling his friends not to come in shooting, which was very wise of him.

Seconds later they did just the opposite, running in from two different sectors. They took a quick look at their boss, then ducked down, scanning the trees. It was too little too late but their lack of combat discipline was just what I needed.

I reached down and grabbed the second tripwire, then lay flat on the ground and pulled.

Two seconds later the flashbang erupted, sending both men into a spin. But it was nothing compared with the explosion that followed from the ammunition dump as something went up, sending a huge gout of earth, mud, foliage and debris into the air and peppering the trees all around with a deadly spread of shrapnel.

I waited for the count of ten before venturing out. I had the Famas ready but there was no need. The two men were on the ground. One was dead, his chest covered in blood, the other was wounded but out of it, breathing in short gasps, his eyes devoid of expression.

I gathered up my gear as quickly as I could and tossed it all in the nearest pond, where it sank without trace in the mud. Then I ran back to the van and drove to the gate heading north and let myself out.

Time to go home.

# FORTY-SIX

On arrival at the FBI office, Bill Warner greeted Callahan and Andrews. He shook hands warmly with them before leading them to a small room set up with an open computer screen on the wall. He was trying to look casual but wore the air of a man on a cloud.

'It's been a while.' The FBI man grinned and waved at them to sit. 'And here we are again with a familiar name. I never was completely sure about Desayeva.'

Callahan nodded. 'Same here. What have you got?'

'You hit us on a good day.' Warner turned to the monitor. 'After what Andrews here found out we had a team running over Ledhoffen's and Dalkin's financial records and phone accounts. Ledhoffen has a business account at another bank which shows an input of two cash transfers totalling eighty thousand dollars.'

Callahan whistled. 'Do you know where from?'

'We do, sort of. One was for fifty grand from an offshore account – but that's all we do know. It's a dead end so far and I don't hold out much hope of going further. My guess is the source is Russian. But the remaining thirty grand came from her favourite cousin, one Bradley Dalkin.'

Callahan was surprised. 'That's clumsy.' Moving too much money around was a risky business, with banks liable to report unusual amounts; some getting nervous at anything more than ten thousand dollars. Maybe Dalkin and cousin Carly were getting carried away with themselves.

Warner agreed. 'They're amateurs, that's why. I asked around the industry but not all banks worry too much about the numbers. We also took a long, hard look at the phone accounts for Ledhoffen and Desayeva. I figured there might be a connection we could follow along that line to see if the money might have Desayeva's fingerprints on it. I figured it was a long shot and it was. No fingerprints . . . at least not there.'

'And?'

'We think Ledhoffen got careless or maybe too clever for her own good. Checking her phone we found a single text message from her to Desayeva in the last twenty-four hours. I figured you might have an idea what it means.' He touched the keys and the screen showed three words.

Callahan's brain fizzed. He recognized them immediately. They were the three-word code location for Portman in the marshland near Beauvais in France.

There it was: the direct link they were after. Carly Ledhoffen had sent Valentina Desayeva, aka Agent Seraphim, Portman's precise location. And if that followed the same path as previously, the Russians would jump on it. He checked his watch. He hadn't heard from Portman, which wasn't good.

'Can I use your phone?' he asked. 'It's important.'

Warner nodded. 'I thought it might be. Go ahead.'

Callahan dialled Portman's number. It rang. And rang. He cut the connection. Portman either hadn't got his phone with him or wasn't in a position to take the call. Neither was potentially great news but he had to believe Portman had the situation under control.

'Problem?' Warner asked.

'I'm not sure. I hope not.'

Warner looked concerned. 'I know what those words mean, by the way. It's a locator reference, right? Ledhoffen was telling the Russians where your man is located.'

Callahan felt guilty for assuming Warner wouldn't realize the significance of the words. 'That's right.' He was about to thank Warner for his work when the FBI man said, 'We found something else.'

'Christ,' said Callahan. 'Better than this?'

'Potentially. We figured there had to have been other calls to Ledhoffen or Desayeva which we hadn't picked up first time round. When we did another trawl we hit on a series of brief calls made to Desayeva's landline. Each originated from five different public pay phones here in DC. They were single calls lasting no more than a minute or so.' He smiled like a magician about to produce a rabbit. 'The kind of calls confirming information with no idle chit-chat . . . or maybe complaining at being cut out of a deal. All five phones are located less than three blocks from Bradley Dalkin's apartment in Rockville.'

'Shazam,' exclaimed David Andrews softly, and blushed when the two older men looked at him. 'Sorry.'

'Shazam's good,' Callahan said, and looked at Warner. 'What do you mean cut out?'

'First of all it's hard to prove it was Dalkin calling unless we can pull up CCTV footage of him at those five locations. If we can tie in the time of the calls and his presence, then yes, shazam's a great word. We'll lean on him a little harder to find out why he was calling.'

Callahan looked at him. 'You're already talking to him?'

'Sorry – didn't I tell you? My bad. We decided to bring him in for a little heart-to-heart – a little preliminary dust-up. He's scared shitless, to use common parlance, or what my young partner, Agent Cahill, calls a weasel scumbag. He's already intimated that it *might* have been him finding your man's code name – Watchman, I believe? – from some papers in his possession, although he hasn't yet coughed to passing it on.' When Callahan nodded he continued, 'And he *might* have contacted Ledhoffen to tap her for a loan.'

'A loan?'

'Yes. He did it a while back. It seems she refused and told him she was nearly broke, too, so no go. That's when we think he came up with the idea of selling the information about Watchman to a third party.'

'Desayeva.'

'Her. And that's where he got all bitter and twisted because he let slip to us that when he mentioned her name to Ledhoffen, she told him she knew Desayeva very well. Eventually Ledhoffen began dealing with Desayeva direct and cut her country cousin out. That might explain the different payments exchanged, where Dalkin got forty-five grand and Ledhoffen nearly double that. She arranged her own sweet deal with probably more to come – and I'm guessing Dalkin knows that.' Warner smiled. 'Spies, huh? It seems you can't even trust your own family not to screw you these days.'

As they walked back to the exit, Warner observed, 'I guess it's not going to be a bundle of laughs in Langley or the State

Department when Ledhoffen and Desayeva's names go public.'

'Serves them right,' Callahan muttered, referring to the State Department. He was remembering that, among others, Walter Broderick had been one of the Russian's main champions for using her as a source. It would have been quite a career-booster for a man on the State Department ladder to have an inside source on all things Russian.

But this bit of news, when it hit the headlines, was going to hit him right where it hurt.

# FORTY-SEVEN

*Moscow*

Two vans stopped outside Building No 3 on the corner of Grizodubovoy Street in the Khoroshyovsky Administrative District of Moscow. Two women and four men got out, each dressed in plain overalls, rubber gloves and carrying boxes of equipment. The woman in the lead ripped away a **No Entry** sticker across the lock and used a key to unlock the door, standing to one side while the others filed inside.

The last man in carried a stepladder and a plastic folding barrier. He stopped to place the barrier across the doorway to deter visitors, and as an additional measure strung a police tape across the door.

Inside, the team moved across the foyer, deactivating the security system and working their way quickly through the floors, checking for signs of use. Most of the rooms were empty and showed a thin layer of undisturbed dust and the kind of chilled feel denoting a lack of any human presence. Only on the fourth floor was there any furniture, this confined to two of the offices and a meeting room – the so-called 'dead room'.

The team sprayed and thoroughly cleaned down every item, every desktop and drawer inside and out. They removed the telephones, three computer terminals and towers, including leads and drives. The first woman in directed a man to check all the door frames and windows and give the glass and sills a careful wipe, and instructed the man with the stepladder to remove a set of recording equipment and a camera from inside the air vent panel in the ceiling of the meeting room. Another man was directed to the washroom at the end of the corridor where he sprayed every surface and wiped them down with strong bleach.

Job done, they retreated, closing the doors and wiping

down the outer frames. One woman went down in the lift, cleaning the call buttons and every surface that might have been touched, while her colleagues saw to the handrails down the stairwell.

Reaching the ground floor they removed the police tape and plastic barrier before locking the door and climbing back in their vehicles and driving away.

When they were gone, so was every trace of the group that had been operating from Building No 3.

# FORTY-EIGHT

I was in Paris. At least, I thought I was – I was feeling a little hazy, dragged from a deep sleep by my phone ringing and unsure of my surroundings. I snatched up the phone and checked the screen. No caller ID.

'What kind of trouble have you started over there?' Callahan demanded with no lead-in. He didn't sound pissed, just loud, like his blood was on fire.

'Wait one,' I croaked, and swung my legs off the bed. I'd called Lindsay on my way in from Beauvais to let her know I was safe and would check in with her later after crashing out. The rest I couldn't recall, but that's what the aftermath of combat can do to you.

'What do you mean?' I played dumb while I woke up fully and drank some water. Dehydration had set in and I hadn't drunk enough to ward it off completely.

'We're getting reports of criminal gangs waging war on each other on the outskirts of Paris. Tell me that's not your doing?'

I gave him the facts, stripping away any emotion because that was all he needed. He didn't interrupt me but I could hear him humming at various points, although whether it was acknowledgement or approval wasn't clear.

When I ran dry he said, 'I'll get someone to take a look at local police and coroners' reports. How's Lindsay?'

'She's fine. Enjoying the sights of Paris on Langley's dollar as far as I know.'

'Good to hear.' He hesitated. 'Is she holding up after the fireworks?'

'She is. But you might want to get a friendly psych to have a talk with her when she gets back.'

'Will do. How close to it did she get?'

'Close enough.' I wasn't about to tell him that she'd actually shot a man dead because Lindsay didn't know and wouldn't want to have that on her record in Langley. Some things are best not publicized if they don't need to be.

'OK. Listen, we've got the leaker.' He gave a long pause.

I got the sense that the pause was deliberate. It certainly caught my attention and I felt a tingle up the back of my neck. 'Are you going to tell me?'

'It began with a former chief of staff in DC for someone you knew. Remember Senator Howard J. Benson?'

Benson. I'd heard of the man but never met him, which was probably a good thing. From what little Callahan had told me before, he'd been a CIA hater who'd latched onto me as a specific target while I was on a contract assignment in Ukraine for Callahan. It didn't matter now because Benson was dead, killed by a sniper at his lakeside home outside Washington. The sniper called himself Two-One, and he'd phoned to warn me off going after Benson because he was already taking care of it. He'd been employed by Benson to dispose of at least two people Benson had seen as a threat to his plans, prosperity and future. In the end Two-One had figured he was likely to be next on the list and had chosen to take care of the senator for good and get out.

'I remember,' I told Callahan.

'The staffer, named Dalkin, had gotten himself into some serious debt, and decided to get creative by contacting a woman here in DC named Valentina Desayeva, and giving her your details. I won't bother you with the rest but the FBI have had a low-level watch on her for some time, and one of their random surveillance teams picked up a photo of her and Dalkin in a meeting at a hideaway a couple of hours out of Washington.' He gave a dry chuckle. 'Sometimes we get lucky.'

'You said three. If Dalkin and Desayeva were on the outside, that means number three must have been feeding my locators to them from inside.'

'Yeah. Something like that. Just when we think we've got the Russians blocked and shocked they go and make a new move. Dalkin made the first approach to Desayeva and she drew him in like warm butter. He would have known everything Benson was working on, including all that business while you were in Ukraine, and saw a way of leveraging some money out of it.'

'So who was the inside leak?'

'A member of our Support Directorate. She's Dalkin's cousin and lives a high life which turned out to be way beyond her means. He's already talking to the FBI and admits he agreed to pay her a lot of money if she gave him information on your real name and current whereabouts.'

'Could she do that? I thought there were firewalls and stuff.'

'She's very smart; she burrowed right inside our contracts files looking for your code name. It didn't include your address details, but all she had to do was look at the last date we had contact with you . . . which showed up your trip to Lebanon. She contacted Dalkin and he did the rest. Unfortunately, even the cleverest people forget that there are always traces left behind, no matter how small. We ran an audit trail and she was done.'

'So that's how they got onto me there.'

'Yes. After that, though, we think Ledhoffen managed to bypass Dalkin and deal direct with Desayeva, who she was already big buddies with.' He gave a brief laugh. 'The Russians were happy to pay Dalkin, anyway, but they probably paid Ledhoffen more. You can imagine how the interrogation team are playing up that one. Dalkin's mad enough to spit shrapnel.'

'Are these people in custody?'

'They've got Dalkin, of course. He's the weak link in the chain. So far he's trying to parlay his way out of a long sentence by offering up his cousin. He claims she's the one who's been giving away your location each time.' Callahan sounded tired, as if the machinations had worn him down. 'Unfortunately Desayeva slipped the net. The FBI was on the point of bringing her in for a little chat when she took off. Her instincts must be well-tuned; she's probably in Moscow by now, cosying up to Uncle Vladimir and looking for the next assignment.'

'What about the cousin?' It really didn't matter to me but I liked to think that all the loose ends had been tied up.

'The FBI is taking care of that today. They've got her on a twenty-four-hour watch while they get all their legal checks done. It's likely to send Langley into a spin when news gets out.'

'And my situation?' None of this told me whether I was clear of trouble yet, whether the people after me had given up for good or whether I'd have to spend the next few years looking over my shoulder.

'That's the good news. I've been talking to Tom Vale, who seems to know a lot of stuff we don't. He tells me the people in Moscow have called off the wolves.'

'The British know things the CIA doesn't? Now there's a thing.' It was a low blow but I figured it didn't hurt for the CIA to have their egos punctured once in a while. If they'd got a leak in Langley it served to show they were not infallible, in spite of what the American public was led to believe. Actually, for that read every intelligence agency in the world; fallibility is built into their very framework because the structures are human. And every now and then proof comes along to show just how susceptible they are . . . and what the consequences are of pretending they're not. 'Did he say who or what kicked it off?'

'It was a pay-back mission. We can't exactly place a smoking gun in Putin's hand but we do know it was organized and run by a secret group in Moscow. And on an issue like this they would have operated only if they'd had the nod from the very top.'

'What was the point – and why me?'

'The aim was simple. It was designed to make up for a number of failed missions by FSB and GRU units in the west, and the expulsion of their sleepers including Anna Chapman and the failure of the Skripal poisoning in the UK. What better way to signal their fight-back and show us they weren't going to take any more of our shit than by knocking off a CIA operative who's been a particular pain in their collective ass for the past few years. I paraphrase, of course, but that operative just happened to be you.'

'Is that all?' I wasn't sure I believed it at first. But given a few seconds of thought I couldn't deny Callahan was probably right: there was a certain tortured Russian logic to it. If taking out a CIA agent could be seen as a face-saver for past fails, then it made absolute sense.

It was all about perceived strength. Being the strong man was Putin's entire game plan and always had been. He'd grown up on it since his days in the KGB, posed picture after picture showing himself as the judo-playing, tiger-hunting man of action, bare-chested and frightened of nothing and nobody – least of all the West. And the people around him would have tapped automatically into the same doctrine because it served them to do so.

'There have been crazier situations,' Callahan continued. 'They don't always make sense to us, but we have to take it at face value. Vale's information is that the group running the operation has been disbanded. We can both guess what that means.'

He was right. The harsh reality of failure in Russian military and intelligence circles was simple. Success brought all the plaudits while failure meant nobody got to hear about it again. Ever.

'You shouldn't throw in the towel,' I said. I wasn't sure where that had come from or even if it was my place to say it. But it was out now. 'Politicians are never around for long. Their turn to go comes sooner or later. And you're the best I've worked with. It would be a waste.' As endorsements went it was unvarnished and down-to-earth, but I figured he'd understand.

'Thank you,' he replied. 'Don't worry – I'm not done yet.' He cleared his throat, then said, 'Send Lindsay home, will you? We have work to do.'

# FORTY-NINE

t was six a.m. when Special Agent Bill Warner unfolded himself from his car and walked into the apartment block where Carly Ledhoffen had her home. The air in the street felt suitably early-morning fresh and he shivered slightly. He nodded at three other agents on the door and stairs, and was surprised at how calm he felt at what he was about to do.

No law officer can feel great pleasure at arresting a spy discovered inside a government agency; it's too close to home and too much of a threat to personal and national security. But Warner couldn't help but feel a quiet satisfaction at being able to finish this. It set the seal on a career which had been long and dutiful, made up of successes and failures, like every other agent he knew. But this one at least made up for the number of cases he'd worked on that had ended in a blank sheet. However, that was the way the cookie rolled, as he was fond of telling his younger colleague Special Agent Charles Cahill.

Cahill was walking several paces behind him with a female colleague alongside him. They were content to allow Warner to go ahead and perform the knock, as it was known. Further back were a number of other agents sent to provide support and keep the press and any early onlookers away, their cars blocking the street at both ends.

Warner knew his job would not end here, in this high-end section of Woodley Park. There would be paperwork, procedures to go through and a host of careful briefings and reports to endure before this reached anything like a court of law. But that was much further down the line and he was happy to wait, to bide his time.

For now he was interested in getting Ledhoffen's first statement, if any, which would open up the game, and making sure he had everything prepared so that some clever lawyer could not wipe the case off the board.

The air inside the apartment block smelled nice, faintly

perfumed with what he thought of as class. The fact that his reason for being here rendered that description largely fake didn't matter. He'd been in too many places where desperation and death had been long absorbed in the brickwork and seeped out at you the moment you walked through the door, invariably following you out as you left and taking a long time to dispel.

He wondered what Ledhoffen would say when she was told cousin Bradley Dalkin had rolled over on her and provided the proof needed that would nail her feet to the floor. She would undoubtedly lawyer-up, which would be interesting to see as it might prove whether she really did have as many close friends in Washington's elite as she had claimed.

His bet was that most of them would run for the hills and want nothing to do with her. The sour taste of treachery was like that; it tested friendships and divided families. It would certainly send seismic ripples through the Intelligence community like no other. The CIA would be the one to suffer most, and he felt for the hard-working and proud Americans who worked there. It wasn't their fault that they had harboured a traitor in their midst, but they were the ones who would have to live with that knowledge.

By the time Cahill and the female agent caught up with him he was leaning on the bell to Ledhoffen's apartment. Seconds later the door opened and the woman herself appeared. She blinked owlishly in the light, looking as if she had been torn from a deep sleep. Her usually immaculate face, which he'd seen from many of the photographs sent to him by David Andrews, was devoid of make-up and looked a little puffy. But along with the faint look of query on her brow was a hint in her eyes of, what – realization?

Being woken at such an early hour when you figured life was yours to enjoy, with all the benefits you had acquired, probably did that to you, he decided wryly. Which was why early-morning arrests were chosen as the most effective by most law-enforcement agencies.

'Miss Carly Ledhoffen?' he asked politely, and held out his wallet and badge.

As he did so, he wondered if, along with giving away the locator information on the CIA asset to the Russian sleeper,

Desayeva, this woman had also sent her the message which had led to Desayeva leaving her apartment and disappearing out of the country just before he and his colleagues had closed her avenue of escape.

If they could prove that, no way would she be able to claim innocence.

Ten minutes later the three Special Agents walked Ledhoffen out in handcuffs and led her along the path to one of the cars. They were watched in silence by the other agents in the street, their faces blank. Ledhoffen looked pale and drawn, stumbling a little with shock as she walked, and staring around as if unable to believe this was happening to her. She was placed in the rear alongside the female agent, who had stayed with her while she dressed in jogging pants and a loose top.

Nobody spoke, nobody showed any emotion. It was their job.

Minutes later they were gone, the street deserted of the agency cars and the atmosphere back to normal. Only a few moved curtains, disturbed by the sight and sound of so much low-level movement at this early hour, were evidence that anyone had seen them.

# FIFTY

Talking to Lindsay proved to be a lot easier while we'd been on the move. Sitting across a lunch table from her in the *Poule au Pot* restaurant near the Palais Royal in Paris was where it all went to pieces.

I mean it was more than pleasant and I could have done it a lot more, soaking in the atmosphere and enjoying her company, satisfied that the events of the last few days were finally over. But somehow, even in this romantic city, facing her with a table set for two between us just seemed to gum up the works, conversation-wise.

There's a no-go area in my business, a line marked in the sand. That line says you don't mix it with colleagues. Not that everyone observes it to the letter; some do and it rarely ends well. But working alone the way I do, I'd never had to worry about it. My closest colleague was usually a voice thousands of miles away, on the end of a comms channel or watching my back from an eye in the sky.

Except now that colleague was right here sitting across the table, not just a remote voice but a living, breathing and attractive being. And the mixer was we'd been through a lot together and that had given us a special bond. Now we were out the other side of the mission and I didn't want to make any stupid mistakes.

'You have to go back to Washington,' I said, as we walked through the Tuileries Gardens afterwards. The sun was warm and the atmosphere a million miles away from what we'd both experienced recently. People around us were laughing and chatting, a typical summer's day in one of my favourite cities in the world. Gone were any thoughts of guns and killers, of being followed and targeted for execution by unidentifiable hit teams; gone, too was a host of work-life habits, of the need-to-do-next thinking that had occupied me for many years. And although I was keeping a weather eye on our backs out of instinct and habit, the trade craft too ingrained to lose completely, my instincts told me we were safe.

My future now, from this minute, was going to be utterly different and unpredictable. An open book to be tested and explored, new pages opened and old ones nailed shut. Even my travel patterns up to now were no longer safe and they would have to change radically, no matter what Callahan had been told.

And that was another odd situation: though Callahan hadn't said so, I figured our conversation yesterday had been our last.

She looked across at me. 'Are you trying to get rid of me?'

The glint in her eye told me she was teasing. It was something else I wasn't accustomed to. Colleagues in my line of business make jokes, usually of the darker kind to alleviate the tension surrounding some of the things we witness. But teasing, not so much.

'No. I'm not. You have a job to do and I know Callahan won't be able to cover for you for ever.'

We were walking a little apart as if by silent agreement that getting too close was not a good idea – that line in the sand thing. Since catching up with Lindsay after the events near Beauvais, we'd been circling around the idea that this was probably going to be the last time we'd see each other. I had no idea what Lindsay thought about that but even with all my instincts about not forming close relationships because of my work, I was finding it tough to contemplate.

I'd taken another room at the same hotel as Lindsay and used the excuse of tiredness and the need for some quiet time to shower, to wash off the tensions and smells that always come with you after a collection of actions and near-misses.

The bit about quiet time was real enough; going through the kind of events I'd seen in the last few days is not something I've ever been able to brush off casually, as if none of it mattered. The adrenalin rush and energy, followed by the inevitable sharp deceleration, even if you survive with a slight leg scratch, can leave you hanging with no easy way of dealing with it. Some would call it a form of withdrawal release, and maybe it is. My usual way of coping was to get away from everyone for a while until I was sure I could string a few words together without sounding as if I might be about to rip someone's head off for being nice. At least, that was the way I felt.

With Lindsay there was no way I could leave her alone any longer than I already had. She had questions I could answer and a lot more I couldn't, and part of her getting over what she'd seen was sharing it. I'd made her come to Paris for her own safety, but now I needed to make her aware that she was safe and secure and not just push her to one side. So, I rested up briefly, followed by some civilized conversation and a walk.

How did that kind of normal human activity suddenly get so tough?

'You're trying to think of a way of leaving.' Her voice was calm, reflective. 'It's all right – I understand.'

I stopped suddenly right in the middle of the path because walking and trying to explain something I could not was multi-tasking. Put a gun in my hand and have me execute a game-plan while entering a building full of danger and watching my back at the same time and I'd be away, no problem. But this was different.

'Yes.' When in doubt, say little.

She tilted her head. I couldn't read her expression but if I could have taken a photograph of it I would have gladly done so. Missed opportunities.

'What are you going to do?' she asked finally.

'Do?'

'You're getting out of the business, aren't you? Now your cover's blown.'

Good question. 'I haven't decided yet. I'll find something.'

She ducked a hand into her purse and showed me the edge of an envelope.

'My tickets back to DC,' she explained. 'And in case you're wondering, part of me wants to stay here for a bit longer . . . maybe a lot longer. But there's also a bit telling me I have to get back to what is normal.' She waved a hand around us, and her smile turned down at the corners. 'This . . . this is not really normal . . . although I'd like it to be. It's fabulous. With you it's . . .' She stopped and took in a small gulp of air. 'I have to go home.' Then, before I could say anything she stepped in quickly and flung her arms around my neck and hung on tight enough to stop me breathing. Her own breath was warm against my skin and I felt a trace of wetness on one cheek.

I could have stood there like that for an hour or two enjoying the moment, no problem.

Two elegant women walked by and smiled approvingly, exchanging a look. That's Paris for you.

Before I could reciprocate with the hug Lindsay let go of me and stepped back, then turned and walked away.

'Don't be a stranger,' I said. At the same time I was thinking there might always be a reason for me to drop by in Washington, and who knew – I was very good at tracing people. One comms operative shouldn't be too difficult to track down.

Or maybe that was a bad idea.

She didn't stop or turn, but bent her head. I wondered if she was having second thoughts. I could cope with that.

Then my phone rang and I swore silently. Callahan, it had to be. Looking to clear up some agency-related mess for the record because someone had their ass in a sling. Well, he was going to have to wait. This was more important.

'Can I call you back?' I muttered without checking the screen. I was busy trying to spot Lindsay.

'You better had.' Lindsay's voice coming out of the phone took me by surprise. It was low and throaty and carried traces of a smile which had me doing the same thing. 'And make it soon, you hear? Citera out.'

I looked up and saw her hand holding her cellphone in the air and waving. Next second she was gone, lost in the crowd.

# ACKNOWLEDGEMENTS

The real Isobel Hunt, whose persona I borrowed with kind permission. Thank you, Isobel. You did just fine!

David Headley of DHH Literary Agency, for his ongoing support and encouragement.

Kate Lyall Grant, for her enormous enthusiasm for my writing.

Natasha Bell for the very best editing and catching all my bloopers; and the rest of the team at Severn House.